HIDING IN PLAIN SIGHT

A DANGEROUS SEARCH FOR JUSTICE IN POSTWAR GERMANY

A GERMAN WIFE NOVEL
BOOK FIVE

MARION KUMMEROW

CHAPTER 1

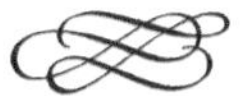

Essen, Germany, Autumn 1947

Roxy walked through the streets of Essen, the cold asphalt beneath her bare feet. The chill didn't bother her. She'd lived through far worse under Hitler's rule.

Since the end of the war, many things had changed for the better, despite the visible scars defining the cityscape: bomb craters, burned-out skeletons of houses, and hastily patched-up ruins.

But Roxy ignored the view, since she was on her way to meet a buyer. In the inside pocket of her worn coat, a silver sugar bowl pressed against her ribs.

"An heirloom. My mother—God rest her soul—brought it out every Sunday," a good customer had confided to her, eyes wet with tears. Then she had squared her shoulders and added, "She would want this. My daughter is very sick. The doctors say she won't make it without penicillin."

Roxy hadn't asked questions. She couldn't afford to. Pity didn't pay on the black market. Good deals weren't made with misty eyes and sobs, especially not with occupation soldiers who had learned to exploit the locals' desperation.

Roxy had a good reputation in the market. She was known for trading the goods fast and not cheating her customers, which meant she could barely keep up with the requests coming in.

"Don't worry. I'll find a buyer for the sugar bowl fast. You should get five cartons of cigarettes for it." That would be enough to procure penicillin from the pharmacy, which was sold exclusively under the counter.

She turned down a side street to meet the British soldier, a collector she'd dealt with several times before. He drove a hard bargain, but at least she could count on him not to have the police in tow.

A man in uniform leaned against the half-collapsed wall of a ruin, smoking his cigarette with lazy confidence. Roxy narrowed her eyes. She knew the major only as Mo. Like her, he didn't work under his real name either.

"Lola," he greeted her, his strong English accent rounding the vowels, and flicked away his cigarette two-thirds smoked. "Punctual as always."

"I have a lovely piece for you." Roxy opened her coat and removed the sugar bowl from her inner pocket. The silver glowed in the foggy autumn light.

Mo took it, turning it in his hands. His fingers grazed the delicate engraving carefully, before he finally murmured appreciatively, "A really fine piece."

"Solid silver. Hallmarked."

He turned the bowl over and pulled out a small flashlight to read the official stamp while Roxy watched his face closely. He seemed to like it.

"Sterling silver. A beauty. How much do you want?"

"Six cartons of cigarettes."

"That's a bit steep." His thumb ran over a scuff on the base of the bowl.

Roxy didn't flinch. She knew this game by heart and anticipated his next offer. Patiently she waited him out until he'd examined the piece from all angles. In a deliberately businesslike tone he said, "There are quite a few scratches. That reduces the value considerably. I'll give you four."

"Four? That's a nice try, Mo. This sugar bowl is worth at least ten cartons, and you know it."

He shrugged. "Possible. In England maybe or overseas. Not here."

Unfortunately, that was true. Back home he could sell the silver piece for twice the price, maybe more, but in Essen? Only the black market existed here, and the British soldiers dictated the prices.

Roxy bit her lip. Despite knowing she wouldn't find another buyer quickly, she lied anyway: "I have other interested parties."

"Five." To underline the offer, Mo opened his leather case and pulled out a carton.

Deducting Roxy's fee, her client would receive just four and a half cartons. But she needed the cigarettes now, not next week. Therefore she nodded. "It's a deal."

The exchange lasted just a few seconds. The valuable sugar bowl disappeared into his leather case, and the cigarettes slid into her coat.

"Always a pleasure doing business with you, Mo." Roxy waited for him to leave, but he lit a second cigarette instead and drew on it leisurely. The smoke drifted into her nose, awakening a sharp longing that burned in her lungs. She'd love nothing more than to follow his example, but cigarettes were currency—much too precious to inhale.

He studied her for a moment. "If your client has more stuff like that, you know how to reach me."

"I'll get word to Lorenz if something comes in." Lorenz, the pianist at a nightclub near the train station, functioned as a human switchboard. Through him you could get messages to the British soldiers.

Roxy turned with purpose to show him she was about to leave, when he said in an uncharacteristically soft voice, "Wait, Lola. I've got something for you."

The hair on the back of her head stood on end. Nobody did anything for free, especially not in her line of work. Slowly, she turned and observed how Mo fished in his trouser pocket and pulled out a tiny carved wooden figure. It was a horse, no bigger than the top joint of a thumb, with a hole at the top so it could hang from a cord. The carving was surprisingly detailed; she could make out the mane and even the hooves.

Spellbound Roxy stared at the tiny horse in his outstretched hand. She knew every cut of the knife, every line. The minuscule nick on the left foreleg where her father's knife had slipped. The way the mane fell to the left. It was her horse. Her pendant. "Where did you get this?"

Mo shrugged. "A German. Like you."

Not like me. A tremor spread through her body as she remembered the day at the camp in Belzec when Kommandant Goslar had taken the only keepsake she had of her late father.

"Do you know his name?"

Mo's eyes narrowed. "Why do you care?"

It had to be Goslar. This was her chance to get revenge at the man who had brought so much suffering to her, to her family, to all Roma. Her stomach fluttered at the thought that he might be here in Essen, perhaps just a few streets away. Should she tell Mo the truth? Should she explain who that German seller really was?

But what would that accomplish? Mo would ask questions she couldn't answer. If he confronted Goslar, the man might vanish before she could track him down.

"It's a beautiful piece," she said finally, and held out her hand. "Maybe he has more."

Mo drew on his cigarette. "No one pays for a wooden pendant. But it suits you. Do you want it or not?"

"Yes. Of course. Thank you." Roxy closed her fingers around the tiny horse. In an instant she was transported back into the past. To a time before the Nazis forced the Roma into camps. She remembered her cousin Tibor, her closest friend during those carefree days in the wagon camp, when her biggest worry had been how to avoid her stern Aunt Gisela. The strength of her emotions took her by surprise and made her sway.

"Are you all right?" Mo asked.

"Yes." Roxy pulled herself together. "I haven't eaten anything today."

"You should smoke more. It keeps the hunger at bay," he said.

"Of course." She managed a weak smile. "I'll be in touch if I find anything of interest for you."

"Do that." With these words, he stomped away.

Roxy waited until he was out of sight, before she bent down and scooped up the butt of the cigarette he'd flicked away at the beginning of their conversation. She pocketed it with the others tucked into her coat. From five to ten butts she could roll a fresh cigarette and trade it for food.

CHAPTER 2

Exhausted, David Goldmann wiped his oil covered hands on his sweat-soaked coveralls. He'd just finished another twelve-hour shift, trying to keep the dilapidated machines for repairing locomotives running somehow.

It was like fighting windmills. Almost every week the British issued new dismantling orders for what was left of the industrial plants so parts could be shipped abroad. Only a small piece of the once-massive cast steel factory had been approved for peacetime production.

"See you tomorrow, Goldmann," a colleague called out. "Give your wife my best!"

"See you tomorrow!" David shouted back with a wave of his hand. After years of persecution, it still felt strange to belong again. When he and Roxy had moved from Berlin to the Ruhr area, they hadn't told anyone about their background. The British knew, of course, and so did his new employer. After the war it didn't hurt to be half Jewish in the eyes of the occupation forces.

To his coworkers he was just Goldmann, the man who could repair any broken machine; the wizard who could work miracles with some wire and a piece of tin. In a time of scarcity, that talent was gold and helped him land a permanent job. The pay was lousy, but it came with some perks. One was that he'd been assigned a flat in the company-owned workers' housing.

Between the buildings, fresh-washed laundry hung on the line. Thin smoke from stove pipes drifted up and mingled with the smell of potatoes and cabbage.

The narrow stairway up to their attic apartment creaked under his weight. In the stairwell, the building's damp wood smell crowded out the aroma of cabbage steam. David fished out the key and unlocked the door. He had to turn it twice, which meant his wife, Roxy, wasn't home yet.

David sighed and flipped the light switch. Nothing happened. So there was another blackout going on. One never knew when or for how long the electricity would be out. Some things had changed for the better after the war, others had stayed exactly the same.

He hung his jacket on the wobbly hook by the door. On Sunday, he'd finally get to fix it, if nothing else came up the way it had for the past few weeks. The tiny hallway was barely big enough for him to stand, no second person, not even his petite wife could fit next to him. The single room in the attic apartment did triple duty as living room, kitchen, and bedroom.

The window glass had broken years ago during the bomb raids, so tar paper had been nailed over the frames to protect the room against wind and rain. Only the window by the stove had cloudy plastic stretched across it, letting in a diffused light. Next to it, the coal scuttle looked alarmingly empty. Even though they used coal only for cooking, they burned through it faster than Roxy could get more. They literally lived on top of coal seams, yet you couldn't buy coal in all of Essen, or the rest of Germany.

Worried, David looked out at the sky, heavy with gray rainclouds. Winter would come soon, and he had no idea how they'd heat the room.

He kindled a fire in the stove and set on the pot of potatoes Roxy had peeled and quartered that morning. If she'd had a good day on the black market, maybe she'd bring home butter or a bit of meat to spruce up the potatoes.

While he waited, he lit the kerosene lamp, pulled off his sweaty shirt, and washed himself at the sink. The cold water raised goosebumps up his skin. Quickly, he finished his cat-lick wash and pulled on a thick, warm, hand-knitted sweater his mother, Helga, had gifted him for Christmas years ago.

He checked his watch. Roxy should have been home by now. She could take care of herself—he knew that—but he still worried every time she was later than usual.

Dealing on the black market was dangerous, not just because the police were cracking down on dealers, but also because of the people she did business with. Desperate people did desperate things.

The water in the pot was just starting to boil when a creak in the stairwell made him pause. A grin spread across his face once he heard the key in the door just moments later.

He went to meet her. "Hello, sweetheart."

"You're already home?" She looked surprised as she wiped her bare feet on the mat.

"It's already late. Way past eight o'clock."

"Really? I'm sorry. I lost track of time." She tried to squeeze past him into the room.

David tilted his head at the strange behavior. "What happened?"

"Nothing." Her gaze turned somewhere far away. "I brought sausage. Did you put the potatoes on the stove?"

"I did." David knew her well enough to know she wasn't ready to talk. Prying would only make her prickly. So he let the topic of her coming late go, at least for the moment.

Half an hour later a heavenly smell of fried sausage filled the room. They sat across from each other at the table, greedily eating the delicious meal. When they were done, Roxy put a small wooden horse pendant on the table.

"A buyer gave me this today," she said, her voice hollow.

"That's nice of him." David picked the pendant up. A lovely little thing, carved with amazing detail, though worn from constant use.

"You don't understand." Her face was turned toward him, yet her gaze seemed to see right through him. His stomach clenched. Something awful must have happened to unsettle Roxy like this. "It's my pendant."

David looked puzzled. "Right. He gave it to you."

"It was mine before." Her small frame jerked, her eyes came back into focus, and she met his gaze. "I never told you. It happened back in Belzec."

As she struggled for composure, he slid his hand across the table until their fingertips touched.

"Goslar took it away from me. He laughed as he did it."

David waited in silence. He'd learned to let her tell a story at her own pace.

"I wasn't registered in the camp because I didn't have papers," she said haltingly. David nodded, sinch he knew that part. "My uncle Gottfried figured it out and dragged me to the camp commandant. As punishment he assigned me to the Sonderkommando, but first he stole my pendant. This pendant." She lifted the little horse, accusation in every line around her pursed lips. "My father carved it for me just before he died. I wore it around my neck for nearly ten years. It was my only link to my parents. And Goslar just took it."

David moved his hand further across the table, sliding his fingers over hers. She looked at him with wounded eyes. "Do you know what he said? 'You'll never see this pendant again.'" She swallowed several times. "In that very moment I swore that one day he'd pay for what he did to me, and to so many other Roma and Sinti."

"That was the day you met Marek, wasn't it?" David asked softly.

"Yes." A nostalgic smile flickered across her face. "Marek

took me under his wing. Without him, I wouldn't be alive today."

"And I'm immensely grateful to him for that." David rose, walked around the table and came to a stand behind her chair, laying his hands on her shoulders. She was the most independent, strongest woman he knew, but in rare moments like this one, she showed him her vulnerability. "What do you want to do?"

"I'm going to find him. And then I'm going to make sure he atones for his crimes."

David thought it was a risky idea, but telling her directly would only stiffen her resolve. "You'll need allies. Men like Goslar don't just disappear. They find new positions, new protectors."

"Do you think I care?" Roxy flared. "You think I'm afraid of him?"

"Of course not," he assured her. "I want him held accountable, too. Report him to the British and they'll deal with the punishment."

"So they can let him go like all the other war criminals?" Roxy seemed to shrink under his hands, like a snail withdrawing into its shell. He knew that response well and had hoped she was past it. "I don't need help. This time I hold all the cards in my hands."

"Roxy," he said, gently kneading her shoulders. "I don't want you to do this alone."

"Why?" She brushed his hands off and stood up. "Because you think I'm too weak? Too stupid? Too—"

"Because I love you, for God's sake!" David turned her to face him and looked into her eyes. "Because I couldn't bear it if that bastard hurts you again."

The words hung in the air between them. Roxy stared at him, surprise flaring in her eyes. Silence bloomed between them while he just stood and waited.

"David," she said at last, quietly. "I'm sorry. I..."

He pulled her into his arms. She pressed her cheek to his chest, a faint tremor running through her. "I want him to be punished, too. But please… report him to the British."

"And if they do nothing? If they let him go like so many others?" Roxy sighed heavily.

David thought for a moment. He sensed her churning thoughts. Too many former Nazis were back in office, protected by old networks, useful to the occupiers. Even Klaus Barbie, the infamous Butcher of Lyon, was under the protection of the American secret service. They were blocking his extradition to France. "Then I'll help you get justice."

She nestled closer against him, and he could feel a smile tugging at her lips. "First I have to find him."

"Knowing you, that'll be the easy part. But promise me you'll be careful. As soon as you find him, you tell me. No solo runs. We do this together or not at all."

An inner struggle played out in the depths of her eyes. The distrust the camps had taught her pitted against the love and trust they'd built together throughout the years. For a moment she drew back, her body tensed as if she might pivot and bolt from the apartment.

"I don't know if I can. Trust. Not after…" she whispered. Finally she nodded, and he saw how much effort it cost her. "I promise. But, David… when we find him…"

"Then we make sure he stands trial. That he pays for his crimes. But not in a way that costs us our souls."

"I lost mine in the Sonderkommando." She shrugged. "You're a much better person than I am."

"Oh, no. You're the most wonderful person I know."

She wriggled free and flashed him a cheeky grin. "That's why I love you so much, because you can lie so shamelessly." Then she kissed him, hot and hungry, and tugged him toward the bed. "The dishes can wait."

CHAPTER 3

A completely ordinary face stared back as Erwin Krüger—
the name he'd been using for nearly two years now—
shaved in the mirror. The gray temples gave him a distinguished
look that suited his new life as an upstanding citizen. Since the
glory years of the SS were over, he'd lost a lot of weight. The
gaunt, almost ascetic appearance underscored his new identity:
an ordinary Wehrmacht soldier, who had been released from
Russian captivity a year ago.

To match the new persona, he sported a mustache on his
upper lip and had even been to the dentist to have four molars
extracted, changing the shape of his face. That, along with the
new haircut, meant not even his own mother would recognize
the once fearsome and well-fed camp commandant of Belzec.

Today was an important day. After a year of patiently
waiting, a former comrade had tipped him off to an open
position in the city administration that matched the
qualifications of his new identity. A clerk in the Department of
Restitution and Compensation.

Erwin smiled at the irony of fate. Restitution for what,
exactly? Those scoundrels and good-for-nothings had gotten
exactly what they deserved. He took a deep breath and carefully

ran the blade along his jaw. Germany's defeat in the war was a regrettable setback, but by no means a final defeat. They just had to keep a low profile for another year or two, then the old guard could regroup and seize power again.

The job in city hall was a first step. When he finished shaving, he carefully wiped away any trace of lather, reached for the tie draped over the back of the chair, and tied it in practiced moves. He studied himself in the mirror with satisfaction and put on his jacket.

Then he opened the top drawer of his bureau and took out a leather briefcase. Inside were the papers he'd rehearsed until they had become second nature. Wehrmacht soldier Erwin Krüger, born 1901 in Königsberg, office clerk, drafted in 1941, wounded twice.

He thought back to the real Erwin Krüger. That man had bled out beside him in a shell crater near Küstrin in April 1945 when the Red Army had launched its offensive on Berlin. Hartmut Goslar had been on the run westward. His SS uniform was supposed to get him through to Berlin, but contrary to his expectations that hadn't worked. Instead, he'd been sent to a front-line unit.

When the grenade had struck and fatally wounded Krüger, Goslar had seized his chance with both hands.

"My… my wife…" the dying man had wheezed, as blood seeped from the corner of his mouth. "Tell her… that I…"

But Goslar hadn't listened. His hands had already been rummaging through Krüger's pockets, lifting the paybook, the identification tag, the personal letters. The man was doomed anyway, so why should his papers die with him, when they could give someone else a new life instead?

When the Soviet troops had found them, Hartmut Goslar had already become Erwin Krüger. Captivity had been brutal. Almost unbearable. It was a disgrace how shamefully those Bolsheviks had treated him. Bile rose in his throat as he thought of the humiliations he had endured.

While most SS men in the camp had been executed, Krüger's papers had saved his life. Later, in the British sector, where the island monkeys had elevated themselves to godhood, Krüger's identity had withstood all checks during the denazification process.

With the help of his old comrades, he had lived a life in the background, earning a living doing odd jobs and waiting for his chance. A few months ago, the authorities had finally issued him a *Persilschein*, certifying him as a politically untainted follower.

Krüger closed the folder and stowed it in his briefcase. He grabbed his worn coat and left the small, terraced house he rented. His neighbor trudged down the street, heavily laden with shopping bags.

"May I help you carry that, Frau Lohne?"

"Thank you, that would be very kind. I got potatoes from my sister today."

Goslar took the heavy bag from her and carried it to the neighboring house.

"Thank you so much. You're always so helpful," said Frau Lohne. The woman's two children had only recently returned to school and her husband was still missing.

"That goes without saying. We have to stick together in these difficult times."

"Yes, that's true." She frowned at him thoughtfully. "Come over tonight and have dinner with us."

"I'd be delighted." Whistling softly, he stepped back onto the street. Life was good.

He took his time because he didn't want to arrive too early for his job interview. On his way, he gazed around attentively: workers hurried to their shifts, women queued outside of stores, children played among the rubble. Essen was slowly recovering from the war, and he would be part of that recovery. A respected civil servant who helped people reclaim their property. The notion amused him.

Of course, this was only an intermediate step; his true calling lay elsewhere. For now, he needed a secure position, a regular income, and above all, the protection of inconspicuousness. In the city administration, he'd have access to lists, files, and information about the people returning to the city. Jews reclaiming their property. Roma seeking compensation. His former victims with the audacity to report to the authorities. He would always be one step ahead of them.

The city hall was an imposing pre-war building that had largely survived the bombings. The foyer was a hive of activity. Officials hurried through the corridors with files under their arms, citizens waited patiently in the hallways. Germany was functioning again, at least on the surface.

After checking in, he sat down on one of the uncomfortable wooden chairs in the corridor. His hands rested calmly on his knees, although beneath the surface he was seething with tension.

His dark suit was of good quality but worn at the elbows after years of constant use. Just recently he'd had the cuffs and collar turned. It projected exactly the impression he wanted to make: respectable, conservative, and modest.

"Herr Krüger?" A young secretary with combed-back hair approached. "Major Lee will see you now."

An Englishman, then. His comrade had warned him; the English liked to trip you up by asking unexpected questions. He forced a charming smile. "Thank you, Fräulein."

Krüger followed her down a long corridor to a spartanly furnished office on the second floor. The walls were decorated with administrative notices and a picture of the English king. He suppressed a mocking smirk.

Major Lee was a slender man in his late forties with sharp blue eyes and a neatly trimmed mustache. "Please have a seat, Herr Krüger." Lee's German was surprisingly good, with only a hint of an accent. "I've reviewed your application. Very nice."

"Thank you very much, Major."

Lee leafed through the papers. "You were a noncommissioned officer in the Wehrmacht, which is unusual for a man with a high school diploma."

"Indeed, Major. I never joined the NSDAP, which, as you can imagine, significantly hindered my career prospects. That's why I wasn't allowed to study and was never promoted beyond the rank of Unteroffizier." He didn't want to lay it on too thick and leaned back.

In situations like this, his many years of experience in conducting interrogations paid off. He waited patiently for the Major's next question, while giving him just the right mixture of attention and subdued nervousness that the Englishman must be accustomed to from former Wehrmacht soldiers seeking an office position.

"You are originally from Königsberg. Why didn't you settle in the Soviet zone?"

"That's a very valid question, Major." Krüger folded his hands and met Lee's eyes. "After my release from captivity, I did indeed spend some time in the Soviet zone. But the situation there..." He paused meaningfully. "I am a man of the law, Major. What I witnessed there doesn't align with my idea of the rule of law."

Lee nodded. "Can you elaborate?"

"Arbitrary arrests, expropriations without due process, people disappearing without a trace." Krüger lowered his voice to a confidential tone. "That's not the Germany I want to live in, Major. The Western Allies are offering us the chance of a democratic future."

It was exactly the answer Lee wanted to hear. Krüger could read it in his expression. The British loved it when Germans confirmed that the West was the right way forward.

"Interesting." Lee made a note. "And why the Reparations Department, of all places?"

Krüger had to tread carefully. "In captivity, I had time to reflect, Major. On what happened in Germany. On the crimes committed in the name of our people." He let a hint of remorse color his voice. "I cannot undo them. But I can help ensure the victims at least receive some kind of justice. That their property is returned, that they're compensated."

Lee leaned back in his chair. "A noble attitude. But are you aware that many of your compatriots think differently? You'll be dealing with people hostile to the victims."

"All the more reason why this department needs to be staffed by people convinced of the need for restitution." Krüger allowed himself a faint smile. "I learned what injustice means while I was a prisoner of the Russians. Nobody should have to go through what I went through. And no one should have to go through what the victims of the Nazi regime suffered." He deftly drew a parallel between himself and the victims. It was a tactic that had often proved effective in post-war Germany.

Lee nodded with satisfaction. "Do you speak any foreign languages?"

"French from school. My English though..." He cleared his throat apologetically. "Well, it needs improvement, but I'm a quick learner."

"That will be necessary. You'll be working closely with us, and not all of our soldiers speak German." Lee leafed through the paperwork again. "Have you completed your denazification?"

"Yes, Major." Krüger opened his briefcase and handed Lee a document. "Category four, *Mitläufer*. A follower. I was never a member of the NSDAP or any of its organizations, though..." Krüger shrugged his shoulders regretfully. "...to my shame I must admit that I wasn't brave enough to join the active resistance. Nevertheless, my conscience is clear."

What delicious irony. His conscience was the purest part about him, simply because he didn't have one. People's need for forgiveness and atonement made them so easy to manipulate.

Lee stood up and went to the window. Outside on the street, even two years after the war had ended, so-called *Trümmerfrauen* were still clearing the rubble. "You see, Mr. Krüger, we need

Germans who understand that the future will only work if we face the past. We must eradicate the roots of Nazism once and for all."

"I couldn't agree more, Major." The lie slid off his tongue with practiced ease.

Lee returned to his desk, jotting down some notes. The silence stretched on, yet Krüger didn't so much as blink.

"One last question, Mr. Krüger. If you discovered a former SS man in your family or among your acquaintances—someone concealing his past—what would you do?"

A trick question. Krüger took a few seconds to think, frowning as if in deep thought. "I'd report him to the authorities, Major. Only if all war criminals are brought to justice does Germany have a future worth living in."

Lee drummed his fingers on the desk. "Good. Very good." He set the papers aside and stood up. "Mr. Krüger, I think you are the right man for this position. You can start next Monday. Report to Mr. Müller."

Krüger also rose and extended his hand to Lee. "Thank you very much, Major. You won't regret it."

Major Lee shook his hand. "Welcome to the Essen city administration."

As Krüger left the office, he cheered inwardly. It was a first step back into the circuits of power. From here on, things were on the uptrend again. He lit a cigarette and mulled over what to do with the rest of the day.

Then he decided to brush up on his knowledge of how the newly appointed city administration functioned. After all, he liked to be well prepared.

CHAPTER 4

For the past two weeks Roxy had been searching for Goslar, chasing every lead, no matter how slim, and exhausting every contact. So far without success. The man had vanished into thin air.

The Red Cross was her last hope. If Goslar was dead, his name would be on one of their lists. If he was alive and had registered somewhere, likewise. It was the last resort.

Inhaling the cold autumn air deeply, she climbed the stairs to the Red Cross office. The building smelled of disinfectant and stale cigarette smoke. Notes with missing person ads lined the walls, mainly women searching for their husbands, fathers, or sons who hadn't yet returned from the war. Others were looking for children who'd gotten lost while fleeing from the eastern territories, or relatives who'd been deported to the camps.

It seemed the whole of Germany was searching for someone. Until now, Roxy hadn't felt the need to visit the Red Cross. After Uncle Gottfried had betrayed her, she didn't want to find out which of her relatives had survived.

Her marriage to David had given her a new family; people who always stood by each other. David's Aryan mother and aunt had protested for days outside the transit camp on

Rosenstrasse, demanding the release of their family members, even when the SS had shown up with machine guns.

No, she felt no desire to reunite with the people who'd sold her to Goslar. Him, on the other hand, she desperately wished to find, so that she could exact revenge. He would pay for his actions. And if no one else held him accountable, Roxy would do it herself, no matter the consequences.

A middle-aged woman with gray hair combed back tightly sat at the reception desk. She looked up as Roxy approached. "Good day, how can I help you?"

"I'm looking for someone," Roxy said.

"Your husband?" the woman asked sympathetically.

Roxy hesitated for a moment. "No, an acquaintance."

"A Wehrmacht soldier?" When Roxy didn't answer immediately, the woman explained, "We have different card indexes for civilians, soldiers, displaced persons, camp inmates... I need to know where to look."

"Oh, I'm sorry." Roxy wondered how much information she should reveal. "His name is Hartmut Goslar and he was a Hauptsturmführer in the SS."

The woman flinched. "I'm afraid the chances of finding him are very slim. Members of the SS hardly ever register with us because they'd be automatically arrested. He has probably long since fled to South America via one of the rat lines."

A prickling sensation in her neck made Roxy fear she'd made a mistake in visiting the Red Cross. But she wasn't willing to give up just yet. "Could you please check for him anyway?"

"Of course. What was the name again?"

"Goslar, Hartmut Goslar."

The woman disappeared and returned with a thick black ledger, which she heaved onto the counter. Roxy recognized the label A-G. While the woman flipped through the pages with nimble fingers, Roxy struggled with her emotions.

The months in the camp had been so terrible, she'd banished the memories from her mind. Now they came rushing back.

Christian's death. The work in the Sonderkommando. The dangling bodies of prisoners who'd been hanged from a gallows as a deterrent. And atop it all, Goslar on horseback.

As if it were yesterday, he raised his pistol and fired.

The shot cracked through the office, so loudly Roxy clapped her hands over her ears.

"Are you all right?" asked a gentle voice.

A dark red pool of blood spread across the light gray linoleum floor. Roxy jumped aside, shouting outraged at the woman: "He just shot him! He didn't do anything! He only stumbled!"

"Fräulein, no one was shot here. You're just imagining things," a monotonous murmur reached Roxy's ear.

The statement enraged her. She hadn't imagined it. All these horrible things had truly happened. There were witnesses. Hundreds. Thousands. But they were all dead. Not one was still alive to confirm her story. Maybe her mind was playing tricks on her. Had it been just a horrible nightmare?

Roxy shook herself and blinked. The puddle of blood had disappeared, along with the dead prisoner and Goslar on his magnificent black horse. Instinctively she reached for her throat, where the wooden horse pendant had recently resumed its rightful place. Not a nightmare at all. The camp had existed. And she had come here to find Goslar and take revenge.

"Here, have some water." The woman handed her a full glass.

Roxy obediently took it and drank.

"You're a survivor of the camps, aren't you?"

Roxy nodded silently.

"We see that a lot. The memories overwhelm people. Some never recover."

"I've put that time behind me," Roxy protested.

The woman pursed her lips, but didn't contradict her.

"Thanks for the water." Roxy placed the glass on the counter. "Have you found Hartmut Goslar?"

"Not yet." A deep crease formed on the woman's forehead. "Are you sure it's a good idea to look for him? Sometimes it's better to let the past rest."

Roxy shook her head. "No. If he's alive, I need to know."

"And what do you intend to do then? Confronting him would only cause problems. He'll deny everything." The woman shook her head regretfully. "Unfortunately, that's how it works. There's not much we can do."

Roxy's mind raced trying to figure out how she might convince the woman to help her. She absolutely had to know whether Goslar lived in Essen. "I don't intend to confront him, I just need certainty," she said, placing a hand over her heart. "In here, I must know what happened to him."

"All right." Once again, the woman set about flipping through the pages of the thick folder.

"Hartmut Goslar," she murmured, trailing her finger down the columns. "G-o-s-l-a-r... Here he is."

Roxy swallowed hard. "You found him?"

"Yes. Hartmut Goslar, SS-Hauptsturmführer, born 1901 in Munich. Killed in action in May 1945 near Küstrin. Confirmed by comrades."

The words hit Roxy like a blow. "Killed in action? Are you sure?"

"It's here in black and white." The woman turned the book toward her. "Two comrades confirmed his death. Hit by a grenade."

Roxy stared at the entry. There it was, neatly recorded in black and white. Hartmut Goslar, died on May 23, 1945. There was no possibility of revenge. No justice. Just a cold, impersonal note in a register. She struggled to pull herself together and said goodbye, "Thank you. You've been very helpful."

Roxy left the Red Cross office as if in a trance. The news echoed in her head: Goslar is dead. Killed in action near Küstrin. Confirmed by comrades. The words refused to penetrate her consciousness, they felt utterly unreal.

She stumbled down the stairs, her feet moving mechanically over the pavement. Passersby walked past her, their voices merging into an indistinct murmur. The city around her blurred into a mush of gray facades and boarded-up windows.

Dead. The man who had destroyed her family and slaughtered countless Roma and Sinti, was simply dead. No justice, no reckoning, no moment of satisfaction in which she could look him in the eye and tell him her name.

Part of her felt relief. It was over. He had gotten what he deserved. But another part felt cheated, as if something essential had been stolen from her. For years she'd imagined facing him. She wanted to see the pain in his eyes when he finally paid for his deeds.

Once again, her hand wandered to the wooden pendant around her neck. How had Mo acquired it? Had one of the comrades who'd confirmed Goslar's death taken his personal belongings and sold them later?

So swept up in her thoughts, Roxy didn't notice that she'd taken a wrong turn until several blocks had passed. She wandered through unfamiliar alleys, past bombed-out houses and piles of rubble.

Suddenly, she stopped. In front of her, between two toppled concrete blocks, a small figure was crouching. A child, no older than eight or nine, nothing but skin and bones. The hollow-cheeked girl in rags looked up at her with eyes that were far too old for her childish face.

"Please," the girl rasped. "Do you have something to eat? I haven't eaten in days."

The scene hit Roxy like a blow to her stomach. Suddenly she was fourteen again, crouching in the dust and begging for bread. The despair in the child's eyes, the sunken cheeks, the trembling hands—it all seemed painfully familiar.

Still dazed by the memories of the camps, Roxy stopped and rummaged in her backpack for something edible, but found only an opened pack of cigarettes, which she always carried with her in case she was offered a good bartering item.

"I'm sorry. I don't have any food." At that moment, alarm bells screamed in her head. Something was wrong. She sensed the presence of others, movements behind her. Too late, she recognized it was a trap.

"Now!" yelled the girl. "Grab the backpack!"

Four or five children jumped out of the ruins, coordinated like a well-rehearsed team. Normally, Roxy would have taken to her heels, because her chances of success if she had to take them all on at once were slim to none.

But for some reason, she froze in her spot, staring at the little girl. Had nothing changed? Did the children still have to steal to survive? A stab of pain shot through her chest. Her favorite cousin Tibor had died after a failed theft in Warsaw.

Meanwhile, the biggest one, a boy with a long scar on his left cheek, reached her and grabbed her backpack. It was too late to save herself and her possessions. If she wanted to get away unscathed, she must sacrifice her belongings. Finally, her brain kicked back in. Instead of fighting the instinct to hold on to her backpack, she slipped out of the straps and threw it to the boy. "Here. Take it!"

The children were stunned.

Roxy took advantage of the moment of shock, spun around, and took off running. These gangs of children were not to be trifled with. Just last week, a man had died from his injuries after an altercation with them.

Gasping for breath, Roxy sprinted as fast as she could. Her bare feet pounded hard on the pavement. Behind her the children shouted and cheered their success. She darted into a side street, then another, racing through alleys and across squares until she was sure no one was following her.

Only when she reached the main street leading to the train station, where there were always passersby, did she slow her pace. Her lungs burned, sweat trickled down her back, and her heart hammered so loudly she was certain the whole street could hear it.

She walked the rest of the way home. Although she was sure none of the children had followed her—why would they, after getting what they wanted? Still, she kept glancing over her shoulder repeatedly, scolding herself for being careless. If she hadn't been overwhelmed by her memories, this wouldn't have happened. Emotions had no place in her life. Not then, and not now.

With shaking hands, she fumbled for the key in her coat pocket, relieved that she always carried money, papers, and valuables in a flat pouch around her waist.

"Roxy? You're home already?" David called out as soon as she pushed open the door.

"Yes, it's me." Her eyes closed, she leaned against the wall for a few seconds. Her whole body was trembling with tension.

"Did you find out anything?" David had offered to accompany her to the Red Cross, but she'd insisted on going alone. He appeared in the doorway, a screwdriver in his hand. His smile faded when he saw her. "For God's sake, what happened?"

Roxy pushed a strand of sweat-drenched hair from her forehead with the back of her hand. "I... it's nothing serious."

"Nothing serious?" David came closer, giving her a once-over. "Where's your backpack?"

Roxy kissed him and slipped off her coat. "Stolen. By a gang of kids down at the harbor."

David hung her coat on a hook. "Why on earth were you at the harbor? I thought you were going to the Red Cross."

"I did." She shrugged wearily. "He's dead. Killed in the last days of the war."

David was silent for a long time. "That's good, isn't it? He can never hurt you again."

"I don't know. It doesn't feel right. I wanted him to be held accountable. I wanted to look him in the eye when he realized he had to pay for his cruelty." Roxy stared at her hands. "Does that make me a bad person? That I'm disappointed because his death was too easy? Because he didn't suffer enough?"

David wrapped his arms around her. "After everything he did to you, that's completely understandable."

"There's something else. Where did Mo get my pendant if not from him?"

David began to massage her tense shoulders. "There could be a thousand reasons. Goslar could have given it away before he died, or someone looted his body. It doesn't really matter, as long as you know Goslar is dead. He's not in Essen. You're free."

"He didn't pay," she whispered. "I wanted to avenge my people."

"I understand. But look on the bright side. You can finally make peace."

Roxy forced a smile. "I don't think I'll be ready for that. Maybe someday."

"That's only natural. You've been through a lot. We'll get through this together."

"Thank you," she said finally.

"For what?"

"For being here. And for always being patient with me."

He pulled her close. "The feeling is mutual."

CHAPTER 5

Out of habit, David woke up before the first rays of sunlight filtered through the milky plastic that served as a makeshift seal for the window. Next to him, Roxy slept soundly, curled up like a cat.

She could sleep anytime, anywhere, no matter what time of day or night, while he was wide awake at six o'clock even on Sundays. Careful not to disturb her, he slipped out of bed.

He put on two pairs of wool socks and his warmest sweater. It was getting bitterly cold in the apartment at night. He lit a fire in the stove and put water on to boil. Then he took out the metal tin of real coffee Roxy had managed to acquire on the black market a few days ago and filled the coffee filter with two heaped tablespoons.

Usually, they traded luxury goods for bread or potatoes, but on Sundays they indulged in real coffee. While he waited for the water to boil, he held his cold hands over the pot. Soon, the delicious smell of coffee filled the room and David heard Roxy stretching beneath the covers.

"Hmm, that smells heavenly," she mumbled sleepily.

"Good morning, sweetheart." David brought her a steaming cup to bed. "Sunday is coffee day."

Roxy sat up and gratefully accepted it. She sipped the hot drink carefully and gave a contented sigh. "Sometimes I forget how beautiful life can be."

David fetched a second cup and slipped under the thick duvet with her. He loved the quiet laziness of Sunday mornings. No factory sirens, no machine noise, no rush. Just the two of them.

"I spoke to a colleague yesterday," David said after a while. "He's planning to go to Berlin to visit his sister for Christmas. The British are issuing travel permits again."

Roxy peered at him over the rim of her cup. "You want to go to Berlin?"

He grinned because she knew him too well. "I miss my family. What do you think about visiting them over Christmas?"

Roxy gnawed her lower lip. Family gatherings were difficult for her. His family had welcomed her with open arms, but he still sensed her unease whenever they visited.

"Only if you want to, of course."

"Why not? A little change would do us both good, wouldn't it?" Roxy frowned. "But we'd have to cross the Soviet zone."

"That's exactly what I meant. Patrick says the British are issuing permits more often again, especially for family visits. We could give it a try."

The thought of seeing his family again warmed David from the inside out. His mother, Helga, had somehow protected her Jewish husband and children through all these years without losing her optimism. His father, Heinrich, still believed in the good in people, even after all the atrocities. And his aunt Feli— party member or not—had quietly helped however she could.

But most of all, he longed to see his younger sister, Amelie, and fall back into their easy bickering.

"We should submit the application as soon as possible," said Roxy, ever the practical one. "If we want to travel before Christmas."

David finished his coffee. "I could take a day off to go to the authorities."

"You don't need to. I can take care of it," Roxy offered.

"That's sweet of you, thank you." Then he reached for the newspaper a colleague had given him last night. He unfolded it while Roxy snuggled up to him and closed her eyes.

He skimmed the headlines until his gaze lingered on an article on the third page.

"Brutal attack in the harbor district," he read aloud. "Two black market dealers found seriously injured."

Roxy froze. "What does it say?"

David continued reading, "The two men were discovered unconscious and severely beaten by a police patrol last night in an alley street near the harbor. The victims sustained multiple injuries. Police suspect a robbery by rival groups fighting over territory."

"Or by the gang of kids," Roxy muttered.

David shot her a sharp gaze. "You mean the ones who robbed you?"

"It fits their modus operandi. First they use a little girl as bait, then they launch a coordinated attack." Roxy shuddered. "Those kids are capable of anything."

David put the newspaper aside and took her hands in his. "Please stop dealing on the black market. It's become too dangerous."

"David, we need the money."

He tapped the newspaper. "The police are cracking down harder, the competition is getting more brutal, and these gangs of kids... I don't want you to be the next one found seriously injured in an alley."

Roxy pulled her hands free. "What am I supposed to do instead? I never learned a trade."

"That's not true." David turned toward her. "You may not have a high school diploma, but you're smart, tough, and you speak English."

"My English might be good enough for the black market. But not for a job with the British. And besides..." She sighed. "Jews have a privileged status with the occupiers. We Roma don't. People still look down on us."

David knew she was right. Prejudice against the Roma ran deep. Even many who were outraged by the persecution of the Jews showed little sympathy for the fate of those they called Gypsies.

"You don't have to tell anyone that you're a Romani woman."

Roxy's eyes flashed with anger. "I should deny my heritage just so I can get a job? Has nothing changed?"

"Not deny it, sweetheart." David tried to limit the damage since this was a touchy topic. "But you don't have to rub it in your future employer's face either. After all, none of us carry that ugly red letter on our identification cards anymore."

Roxy jutted out her lower lip and chewed on it. "But who's going to hire a woman with no formal education? At best, they'd take me on as *Trummer* clearing rubble, and I'd rather deal on the black market. It pays a lot better."

David furrowed his brow. Many companies were desperately looking for workers. "What about manual labor? You love carving, and you're really talented at it."

Roxy snorted. "Carving is a hobby, not a profession."

"Why not? Carpentry shops are hiring again. Almost everything needs to be repaired, especially furniture. That skill is in high demand."

"You really think so?" For the first time since she'd gotten her horse pendant back, hope flashed in Roxy's eyes, but then she pouted again. "They only want men anyway."

"There aren't that many men left. If you want, I'll ask around among my colleagues."

Roxy wrinkled her nose. David could literally see the wheels turning in her brain. Finally, she nodded. "Maybe... maybe I could try. But I don't want to get my hopes up."

David pulled her into his arms. "It's worth a try, isn't it? Better than risking your life on the streets."

She nestled against him. "You're right. I'd like a real job, too."

"So it's decided?" David lifted her chin so she'd meet his eyes. "No more black market?"

Roxy hesitated for a moment, then nodded firmly. "I'll try to find honest work. But I'm not quitting black market trading until I've found a job." She snuggled up to him and asked quietly, "David?"

"Yes?"

"Do you ever wonder what our lives would have been without Hitler's rise to power?"

"I used to think about it a lot, but not anymore." He gently cupped her chin. "You and I would never have met. You'd be traveling around the country with your family, and I'd be working in the locomotive workshop in Berlin. Our paths would never have crossed."

"That's a strange thought." Roxy seemed to think. "Of course I'm glad we found each other, but that doesn't mean I'm grateful for the horrible things that happened to me."

"Don't tell me you could be happy without me?" he teased her.

"Hmm... let me think..."

She gave him a mischievous gaze, and a wave of love washed over him. He kissed her deeply.

CHAPTER 6

On his first day at work, Erwin Krüger—he addressed himself by his new name without fail—entered Essen City Hall exactly at eight o'clock. His worn shoes clattered on the stone floor of the foyer, a satisfying sound radiating authority. After years of deprivation, it felt good to be someone again.

"Good morning, Herr Krüger," the receptionist behind her desk greeted him cheerfully. "Herr Müller is expecting you."

"Thank you. On the second floor, right?"

"Yes. Shall I show you the way?" she asked helpfully.

"That's very kind of you, but it won't be necessary." He nodded politely and added, "Have a pleasant day."

She stared at him in bewilderment, clearly unaccustomed to the courtesy.

He climbed the stairs to the second floor and walked down a long corridor lined with offices on both sides. The clatter of typewriters and muffled voices echoed through the closed doors. Germany was functioning again, the administration was up and running—and he was part of it.

A smile tugged at the corners of his mouth, because he was well aware of the irony of the situation. A former camp commandant at Belzec was supposed to help the victims of the Nazi regime obtain justice. It was downright delicious. Too bad he wasn't allowed to tell anyone about it.

"Herr Krüger?" A bloated middle-aged man approached him, his hand outstretched in greeting. "Friedrich Müller, department head. Good to have you here, we're drowning in work."

Krüger shook the soft, sausage-fingered hand. It was the sign of a classic bureaucrat who'd spent his life behind a desk while the best men fought and died. Regrettably, since the collapse of the Third Reich, physical fitness no longer held much value. "The pleasure is all mine, Herr Müller."

"Come, I'll show you your desk." Müller led him to an office where three desks took up almost the entire room. "This is where you will work. Reviewing restitution claims, drafting opinions, interviewing applicants."

A chill ran down Krüger's spine, since he hadn't expected in-person contact. Despite his changed appearance, a former inmate might recognize him. "I wasn't aware we had walk-ins."

"We usually don't. Normally, we conduct the initial interviews on the phone and prepare a decision template. The personal interview and the final decision are handled by another department."

Krüger nodded with relief and looked at his desk, which was completely empty except for a black telephone. Müller followed his gaze. "Don't worry. You'll be swamped by files soon enough." He pointed to a thin man in his early sixties. "Herr Weber will teach you the ropes. Please feel free to ask him any questions you may have. He's been in this department since the beginning."

Weber peered at him through his thick horn-rimmed glasses. "Finally, we're getting reinforcements. The applications are piling up to the ceiling."

Next, Herr Müller pointed toward a fine-boned blonde nearly

hidden behind a cast-iron Olympia typewriter. Her fingers flew across the keyboard. "This is the secretary, Frau Hoffmann. She'll do your typing and take you later to pick up office supplies."

Frau Hoffmann pressed the lever to move to the next line before looking up. She was the epitome of a good Aryan woman. "Welcome, Herr Krüger." Without waiting for his reply, she continued typing at breakneck speed as if she were competing in a race.

Krüger immediately took a liking to her. Order and discipline were the fundamental characteristics of the master race. Someone so absorbed in their work was prime material. He smiled warmly. "Thank you very much. I look forward to making my contribution."

Müller then led him to a filing cabinet that took up the entire wall. "This is where the open cases are. Mainly Jewish families reclaiming their property—houses, businesses, jewelry, works of art. But also other victims of persecution by the regime." He lowered his voice and said with obvious disdain, "Sinti and Roma, Jehovah's Witnesses, political prisoners, and the like."

"Important work," Krüger murmured as his gaze wandered over the countless files. Each one represented people who'd been considered vermin. Rightfully so, in his opinion. Unfortunately, too many had survived and now had the audacity to make demands. He went to great effort to keep his expression neutral. Soon, it would be time to show his true colors and resurrect the movement. "How do we proceed?"

"Systematically." Müller pulled out a file. "Every application will first be reviewed for formalities. Are the documents complete? Can the property claims be substantiated? Are there any witnesses? Once we've established that, we'll evaluate the case and recommend restitution or compensation."

Krüger nodded thoughtfully. "What do we do if the evidence is insufficient?"

"Then we reject it. We can't approve every claim just because someone says their property was stolen." Müller shrugged.

"There are charlatans wanting to take advantage of the situation, and others trying to get more than they're entitled to."

Excellent. Krüger struggled to suppress his satisfaction. He'd have to approve some of the cases, but he could certainly delay others. Given the poor health of most of the returnees from the camps, some cases would resolve themselves if the process took long enough.

"I see. Do we make the decision ourselves?"

"Our department prepares the decision template, which is then sent to a committee that determines the final amount."

Müller led him back to his desk. Before leaving the office, he said, "Today you'll shadow Herr Weber, starting tomorrow you'll be on your own."

Weber seemed moderately enthusiastic about having someone sitting next to him to whom he had to explain every step. Eager to make a good impression on his new colleague, Krüger said, "I don't want to get in your way."

A hint of gratitude appeared in Weber's eyes. He pushed the file in front of him over to Krüger. "Herr Rosenberg from Düsseldorf is reclaiming his textile business, which was Aryanized in 1938. Familiarize yourself with the facts. Then we'll go over your findings."

"Gladly."

Weber reached for a second file from the stack and immersed himself in it without giving Erwin another glance.

Erwin was fine with that. In his former life as Hartmut Goslar he'd studied law and gained sufficient experience with official files while working in the camp administration, even if his knowledge had become somewhat rusty since the escape, collapse, and captivity as a prisoner of war.

The file on his desk belonged to Mordechai Rosenberg, born in 1895, married, two children. The textile business had been of considerable value when it was sold to a party member in 1942 for a fraction of its worth. In 1943, the entire family had been deported.

"It's a shame he came back," he muttered, barely audibly.

"Excuse me?" Weber asked.

Erwin bit his tongue, vowing to be more careful. "I was wondering if any other family members had returned besides him. You know." He made a vague gesture with his hand.

Weber nodded understandingly. "It's hard at first. Most didn't survive, especially the children. You'll get used to it soon."

"We're doing something good here." Frau Hoffmann glanced up with a brisk nod. "A little measure of justice for the victims of the regime."

Erwin studied her features. Her eyes shone with determination, a deep furrow etched in between them. She wasn't Jewish. If he had to guess, he'd say that either a close relative or she herself had been involved in the resistance. Or she'd fallen in love with one of those ugly old Jews who preyed on pretty young girls. If Erwin were still camp commandant, he'd have found out in minutes why Frau Hoffmann sympathized with such scum.

"Of course." He returned to the file. If only one Rosenberg was alive, proving ownership claims would be complicated. Missing documents, deceased witnesses, unclear inheritance relationships—these were all excellent grounds for delay.

He spent the next few hours familiarizing himself with the file and studying the department's procedures. It was fascinating to see how the system worked. On paper, everything was meticulously specified. In practice, however, there were countless ways to stall applications, request additional evidence, or craft rejections based on formalities.

Around noon, Frau Hoffmann said, "Herr Krüger, would you like to join us for lunch? There's a nice, inexpensive restaurant around the corner."

"I'd love to." Erwin stood up and grabbed his coat. Sharing a meal was the best opportunity to learn more about his colleagues.

The restaurant was a decent place. It was clean, warm, and filled with the smell of home cooked food. They sat down at a table by the window, and Krüger listened as Herr Weber and Frau Hoffmann discussed a case.

"The Weiss family is going to have problems," Weber said between two spoonfuls of hearty potato soup with sausage. "The current occupant of their house refuses to move out. He claims he bought it legally."

"Ten thousand marks for a house that was easily worth twenty times that," snorted Frau Hoffmann. "And he calls that legal!"

She was clearly on the side of the victims, so Erwin had to be careful with her.

Weber shrugged. "It could take years to sort out. The appraisers are overloaded, and so are the courts."

"It must be frustrating for the claimants." Erwin wanted to gauge Frau Hoffmann's opinion more precisely.

"Indeed. Some give up and accept symbolic compensation." She sighed. "Understandable, after everything they've been through."

After lunch, Krüger immersed himself once more in the Rosenberg file, jotted down notes, and drafted a letter, requesting additional papers: business records, tax documents, witness statements. Everything was formally correct, and time-consuming.

Late in the afternoon, a knock sounded at the door. A scrawny man with gray hair and deep-set eyes entered, placing a stack of papers in the mail basket. "These are the new claims. Do you have anything for me?"

Erwin looked up. For a moment, he glared at the disrespectful man, then he remembered—he was no longer Hauptsturmführer Goslar, but clerk Krüger. He extended his hand in greeting. "Good afternoon. I'm Erwin Krüger, the new colleague. I look forward to working with you."

Like the receptionist that morning, the mail carrier seemed

perplexed by the friendly treatment. "Very pleased to meet you. I'm Hansmann. If you need anything, please just ask."

"Thank you very much." Most people tended to underestimate mail carriers, janitors, and cleaning ladies, but Krüger had discovered that these employees were often best informed about the latest office gossip and, above all, knew everyone in the company.

Meanwhile, Herr Weber rose and handed Herr Hansmann a pile of files before turning toward Erwin: "What about your drafts?"

Erwin hesitated. "I... I'm sorry. Today is my first day and this case is difficult. I'll need more documentation."

"Then I'll take these. See you tomorrow." Hansmann continued his rounds.

Frau Hoffmann explained: "He delivers internal post every afternoon. In the mornings he runs errands to other government agencies."

Herr Weber frowned at Erwin. "It's understandable that you need time to get up to speed, but we are expected to deliver results."

Erwin was close to losing his temper. Who did this armchair warrior think he was? Nevertheless, he feigned contrition. "I'm sorry. I didn't want to immediately propose a negative decision, but rather give the applicant the opportunity to submit more information." That wasn't true, because Rosenberg's case was crystal clear.

Out of the corner of his eye, he noticed Frau Hoffmann raising her eyebrows in appreciation.

Herr Weber sighed. "Understandable, but please don't spend too much time on any one case."

"I'll do my best." Erwin leaned back in his chair. He'd drag out the proceedings, requesting additional documents until the old man either gave up or died.

As he left the office, he hummed softly. The new job wasn't what he was used to, but it was a good start. Many of his old comrades had managed to clear their names and now worked in the administration. None of them were happy about the new British rulers, and even fewer appreciated the fact that Judaism was on the rise again and was cunningly stealing back their old fortunes.

CHAPTER 7

I n front of the brick building housing the Bosch carpentry shop, Roxy paused to eye the weathered sign above the entrance door. She smoothed a hand over the coarse fabric of her navy blue cotton dress, which she'd washed and ironed especially for this occasion. She'd braided her wild black curls into two plaits because she wanted to make a respectable impression.

Squaring her shoulders, she opened the door. The entry bell jangled. The smell of sawdust and glue hit her. She took a deep breath. Memories of the caravans of her childhood came flooding back, of how her father had taught her to carve before he was hit by a car and died.

A shiver ran down her spine. Although she'd grown up relatively carefree in the circle of her extended family, she didn't want to think about that time anymore. Because then her thoughts inevitably led to the labor camps, where her family had ultimately betrayed her.

"How can I help you?" The voice of a woman in her midfifties rasped through the dusty air like a rusty saw.

"I'm here about the job." Roxy stepped closer to the desk.

The woman's head snapped up and she scrutinized Roxy

from her head to her bare feet and back again. "Oh, really? And where did you leave your shoes?"

"I don't wear any." Roxy had never understood why people placed so much importance on shoes when you moved with more agility barefoot.

"I see." The woman leaned back in her chair. "And I presume you don't have papers either?"

"In fact, I do." Roxy pulled the identification card out of her pocket. It had been issued after her marriage to David. Real papers without the ugly Z for Gypsy broadcasting her ethnicity to every casual observer.

The woman skimmed it. "Roxana Goldmann... You're Jewish?"

"Not me, my husband." As a precaution, she didn't mention that she was a Romani woman, because you never knew how the other person would react.

"Tell your husband that he has to come by in person if he wants the job."

Roxy shook her head. "It's for me."

The woman's face puckered as if she'd bitten into a lemon. "We don't hire women."

"I'd like to speak to the boss."

"He doesn't have time for—"

"I'll wait." Roxy sat on the wooden chair next to the door. She'd spent plenty of time waiting over the past years. In hiding, for food, for the end of the war. She could be very patient. She'd sit there all day if she had to.

The woman sighed theatrically and disappeared through a door leading to the workshop. Roxy heard voices, followed by heavy footsteps.

Master Bosch was a burly man with beefy hands and a ruddy face. He eyed Roxy with undisguised curiosity. "You want to be a carpenter?"

"Yes."

"It's hard work, not for half-pints like you."

He didn't say it unkindly, but it stung anyway. "Believe me, I worked harder in the labor camp than you can imagine."

His eyebrows shot up. "My wife said you're not Jewish."

"As if Jews were the only ones persecuted by the Nazis." Roxy's temper got the better of her and before she could bite her tongue, the words tumbled out of her mouth. "We Roma were also on the hit list. Out of my whole family, I'm the only one who survived."

His expression darkened. "A Gypsy, then. No, I really can't hire you, young lady." The condescension dripped from his words.

"You can't be serious, can you? Germany has just lost the war and no one seems to have learned anything," Roxy grumbled. She was so tired of being constantly discriminated against for who she was.

"That's not the point. I was never a supporter of Hitler. I even slipped food to Jewish acquaintances whenever I could," he protested. "But there are men who need this work much more. Soldiers who have returned from the war and have families to feed."

An irrepressible rage tightened Roxy's throat, which was probably for the best; otherwise she might have told this pompous man exactly how fed up she was with his nonsense. After she'd escaped from the camp, she'd dreamed of vengeance for the injustices she'd endured. But satisfaction had not materialized: Nazis were back in office in droves, Roma were still marginalized, and the women who'd kept the country running for years were banished back to the kitchen as soon as the men returned home from the battlefields of Europe.

As her anger ebbed, a paralyzing fatigue settled in. Nothing had changed. Nothing at all.

"I'm truly sorry. Why don't you ask at the German Coal Mining Authority; they're always hiring young women for the typing pool."

"Thanks." Roxy didn't bother explaining to him that she'd

never attended a proper school and was unsuitable for office work for that reason alone. "I'm looking for a job where I can be active and create things. I'm really good with wood. My father taught me how to carve. And later I helped repair our caravans."

"Yes, the traveling folk. Do you even have a school diploma?"

Roxy slumped her shoulders. "The war got in the way."

"I really can't hire anyone without a diploma, I'm sorry." He was clearly in a hurry to get rid of her, but Roxy didn't want to leave without a fight.

"Do you say the same to the soldiers who return home after many years at the front and in captivity?"

"That's completely different." He looked down his nose. "Listen, Frau Goldmann. First of all, you're a woman. Second, you don't have a graduation certificate. Third, you're walking around barefoot like a beggar. And fourth..." He paused briefly. "Fourth, you're a Gypsy."

"I'm a good worker. Please give me a chance."

Bosch snorted. "I run a respectable business. Not a Gypsy shop." He turned away, signaling the end of the conversation.

Roxy left the carpentry. Outside, she felt the cold pavement beneath her soles, and with it rose the familiar fury she'd suppressed since the end of the war. A few meters further on, she stopped and slowly turned around to glare at the building. The anger boiled inside her like hot water in a kettle. Shivering all over, she clenched her fists.

"Gypsy shop," she repeated, his words leaving a bitter taste in her mouth. That was typical. Always the same prejudice, the same hatred, just now no longer openly expressed, but hidden behind pious excuses.

She walked around the building to the backyard, finding stacked wood and a pile of tools. A crooked handcart leaned against the wall, its wheels encrusted with sawdust. Next to it lay a stack of freshly sawn boards, neatly stacked and ready for further processing.

The injustice burned hot in her chest. She had worked harder than most ever would. She had survived horrors that had claimed so many lives. And still they treated her as lesser just because she was Roma.

"This is a proper business," she hissed through clenched teeth. "Not a Gypsy shop."

Before she could stop it, her foot lashed out and kicked the handcart. Rotten wood splintered with a satisfying crack. A spark of guilt flashed through her mind. But years of pent-up anger burst through the dam of practiced indifference that Roxy had wrapped around her feelings like a cloak.

There was no stopping her now. She grabbed one of the boards from the pile and smashed it against the wall. Once, twice, again and again, until the wood broke in her hands. Splinters flew through the air, and at last she could breathe freely again.

"What the hell is going on here?" a voice behind her bellowed.

Roxy spun around. Master Bosch stood in the back door, his face the color of a beet. Behind him, two journeymen peered out curiously.

"You... you destroyed my materials!" he gasped, pointing an accusing finger at the broken board in her hand. "I'm calling the police!"

Roxy dropped the board and backed away. Panic squeezed her chest like a vice. Police meant questions upon questions. The authorities wouldn't believe a Roma anyway, so she'd probably end up in jail.

"I'm sorry," she stammered, but Bosch was already charging toward her.

"Grab her!" he yelled at his men.

Roxy's survival instinct kicked in. Within a heartbeat, she was back in the war. Living in hiding for years had taught her to vanish at will, to steal food and clothing to live, to sleep in places where no one would find her.

Her legs moved even before her brain gave the command, and she sprinted out of the yard. Footsteps and shouts sounded behind her, but she knew the alleys better than they did. She turned sharply to the right, then to the left, slipping through a gap between two houses. Her feet found secure footing in the rubble of a ruin as she climbed for her life.

On the other side, she jumped onto the street and kept running. On and on. Only when she was sure no one was following her did she slow her pace. Her heart pounded violently against her chest. An unfamiliar dizziness washed over her. Gasping, she bent over to catch her breath.

After a while, she straightened and pricked up her ears. Nothing. She leaned against a wall and closed her eyes. What had she been thinking? She couldn't afford such outbursts of anger. She was no longer the desperate girl in the camp with nothing to lose. She'd become a law-abiding citizen with a clean record—until now. David's wife.

The thought of David hit her like a blow. He'd be horrified. He'd wanted a fresh start for her. Instead, she might have ruined any chance of ever getting a job in this city. News traveled fast. She could already see the headline: "Gypsy destroys property and flees from police."

She took a detour home, her enthusiasm evaporated. The streets seemed grayer than usual, the people more suspicious. Or was it just her?

David would be home from work soon, and she'd have to confess what she'd done. But he was a man and not a gypsy. No one questioned his mechanical skills. As a half-Jew with victim status, they'd hired him with open arms and soon put him in charge of the heavy machinery.

It was so unfair! Anger—and envy—choked her throat until she had to stop by the side of the road. It wasn't David's fault, so she mustn't be mad at him.

She arrived home to an empty apartment. That was lucky, because she needed time to figure out how to explain her actions. She set the potatoes on to boil and stared at her hands. The same hands that could so skillfully carve figures out of wood had just destroyed her future.

The truth was inescapable: the black market was the only way for her to earn money. Nobody would hire her, or give her a chance. She would always remain an outsider, no matter how hard she tried to belong.

An hour later, David came home and greeted her cheerfully, but his smile faded when he saw her expression. "No luck again?"

She shook her head and helped him out of his jacket. "Woman, gypsy, no degree, no shoes. Take your pick."

David put his arm around her shoulders and kissed her. "You have to be patient. It'll work out."

"When?" The words burst out of her. "When will things finally get better? The war is over, Hitler is dead, but it's still the same. We're still the wrong kind."

"You're alive," David replied quietly. "That's a lot."

Roxy stayed silent. He was right, of course. She was alive, while millions were dead. Marek, Tibor, Livia, Christian, almost her entire extended family, half a million Roma and Sinti.

A heavy weight squeezed her chest until she gasped. Suddenly, she felt like she was going to vomit. Her vision went black. She struggled to swallow her disgust, disappointment, and rage until two strong arms wrapped around her. David held her tight. Relieved, she leaned into him. David was different. He loved her for herself. In the past, he'd have stood by her instead of betraying her for his own benefit.

Just like Marek. The cynical, jaded Marek, who'd still sacrificed his life so that she could escape. Her eyes welled up and she buried her face deeper into David's chest so he wouldn't notice.

What the hell was wrong with her? First the outburst of anger and now this? She didn't recognize herself anymore.

Once she regained control, she said, "Maybe I should wear shoes when I apply for a job."

David glanced at her narrow, delicate feet, the soles of which were tough as leather from years of walking barefoot. He knew how much she hated shoes, how cramped and cut off from the earth they made her feel.

"At least then you wouldn't stand out right away." In his expression, she saw love, hope, and an unshakeable belief in a better future. She'd keep trying for his sake, even if she no longer believed it herself.

CHAPTER 8

David lay awake at night, listening to Roxy's restless breathing. She tossed and turned, muttering incomprehensible words. He knew her memories tormented her —dreams of her time in the camps, of persecution, of the eternal search for a place in a world that didn't want her.

He was up even before the alarm clock rang at five in the morning, an idea taking shape. Roxy needed shoes, but not just any shoes. She needed shoes that suited her.

After breakfast, Roxy kissed him goodbye. "Have a good day."

"Exhausting will be more like it." He studied her face. The traces of disappointment were still visible. "What are you going to do?"

"Apart from housework and shopping?" She shrugged and sighed.

Since yesterday, she had been quiet and withdrawn as if she were brooding over something. David wished he knew what had really happened at the carpentry shop, but he knew Roxy well enough to accept that she wouldn't talk before she was ready. Until then, he'd worry.

Roxy was a free spirit who refused to be forced into

conventional paths. This quality had helped her survive the war. It had also provided invaluable services to him and his family in the chaos following the collapse of Hitler's regime.

But in the new Germany, these abilities were no longer in demand, and it depressed him to see her withdrawing more and more every day, her old spirit of adventure, which he loved so much, fading away.

He quickened his pace toward the entrance gate of the cast steel factory as it hummed to life. In the two years since the war, David had risen from an unskilled worker to foreman for machine maintenance. His mechanical skills and his diligence in learning English had earned him respect, even if some of his colleagues called him "the Jew" behind his back.

"Good morning, Goldmann," the workshop manager greeted him as David entered the hall. "The turbine is acting up again. Take a look at it right away."

"On it." David wanted to ask a favor, but Murr was already gone. So he headed to the changing room, put on oil-stained overalls, heavy boots, a discarded Wehrmacht helmet, and thick gloves before making his way to the giant turbine.

Despite its size, the turbine was finicky, behaving almost like a human being, sulking when something displeased it. He knelt down and pressed his ear to the housing, listening to the irregular sound of the motor.

He soon found the problem. While he fixed it, his thoughts wandered to Roxy and the surprise he was planning for her.

Gradually, his colleagues, who worked at the various locations of the cast steel plant, arrived. Although some occasionally met for a beer, he hadn't really warmed up to them. He missed the close-knit camaraderie of his old workplace, a locomotive workshop in Berlin. He sighed. He never thought he'd miss anything from the war years.

"Hey, Goldmann, are you coming to lunch?" asked an older engineer with a wooden leg.

"Just a minute, as soon as this beauty is up and running again."

"You and your machines," grumbled the other, even as he stood next to David watching curiously. "You've got a knack for it."

"Thanks. All done." David peeled off his gloves and straightened. "I'm starving." One of the perks of working in the British-controlled steel plant was the free meal in the factory canteen. Made all the more valuable because in the second post-war fall, there was hardly any food to buy, even with ration cards.

Over lunch, he finally had the opportunity to talk to his boss. "Murr, I have a favor to ask."

"Let's hear it, Goldmann."

"Could I stay longer tonight? I'd like to use the rubber press and some scraps of fabric."

Murr raised an eyebrow. "What for?"

"I want to make shoes."

"Shoes? Go ahead." Then he hurried off, always in a rush.

All day David thought about his project. While he adjusted valves and repaired pipes, he sketched the shape of the shoes in his mind.

After the shift, with most of the workers gone, he set to work. First, he gathered the materials: rubber scraps from the production of seals, fabric from a pair of torn work pants, thread and thin wire from home.

With the same precision he used when repairing machines, he began to construct a pair of shoes. He made the soles from flexible rubber, which he carefully cut into the correct shape. They had to be soft, flexible, like a second skin. Roxy should still be able to feel the ground through them, yet be protected from cold and dirt, as well as the disapproving looks of other people.

Then he cut the dark blue fabric. He formed eyelets for the laces out of wire and punched them into the fabric. He glued the fabric to the rubber sole and sewed it with strong thread. The sewing was harder than expected, but he persisted.

Near midnight, as he looked at the finished shoes, which only needed laces, Murr came by. "Well, show me your masterpiece."

David pushed them toward him.

Murr took them in his hand and examined them from all sides before bending the sole in the middle. "I get it, times are tight, but why with such a flimsy sole?"

A colleague from the night shift peered over. "Those are supposed to be shoes? They look more like... I don't know. Rubber slippers maybe."

"They're meant to be comfortable." David proudly examined the result of his work in Murr's hand. Indeed, they looked rather strange, even ugly. But David was sure Roxy would love them once she tried them on. That was the only thing that mattered.

"No proper sole, no firm grip," Murr commented, shaking his head. "You can't walk in those."

"My wife prefers to go barefoot," David explained. "These are for winter, when it's too cold outside."

"The things people do." Murr scratched the back of his head. "My wife wouldn't talk to me for a week if I brought home something like that."

"Total waste of time," said another colleague. "Women want proper shoes. With heels and stuff."

David didn't bother to reply. Roxy was different. She was a truly special person and he loved her for it.

When he finally got home way past midnight, Roxy was already asleep. He hid the shoes in his toolbox and slipped under the warm blanket next to her. She murmured something in her sleep and snuggled up to him. Tired but content, David closed his eyes.

The next evening, after dinner, he brought out his surprise.

"I have something for you." He set the shoes on the table.

Roxy stared at him as if he'd placed a dead rat in front of her. "What is that?"

"Shoes. For you."

"You're giving me shoes?" Her voice became unusually shrill. "David, you know very well that I hate shoes."

"These are different," he insisted. "Try them on."

"No." Her eyes flashing with anger, she crossed her arms over her chest. "I don't want shoes. I've walked barefoot my whole life and I'm not going to change that now."

"Roxy, please. The day before yesterday you said you'd try. Just once."

Her shoulders began to shake and he wondered what he'd done wrong. It wasn't like her to have an outburst of anger. "David, you don't understand. Shoes are like... like prison for my feet. I... Goslar..." Tears spilled down her face, and she defiantly wiped away. "In the camp, they forced me to wear wooden clogs. I swore that I would never again..." Her voice broke.

These current mood swings weren't like her, which seriously worried David. He took a step toward her and put his arms around her. She stood stiff as a board in his embrace as if she'd rather be anywhere else in the world than with him. Her rejection pierced his heart.

"I just wanted to make you happy," he said helplessly. "I made them with my own hands."

"You did?" Slowly, her body relaxed.

They stood like that for a few minutes until he tried again. "Please. I made the soles out of very thin rubber. They're as soft as socks, and you're not barefoot."

"Then I guess I'll have to try them on." He believed to hear an amused smile in her voice as she pulled away from him.

"If you don't like them, we'll never talk about it again."

Reluctantly, Roxy sat down and slipped on the left shoe. Surprise flickered across her face. Then she put on the right one.

"They fit like a glove." As she stood up and took a cautious step, her eyes widened. "I can feel the ground."

"Of course. That was the idea," David replied proudly.

She took a few more steps, jumped up, crouched down, and flexed the soles of her feet in all directions. "It's like wearing thick socks."

David beamed. "Do you like them?"

She didn't answer, instead she twirled, climbed onto a chair, jumped down, walked across the bed, and stood on her tiptoes.

"Well?" David could barely stand the suspense.

"They're... perfect." Roxy threw her arms around his neck. "How did you do this?"

"With a lot of patience and a few sleepless hours," he laughed. "But it was worth it. Now you can go to job interviews without people giving you the side-eye."

Roxy kissed him passionately. "You're the best man in the world," she murmured against his lips. "No one has ever given me anything so wonderful."

CHAPTER 9

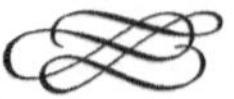

Roxy sat on the hard wooden bench in Essen City Hall and waited. It was already her third visit. Finally, she'd gathered all the necessary forms, signatures, and documents and could submit the application for travel permits from the British zone to the Western sectors of Berlin for herself and David.

The large entrance hall was filled with the echo of hurried footsteps and muffled conversations. The smell of wet wool, ink, and tobacco hung in the air. Officials hurried through the corridors carrying stacks of files, while citizens waited patiently on the benches.

"Have a seat. It'll take a while," the clerk had said. That had been two hours ago. People came and went. Only Roxy seemed to have been forgotten. Just as she was about to knock and ask about the status of her application, a door further down the corridor opened.

A man stepped out, a leather briefcase under his arm. Something about the way he moved caught her attention. She tilted her head, watching as he said goodbye to someone inside.

His coat was as shabby as everyone's, except the British. His hat was pulled low over his face. He wasn't young anymore, yet he stood very straight and radiated an authority she recognized from another time.

Roxy looked down at her English book, forcing herself to focus on memorizing the vocabulary. But the man magnetically drew her gaze, as if he exerted a secret power over her she couldn't break.

He walked down the corridor with measured steps. Her gaze dropped to his shoes, clicking softly on the stone floor. They were worn, yet impeccably clean, almost shiny. The image of polished boots flashed through her mind and an icy chill settled in her bones.

As he walked past her, she smelled his aftershave—a tart, spicy scent that sent her insides into an inexplicable turmoil. She turned her head to watch his back. The squared shoulders, the upright gait. Suddenly, the hairs on the back of her neck stood on end.

At the end of the corridor, the man stopped and spoke to someone. Although she couldn't make out the words, the sound of his voice made her blood run cold.

Her mind flashed back as if it had only been yesterday. She'd been standing at a safe distance when a group of new arrivals entered the camp.

"You are my prisoners, and I decide whether you live or die."

As if pulled by invisible strings, Roxy stood up and followed him through the hallway, her eyes fixed on his back. It was impossible. The Red Cross had confirmed Goslar's death. Killed in action near Küstrin, confirmed by comrades.

But that voice... that damned voice she'd never forget even if she lived to a hundred years.

Pretty pendant. Let me see it. Goosebumps had risen on Roxy's arms. *You'll never see this pendant again.* Then he'd pocketed her beloved necklace and had assigned Roxy to the Sonderkommando as punishment. The horrible memories she'd so carefully locked away deep in her soul burst forth and choked her. Desperately she fought against the black vortex that threatened to pull her under.

A door at the other end of the corridor opened and the secretary called out, "Roxana Goldmann. Your travel permit is ready."

Roxy ignored her. She had to follow this man. She had to be sure. He was heading down the stairs and would soon disappear forever if she didn't act now. Seconds later, he vanished from sight.

"Frau Goldmann!" the secretary called.

Roxy turned her head, even as her feet carried her toward the stairs. "I have to go. I'll come back later." She hurried down, catching a glimpse of Goslar leaving the building.

If it was him—and she was sure it was—she had to confront him. He should finally pay for his actions. Ignoring the disapproving glances of those waiting, she cut through the hall. Finally outside, she spotted Goslar turning the corner.

In her new shoes, she followed him. He walked without a care in the world, his hands clasped behind his back. Roxy snorted; this man was cold and calculating. He divided humanity into two groups: masters and slaves. Feelings were foreign to him, at least when it came to slaves. He'd proven this again and again in Belzec, imposing draconian punishments for the slightest infraction or shooting prisoners in cold blood because they'd stepped across an imaginary line on the ground.

A wave of hatred boiled up inside Roxy. She imagined her fingers tightening around his neck and squeezing until he gasped for air and begged for his life. Then she pushed the deeply satisfying fantasy aside while she concentrated on staying out of sight.

Since childhood, she'd perfected the ability to remain unnoticed. For David's sake, she tried not to suddenly appear at his side and startle him. For tailing Goslar however, she kept a respectful distance, using house corners, piles of rubble, and parked cars as cover.

Goslar turned into a quiet residential street. The terraced houses with tiny front yards were mostly intact. The flower beds of the pre-war years had given way to more practical produce: beetroot, savoy cabbage, and kale. Here and there, lamb's lettuce peeked out of the ground.

He stopped in front of one of the houses, fumbled for a key, and unlocked the door. Before entering, he turned and looked down the street. Roxy ducked behind a wall just in time, her heart pounding.

Finally, she caught a glimpse of his face. He no longer wore a military-style short haircut; instead, his now brown hair fell in a gentle wave over his forehead. His eyebrows and cheeks didn't match her memory either. But his eyes... those cold, merciless eyes hadn't changed. Neither had the narrow, straight lips that had pronounced death sentences without any emotion. There was no doubt.

This man was Goslar.

Roxy waited until the lights in the house came on before creeping closer. The nameplate on the mailbox read: Erwin Krüger.

Her whole body trembled under the force of her emotions. For a few seconds she stared spellbound at the name. She'd been wrong. This man wasn't Goslar.

Lost in her thoughts, she realized too late that the curtain was moving. A beam of light fell on the path from the garden gate to the house. After her head snapped up, she froze. Those features. They were so familiar and yet so strange. Instinctively, she ducked down, so she wouldn't be spotted.

Quickly, she stepped out of the light into the darkness and watched as Goslar—or Krüger—pivoted his head back and forth as if searching for her. Then he shrugged, stepped away from the window, and drew the heavy blackout curtains, which must have been left over from wartime.

Deeply shaken, Roxy set off for home. Her thoughts spun, trying to make sense of what she'd witnessed. Halfway there, she remembered that she had left the city hall in a hurry without picking up the travel permits. Automatically, her feet changed direction while images from the past swirled around in her head.

Marek sacrificing his life so she could escape. Dead bodies alongside the camp road. Collecting them each morning. Goslar on horseback, whip in hand. His cold, emotionless gaze.

It was him, definitely. Or was it? The evidence suggested otherwise. He'd changed his appearance and called himself Erwin Krüger, but deep down Roxy knew it was him. Her eyes might be fooled, but her body had recognized him.

Shortly before she reached the city hall, everything clicked into place: a new name for a new life. How long had it been? How long had he been leading this respectable bourgeois life while his victims suffered the consequences of his crimes and thirsted for justice?

At the city hall the doorman balked because the building was about to close.

"Please, I was here before. I just need to pick something up quickly," she pleaded with him.

"Fine. I'll lock up in ten minutes. Then you have to be gone."

"Thank you so much." Roxy flashed him a grateful smile.

The secretary eyed her sternly. "You can't just run off and expect us to—"

"I'm sorry," Roxy interrupted her. "It was an emergency. Please, can you give me the travel permit?"

Grumbling, the woman handed her the form. As Roxy signed the receipt, her shaking hand distorted the letters. Again, the secretary cast her a stern look.

On the way home, Roxy struggled with conflicting emotions. Part of her wanted to run straight to David and tell him everything. The other part—the one that had survived years in hiding—warned her to be cautious. She needed time to think.

CHAPTER 10

In the darkness of his living room, Erwin Krüger peered out through a pinhole in the curtain. Down at the intersection, a single streetlight cast a pale glow on the tree stumps, whose branches had been turned into firewood last winter. Nothing moved. Yet he couldn't shake the feeling he was being watched.

Ever since he'd left city hall, unease had been gnawing at him. Several times he'd turned around, stopped, and stared into the twilight, listening. But there'd been nothing. No footsteps behind him, no suspicious figures in the shadows. And yet...

"Paranoia," he muttered, stepping away from the window. "Bloody paranoia."

Taking the new job had been a risky move: out of the anonymous life of a day laborer into the public eye of city government. It had been necessary because he needed to earn money.

Of course, he'd been prepared for Germany's downfall. He'd stashed gold and jewelry belonging to the murdered gypsies, as well as personal keepsakes, with several comrades loyal to the cause. But these savings were depleted. False certificates, the dentist, this house—creating a new identity was expensive.

At the same time, his position meant visibility, and that was dangerous. Despite his altered face, the new name, and the carefully constructed biography, someone might still recognize him.

He lit a cigarette, drawing the smoke deep into his lungs. In Belzec, he had been a god ruling over life and death. With the collapse of the regime, everything had changed. As he considered the past, the tobacco calmed him.

Life was unfair! He, the once highly paid lawyer with a brilliant SS career, had been demoted to an insignificant clerk with no decision-making authority.

One last glance through the pinhole confirmed what he already knew: there was no one out there. The street lay peaceful in the dim glow of the streetlight. A dog barked in the distance, but otherwise everything was quiet.

Krüger stubbed out the cigarette in the ashtray before reaching for his coat. He craved human company, a few beers, and conversations that would distract him from his nerves. At Zur Eiche, a nondescript pub on the outskirts of town, men like him regularly gathered. Some had new names, but all kept to the same old convictions.

The cold night air cleared his head. He crossed the city with quick steps, turning into carefully selected side streets. He never took the same route twice in a row. These precautions had become second nature to him.

Zur Eiche was located in a basement beneath a watchmaker's shop. The neon sign flickered as Krüger entered.

"Hartmut," greeted the owner, a former Gestapo man and friend of his who was missing two fingers.

"I'm Erwin now, don't forget that."

"Sorry, old habit."

"The others don't know my old name, and that's how it should stay." Erwin lowered his voice. "I think I'm being watched."

"You and your paranoia. Who's supposed to be watching you, a city clerk?" Gunther replied.

Smoke hung thick in the low-ceilinged room. Several middle-aged men sat at the tables. Empty beer glasses and the jovial mood suggested they had been there awhile already.

"Erwin! Over here!" Heinrich Brandt waved to him. It was a mystery to Erwin how he'd managed to continue running his family's textile factory, since the occupiers knew he'd worked in the department organizing the deportations from the Rhineland.

"Evening," Erwin greeted the group. Before he could even order, Gunther placed a glass of beer in front of him.

It still seemed absurd to him that the seasoned, admittedly sometimes brutal, Gestapo interrogation expert ended up a pub owner. But these days, you couldn't choose your position if you had a past to hide

"How are things going at city hall?" Bernd asked.

"Frustrating." Erwin took a large sip. "I sit there all day helping these parasites grab our property."

"At least you're right in the thick of it," said Gunther, who'd joined them. "You know who's coming back, who's filing claims. That's valuable information."

The others nodded in agreement. "The time will come when we can put that information to good use. When the occupiers finally leave and we take our country back."

"That'll take a while," Erwin muttered. "They're getting very comfortable here. And the people..." He grimaced in disgust. "The people are groveling at their feet."

"Understandable after the brainwashing," Bernd interjected. "That'll change. The Russians scare them, you can feel it. Soon they'll need us again."

The men nodded. It was a familiar ritual, these conversations about a future in which Germany would regain its glory. Erwin listened with only half an ear as his thoughts wandered to the eerie feeling he'd had that afternoon.

"Do any of you feel like you're being watched?" he asked abruptly.

The others looked at him in surprise. Bernd said, "No. Do you?"

Erwin rubbed his cheek, which still felt unfamiliar without his molars. "Today I had the feeling I was being followed."

"Probably just a thief sizing you up."

Erwin flinched and made a mental note to hide any documents referring to his true identity.

"You're jumpy," said Gunther. "That's normal. If you want, I'll tail you for a few days, just to be sure."

"No need," Erwin protested, not wanting to show weakness in front of his comrades. They were probably right, and he'd imagined it.

Bernd leaned forward. "The danger doesn't come from pursuers on the street, but from traitors. From people who think they recognize you and report you to the occupiers."

The conversation was interrupted when the door opened and two women entered. They sat down at the bar and each ordered a shot of schnapps.

"Those women are Sonja and Karola," Bernd explained quietly. "Both war widows. They come here almost every week. Have a shot of schnapps and go home."

Erwin studied them with interest. The dark-haired one wasn't his type, but the other one... In her late thirties, carefully styled blonde hair. Thin from hard years, but still busty and with healthy, wide hips.

It had been a long time since he'd been interested in a woman. The years of hiding had called for other priorities. That had changed with his new identity and job.

"Excuse me for a moment," he said and stood up.

He went to the bar and sat down on the stool next to the blonde woman, introducing himself, "Good evening, ladies. Erwin Krüger."

"Sonja Schenk." Her soft voice featured a Rhineland accent. She offered him a well-groomed hand. "And this is my sister-in-law Karola Gauss."

The dark-haired woman nodded shyly. "Pleased to meet you."

"May I buy you a drink?" Erwin asked gallantly.

Sonja hesitated for a moment, before she nodded. "Why not? It's been a long time since anyone bought us anything."

He signaled to Gunther to bring three schnapps. "These are hard times for all of us."

"You can say that again." Sonja downed the schnapps in one gulp. "But you're probably not interested in my story."

"Yes, I am." Erwin signaled Gunter for another round. "We've all suffered terrible losses. Sometimes it helps to talk."

Sonja looked at him, her gaze intense. "You were at the front?"

"Yes. Wehrmacht." The lie came easy. "Then Russian captivity. I've only arrived in Essen at the beginning of the year."

"I'm sorry to hear that." Her voice warmed. "At least you came home. Many weren't so lucky."

"Luck is relative," said Erwin. "Sometimes I wonder if the dead aren't the luckier ones. They don't have to see what's become of our country."

Sonja nodded thoughtfully. "I believed in the Führer at the beginning. Truly believed. Germany was supposed to become great again. We were supposed to find our place in the world, be respected by other nations." She stared into her glass. "Then came the war, the bombs, it was one big lie."

"The Führer was a good man," Erwin said cautiously. "But he was surrounded by traitors and incompetents. That was his downfall."

Sonja shot him a sharp look. "Do you really believe that? That he didn't want all this..." She made a sweeping gesture with her hand. "...the camps and all that?"

The question was leaning toward dangerous grounds. Erwin didn't know if he could trust her, so he stuck to platitudes. "The Führer loved his people above all else. In the end, he even died for us."

She tilted her head, disillusionment reflected in her eyes. "I don't know. His suicide was cowardly; he shied away from the consequences of his actions."

"The Führer wasn't a coward!" Erwin snapped, then immediately lowered his voice again. "I'm sorry. My nerves aren't the best after the terrible experiences in captivity."

"Understandable." She sighed. "My husband didn't come back. Neither did my two sons."

Her sister-in-law cut in, "I thought we agreed to let the past rest. It's time to look forward."

"That's easy for you to say." Sonja sounded bitter.

Erwin seized the opportunity to make a move. "May I invite you to dinner? I know a very nice little restaurant."

Sonja sought her sister-in-law's gaze before nodding. "Why not? It's time to look forward, isn't it?"

They settled on a place and time, then the women said goodbye. Erwin watched Sonja leave the bar, feeling something like joy for the first time in a long while.

Once he returned to his table, the others grinned at him.

"Any luck?" asked Bernd.

"We'll see," Krüger replied. "It's time to let the past rest, isn't it?"

"Well, if you say so." Gunther returned with a round of schnapps and raised his glass. "To beautiful women."

CHAPTER 11

David arrived home to a pitch dark apartment. He hung his coat on its hook, put on his cozy house slippers, and shuffled into the living room. When he turned on the light, he spotted Roxy curled in the patched plush armchair with her knees pulled up.

"Oh, hello David. I didn't hear you come in."

Immediately, alarm bells shrilled in his head. Roxy never missed a thing. She had eyes like an eagle, ears like a lynx, and an almost uncanny ability to perceive things that remained hidden to others.

"Are you sick?" He kissed her on the lips, but she didn't kiss him back like she usually did.

"No. Just tired."

"Have you eaten?" He glanced at the empty stove, which wasn't radiating its usual warmth.

"No."

"Are we out of coal?"

"No. Why?" She asked puzzled.

"Because the stove is cold."

"I'm sorry, I must have forgotten." She rubbed her forehead.

His worry deepened. Roxy never forgot her chores. She was

conscientious to a fault. He was about to stoke the stove when he noticed a piece of paper on the kitchen table. "What's that?"

"Our travel permit." Instead of waving the document at him, beaming with joy, she looked like someone died.

"Aren't you happy?" he asked.

"Yes, I am." Her voice sounded strangely hoarse.

David knelt down next to the armchair and studied her expression. "What's wrong?"

"Nothing." She shook her head mechanically. "I'm just tired."

He didn't buy it. He knew Roxy well enough to know when she was lying. But he also knew that pushing her wouldn't help. "I'll call my father and let him know. Do you want to walk with me to the phone booth?"

She looked up as if she were seeing him for the first time.

"A little fresh air will do us both good."

"Maybe." She slowly got up, put on her jacket, and slipped into the shoes he'd made.

The nearest public phone was a fifteen-minute walk from their apartment. David had scraped together every coin he could find—a long-distance call to Berlin was expensive. As they walked through the streets, he tried several times to strike up a conversation, but Roxy responded only in monosyllables.

As they reached the phone booth, David looked at his watch; his father usually worked late and would still be at Falkenstein Bank. He gave the operator the number and waited patiently for the connection. Roxy stayed outside.

"Heinrich Goldmann."

"Father, it's David."

"David! What a surprise." Joy warmed his father's voice. "Is everything all right?"

"Yes, everything's fine with us. I just wanted to confirm that we're coming to visit over Christmas. Roxy finally got our travel permit today."

"That's wonderful! Your mother will be delighted. She misses you very much."

David smiled. His mother was the backbone of the family. She'd fiercely protected her Jewish husband and their children from the worst during Hitler's reign. "How are you all? How's work?"

"Good, very good indeed. The bank is recovering. However, Julius isn't in good health. His leg still troubles him, and it gets worse in the cold season. I'm worried about him."

"I'm sorry to hear that." David's parents had hauled Julius Falkenstein, the bank's former and current owner, in a handcart with a broken thigh through bombed-out Berlin. It had taken them two days to make it to Aunt Felicitas' mansion in Oranienburg. David's aunt had sheltered the entire family and the Falkensteins there during the last weeks of the war. "And Mother?"

"She's working herself half to death at the reception camp at Anhalter Bahnhof, helping returning soldiers. You know her, she can't sit still, always has to be on the move."

"That sounds just like her." A wave of longing washed over him. He missed his family more than he wanted to admit. "Tell her Roxy and I can't wait to finally visit you."

"I will. How are things going with you? Has Roxy found a job?"

"Unfortunately not." David looked at his wife as she leaned against the glass pane. "It's not easy for her."

"The prejudices against Roma are deeply ingrained in people's minds." Heinrich sighed. "Shall I ask Julius for a favor? He has connections in practically every corner of Germany."

"That's a generous offer, but I'll have to ask her first," David hedged.

Heinrich chuckled. "She's a headstrong woman. Let's talk about it in person when you're here."

"I'm running out of coins anyway. We'll call when we know our exact arrival date."

"See you soon."

David watched Roxy's back for a few seconds before hanging

up too. Her rigid posture revealed that something was bothering her. He pushed open the door of the phone booth. "My parents are excited to see us again."

"That's nice." Unusually quiet, she walked beside him until her hand found his. "David, I have to tell you something."

Finally. To give her the space she needed, he continued walking without turning to face her. "I'm listening."

"Today at city hall... I saw someone." She drew a deep breath. "Goslar isn't dead."

David's stomach clenched. "What?"

"He works there. In the city administration. He calls himself Erwin Krüger, but I'm sure it's him." The words poured out of her. "I followed him, David. To his house. It's him. I'm sure of it."

David stopped and searched her face. An icy wind blew through his heart. "Did he recognize you?"

"No, I was careful. He didn't see me. Although..." She frowned. "I think he sensed he was being followed because he kept turning around."

"Are you sure he didn't see you?" The chill penetrated deep into his bones. If this Erwin Krüger really was Goslar, the man was dangerous. He was a cold-blooded murderer, who would do anything to keep his new identity from being exposed. Roxy was in grave danger.

"David, if I don't want to be seen, no one will spot me. You should know that by now." At last she smiled, crooked and fierce.

He nodded, because he'd been startled by her skill more than once. However, it didn't particularly reassure him. "And you're sure it's him?"

"His face looks different, but his posture is the same. And his voice, David! I'd recognize it among a thousand others. It's him." She leaned against him. "What do we do now?"

Despite the danger, his heart leapt because she'd said "we." Although he'd fallen in love with her at first sight, back then on that train car, their relationship had been rocky at first. This was largely due to Roxy's experiences in the camp and her inability to trust another person.

"You have to report him," he finally said. "To the British. Preferably tomorrow."

"With what proof?" Roxy laughed bitterly. "I'm an uneducated Roma woman who claims to have recognized a supposedly dead SS man. Who will believe me?"

"You were in his camp. You know details only someone who was there would know."

"Details anyone can read in the newspaper." Roxy shook her head. "No, David. It's not that simple."

They continued walking while David's thoughts raced. "You're right. It's going to be difficult. But you have to try anyway. Let's go together. I'll support you."

"What if they don't believe me? Then he'll be warned and disappear. For good."

"We have to take that risk, then at least we'll have tried."

Roxy avoided his gaze. "I can't bear the thought of him living as if nothing ever happened. The deaths of practically my whole family are on his conscience."

On their doorstep he asked, "Promise me you won't do anything rash. That you'll talk to me first."

Roxy met his eyes for a long moment. He noticed the struggle between reason and the thirst for revenge. Finally, she nodded slowly. "I promise. I'll go to the British tomorrow and report him."

CHAPTER 12

Standing in front of the austere brick building of the British military administration, Roxy took a deep breath. The Union Jack hung limp in the cold morning wind, and the two guards eyed her suspiciously. She was wearing her best dress, David's homemade shoes, and had braided her hair into a single plait.

"I want to report a war criminal," she said to one of the guards in her best English.

The soldier looked her up and down. "Wait here," he ordered curtly and disappeared into the building. After a while, he returned and asked her to follow him. Her heart pounding, Roxy followed him, the clatter of typewriters seeping through the closed doors.

He knocked on a door marked "Sergeant Wilson" and waited for the "Come in" before opening the door and saying to the burly man behind the desk, "This is the woman who wants to denounce a war criminal."

"Thank you." Sergeant Wilson motioned for Roxy to sit down in a chair facing his desk while the guard closed the door behind her.

Roxy looked at the sergeant with fascination.

Wilson noticed and asked in excellent German, "Haven't you ever seen a black man before?"

"Not up close." She knew it was rude to stare, but couldn't force herself to look away.

"I'm just a person, like you."

His uniform triggered memories she'd rather forget. Tears welled up in her eyes, followed by a hot flash that slowly ran from her head to her feet—what the hell was wrong with her? "Certainly not like me."

A hurt expression she knew too well flickered across his face. "You still believe that Germans are superior? Do you think I'm subhuman just because I'm black?"

Dazed, Roxy shook her head. Her mind seemed to fill with fog as she tried to figure out a way to get herself out of this mess. "I'm sorry. No. I don't. I was thinking that nobody deserves to be treated the way I was."

"Oh, really?" He quirked one eyebrow. "What awful things happened to you? Besides, you Germans brought this on yourselves..." He gestured toward the window, through which the ruins on the other side of the street were visible. "...after all, you started the war."

Roxy glared at him but bit back a reply because she didn't want to antagonize him.

Wilson, on the other hand, seemed to have been waiting for an opportunity to vent. "I was there when we liberated Bergen-Belsen. It was pure horror. That day was the worst day of my life. People reduced to skeletons, apathetic from hunger, barely resembling human beings. Thousands of them. Lice-infested, dirty figures, more dead than alive. Compared to that, everything you're complaining about is a speck of dust."

She stared open-mouthed while he talked himself into a rage.

"Every German is complicit. You all turned a blind eye and kept your mouths shut. Nobody rebelled. But now suddenly nobody was a Nazi, nobody knew one, and everyone acts shocked about the atrocities. They claim they knew nothing, noticed nothing, saw or heard nothing. Just like the three monkeys."

Roxy frowned at the reference, wondering why he'd brought monkeys into the conversation, but she didn't dare interrupt his flow of words.

"Have you suddenly had a pang of conscience and want to wash your hands by reporting a war criminal? Did you also denounce your neighbors to the Gestapo? Did you enjoy seeing these people tortured? Were you involved yourself? Are you perhaps trying to cover up your involvement with this report?"

"Now wait a minute!" Roxy had heard enough. Occupier or not, she wasn't going to let this man insult her. "You don't know me."

Wilson's eyes narrowed to slits and he looked as if he wanted to pounce on her. She instinctively pressed herself against the back of the chair, her eyes searching for cover to dive behind if she had to run.

"I know enough Germans to know what kind of people you are." He curled his lips mockingly. "But maybe you're the exception. Let me guess, you led a resistance organization?"

"No, I didn't," Roxy said quietly. She had been too busy fighting for her survival.

"There we have it. A follower who closed her eyes to the Nazis' atrocities." He accused her with triumph in his voice.

She shook her head. "I was many things, but I certainly wasn't a follower."

Something in her voice made him pause. A little calmer, he asked, "What did you do during the war, then?"

"You really want to know? It might shake your conviction that all Germans are bad."

"Or it could confirm my opinion." He leaned back, folding his hands in front of his stomach. "Try me."

Roxy's gaze turned flat. "If you really want to know: every morning I collected the dead, pulled out their gold teeth, and hauled them by cart to a mass grave. I also rummaged through their possessions and sorted them for reuse."

He grew ashen beneath his dark skin. "You were in a camp?"

"In a Gypsy camp, to be precise." She tilted her head. "There was no happy ending for us, as you so nicely put it. We Roma are still marginalized, spat on, and mocked."

"I'm sorry to hear that."

"You don't have to be. It's not your fault," she said generously.

Silence hung between them until he said, "I think I owe you an apology. I was a little too quick to judge."

"Put a sponge over it."

Puzzled, he raised his eyebrows.

"That means. Let's forget about it." Roxy took a deep breath. "I'm here because I want to report my former camp commandant."

"That's big. I'll have to consult my superior." He picked up the phone and dialed a number. Shortly after, the door opened and for the second time Roxy stared with fascination at a uniformed man.

"Lieutenant Morrison, this is Roxana Goldmann. She wants to report a war criminal," Wilson explained to his superior.

"Mo..." Roxy swallowed hard under his warning gaze. "Lieutenant Morrison."

His face showed no trace of recognition as he looked at her.

"Wilson, please fetch another chair." As soon as his subordinate had slipped into the next room, Mo hissed at Roxy, "We don't know each other. We've never met. Understood?"

She nodded. "Of course, Lieutenant."

Wilson returned and sat down next to his boss, opposite Roxy.

Morrison led the conversation. "Why didn't you go to the German police?"

A lump formed in Roxy's throat. She cleared her throat before answering, "The man works for the city administration. I was afraid. That's why I came straight to you."

Morrison frowned. "Tell me what you know."

Roxy took a deep breath. "He calls himself Erwin Krüger now, but his real name is Hartmut Goslar. He was camp commandant in Belzec."

"Frau Goldmann was an inmate in the Gypsy camp there," Wilson explained.

"A Gypsy." Morrison rubbed his chin. "That explains a lot."

Roxy clenched her teeth in anger.

"Please, tell us your story," Wilson urged her kindly.

She shot him a grateful gaze, and he winked in response. Encouraged by the silent support, she described how she'd run into Goslar by chance.

Morrison took notes while watching her closely. Once she'd finished, he looked her straight in the eye. "Thank you very much, Frau Goldmann. If what you say is true, we are indeed dealing with a serious case. In such cases, we don't investigate it ourselves, but refer it to a special unit."

"Of course it's true," she burst out.

"What I meant to say is that the case is complicated. Nobody denies that Hartmut Goslar is a war criminal. Erwin Krüger, on the other hand works in the city administration. Thus he has undergone a denazification along with a thorough vetting, proving he's an upstanding citizen with a clean record."

"They're one and the same person," Roxy growled.

"Well, that's what we need to determine. We can't prejudge someone based on a single statement."

Blood boiled in her veins. Did Morrison mean this criminal's word still carried more weight than hers? Had nothing changed?

Sergeant Wilson seemed to sense her tumbling thoughts. "Frau Goldmann, we just want to make sure the case is watertight, and Goslar is put behind bars. To do that, we need evidence."

"I recognized him, even though he has slightly changed his appearance. That's the only proof I can offer."

"That alone is very thin," Morrison interrupted. "Do you have documents? Photographs? Witnesses?"

Roxy's hope began to fade. "Hardly anyone survived, you know that yourself."

"Krüger will deny being the Goslar we're looking for. Then it's your word against his. That's not enough."

Wilson glanced at his superior in surprise. He'd obviously expected a different reaction.

"I know it's him," Roxy insisted. "I'd recognize that voice anywhere."

"I'm sorry, Frau Goldmann, but without concrete evidence, there's nothing we can do," Morrison said coolly.

The disappointment hit Roxy like a punch to her gut. "So you're not going to do anything? He murdered hundreds of people, and you're letting him go?"

Morrison sighed. "It's not that simple. After the war, many people disappeared and assumed new identities. We investigate every credible allegation, but we need evidence."

"My entire family is dead!" Roxy's voice cracked. "He shot people for fun because they stepped across an imaginary line on the ground. And now I'm supposed to just forget? Let the past rest?"

Wilson looked stricken, but Morrison remained impassive. "I understand your anger, Frau Goldmann. But we need evidence. Come back when you have some."

Deeply disillusioned, Roxy reached for the wooden horse pendant around her neck. She instantly calmed down. The next moment an idea struck her. She took off the necklace and held it out to Morrison. "Goslar took this pendant from me at the camp."

Morrison turned pale as a sheet. "That proves nothing." Hectic red spots bloomed on his cheek as he turned to Wilson.

"Something just occurred to me. Fetch the Henderson file. That might help us."

"Sir, of course," Wilson replied in surprise, stood up, and left the room.

As soon as the door shut behind him, Morrison's demeanor changed. He leaned back, eyeing Roxy with a blank expression. "You should never be nice to anyone, it just comes back and bites you in the ass, Lola."

Roxy took a deep breath. "That's why you won't pursue my report?"

Morrison rubbed his chin. "This case is complicated. If my superiors find out that I'm trading on the black market, I'll lose my job. I might even go to prison."

Roxy's eyes widened. "You're willing to let a ruthless mass murderer roam free to save your own skin?"

"The Nazi era is over. He can't hurt people anymore," Morrison said.

"So he won't be held accountable for his crimes? Is that fair?" Anger snaked up her spine. "You British come along on your high moral horse, acting like you're so much better than us Germans. And then you just look the other way while one of the worst Nazis lives a happy life right under your nose?"

"No, it's not like that... but in this one case, there's nothing I can do. I want to keep my job."

"And I want justice," Roxy replied. "I'll hunt him down. You can bet on that."

"As long as you keep me out of it." His tone turned threatening. "Do not ever mention who gave you that pendant. The word of a Gypsy against that of a British officer. Who do you think they'll believe?"

"You, of course." She squared her shoulders. "Don't worry, Lieutenant Morrison, I'll keep you out of it. The Nazis taught me how to survive under a criminal regime. It seems that nothing has changed since the end of the war except the name of the government."

She ran into Sergeant Wilson in the hallway. "Frau Goldmann, you're leaving already? What about the file?"

"Ask your boss."

"I'm sorry. I've never seen him like this."

"No need to apologize. It's not your fault." Roxy was close to tears of disappointment.

"If there's anything I can do for you, in this case or with something else, let me know." He held out his hand. "You're a better person than most Germans."

"Thank you. It was a pleasure meeting you." Roxy bolted outside before she lost it. On the way home, she thought about David, his faith in the system, his belief that justice was possible.

How could she explain to him the world didn't work that way? That the good guys didn't always win and the bad guys didn't always get punished?

CHAPTER 13

Erwin Krüger picked up the phone and answered it in his usual professional calm. "Krüger, Restitution Department."

"This is Lieutenant Morrison, British Military Administration. I need to speak to you urgently. Can you be in my office in an hour?"

Erwin's pulse quickened. A call from the British was never good. "Of course, Lieutenant. May I ask what this is about?"

"We'll discuss that in person." Morrison hung up.

Erwin stared at the receiver in his hand while his thoughts raced. What did the British want? Had his cover been blown? Had someone become suspicious?

He closed the file on a Jewish antiques dealer that he'd been reviewing and said to Frau Hoffmann, "I have an appointment. If anyone asks, I'm with the British Administration."

"It must be an important case if they're getting involved."

"I'm sorry. I haven't been given any information, only that it's urgent."

An hour later he stepped into Lieutenant Morrison's office. For a second he was taken aback. The Brit was none other than

Mo, uncrowned king of the black market, with whom he'd done many lucrative deals.

"Herr Krüger," Morrison didn't reveal whether he'd recognized him, "a complaint has been filed against you for war crimes."

Krüger's blood ran cold. Summoning superhuman willpower, he kept his composure. "With all due respect, Lieutenant, that is an absurd accusation. I was a simple soldier who..."

Morrison waved him off. "Someone recognized you."

"Someone from my old home town of Königsberg?" Erwin was groping in the dark. Gunther had vetted the real Krüger's background, there was nothing anyone could pin on him. "I have nothing to hide."

Under Morrison's intense scrutiny, he felt alternately hot and cold, but somehow kept a straight face.

Finally, the Brit seemed to come to a conclusion. His hand dropped casually to his hip. "You're actually from Munich, aren't you? You're SS-Hauptsturmführer Hartmut Goslar, former commandant of Belzec."

Erwin's heart skipped a few beats. He forced himself to snort in disbelief. "That's ridiculous. I submitted all my papers for denazification. I was a simple Wehrmacht soldier, classified as category four."

Morrison leaned back. "Look, Herr Krüger, we take such accusations seriously. Camp commandant, that's a as bad as it gets. Normally, we refer such cases to the special unit."

Erwin pricked up his ears.

"But in your case..." Morrison let the pause draw out. "You are a citizen with no criminal record, and the evidence is thin. Very thin."

"Then why did you ask me to come?" Erwin knew an interrogation ploy when he heard one. Morrison wanted something.

The lieutenant stood up and walked to the window. "I'm a

pragmatic man. If you actually were Goslar, you'd have a serious problem."

And so would you. "As I've said, I'm not. Your witness must have mistaken me," Erwin hastened to assure him.

"Perhaps... or not." Morrison turned, locking eyes with him. "Our special unit can find that out. They'll dig into your past, question schoolmates, former neighbors, relatives. A false identity never stands up to careful scrutiny. Even if you were innocent, embarrassing things might come to light, which you'd rather keep under wraps."

"What exactly are you proposing?" Erwin deliberately played naive, although he had a pretty good idea what the Brit wanted.

Morrison returned to his seat. "You are a capable man. I hear you're respected at the city hall, even after a short time. It would be a shame if false accusations destroyed your career, wouldn't it?"

"Indeed." Erwin rubbed his nose as if considering the man's words. It was crystal clear that Mo wanted to save his own skin. "Why are you interested in my career?"

Morrison paused, clearly not having expected questions.

"Let's lay our cards on the table." He took his hand off his hip and placed both palms on the desk. A peace offering. "Your position at city hall can be useful. A lot of information passes across your desk. Valuable objects slated for return. Sometimes these items get lost before they reach their rightful owners."

"That would be abuse of office."

"I'd call it pragmatism." Morrison's smile was cold. "In return, I'll make sure this inconvenient accusation disappears."

Erwin's mind raced. He had no choice, but perhaps he could use the situation to his advantage. "This witness who supposedly recognized me... how credible is he?"

"Very credible. She even has..." Morrison cut himself off.

So it was a woman, interesting. Women were often tougher

than men, once they sank their teeth into something, they rarely let go, much like a trained dog. "What does she have?"

"A wooden horse pendant, which Goslar allegedly took from her."

Erwin's gut twisted. A horse pendant. The memory returned in a rush. A young girl, grimy to the bone, her eyes terrified and defiant at once. A Gypsy without papers who'd been foolish enough to sneak into the camp to join her clan. Into his camp! She'd seriously believed she'd get away with it. He should have shot her then instead of putting her in the Sonderkommando.

And he should have burned that damn pendant instead of selling it on the black market.

"That pendant," he asked, "how come it's in her possession, if Goslar supposedly stole it from her?"

"It's complicated." Morrison shifted uncomfortably.

Erwin leaned forward. "Not for me. This woman..." If only he could summon her name. "You gave it to her, didn't you? It would be interesting to find out what your superiors think about a British officer not only controlling the black market, but also hawking evidence of war crimes."

Morrison turned pale. "That's a lie! Nobody will believe you!"

"Are you sure?" For the first time since the conversation started, Erwin held the upper hand—and the lieutenant knew it. He just had to keep him on edge a little longer, and soon the Brit would be eating out of his hand. "It would be a huge scandal. Even if, contrary to expectations, you're cleared in the end, your reputation would be ruined... and your career."

"Are you threatening me?" Morrison's voice trembled beneath his feigned indignation.

Erwin drank in the smell of fear, a familiar rush lifting him into near euphoria. Power over another human being—how long had it been? The thrill came close to the old days, when prisoners had quaked under his gaze, when he could punish at will, or snuff out a life simply because he felt like it. "Not at all. I think we can be very useful to each other."

Relief washed over Morrison's face. "What do you have in mind?"

"Here's my proposal: you make sure this accusation vanishes. For good. In return, I'll forget our little conversation."

"And the information?"

"You'll get that anyway. As a favor between friends, generously compensated."

"You want money?"

"Life in Germany is expensive as you know. Fifty percent."

"Fifty percent? That's... extortion." Morrison's eyes nearly popped out of his head.

"Or I'll talk to your regional commander."

Morrison seemed to regain his composure; he was an opponent not to be underestimated. "That would incriminate you as well."

"Thirty percent and we remain friends."

"Deal." Morrison stuck out his hand and Erwin shook it.

He already had his hand on the door handle when a thought occurred to him. "By the way, this woman... what's her name again?"

Morrison hesitated. "Why do you want to know?"

"Just out of curiosity. If someone falsely accuses me, I want to know who it is."

"That's not a good idea, Krüger."

"Leave it to me." Erwin's voice grew cold. "You keep your end of the bargain. I'll take care of loose ends."

"Roxana Goldmann."

"Thank you very much. Here's to a fruitful partnership." On the way back to city hall, his mind raced. Roxana. The girl from Belzec. He remembered her now clearly—the odd mixture of defiance and fear when she stood before him. She'd survived. Worse, she'd recognized him. And now she posed a threat to his new life.

His steps quickened. He had to act. First, he'd erase any trace of his past. The few documents referring to Hartmut Goslar had to be destroyed. Next, he'd go to the pub tonight and tell his old comrades that a Gypsy woman was spreading lies about him. They'd help him.

The rest of the day was torture. The letters in the files blurred before his eyes. He read each sentence three times and still couldn't recall what it said.

"Are you all right, Herr Krüger? You look a bit under the weather," asked Frau Hoffmann with concern.

He coughed, touching his forehead. "I'm afraid I'm coming down with a cold. Nothing serious, I hope."

"No wonder, in this dog-cold." She tipped her head. "Go to bed early and make yourself a hot grog, with honey if you have some. It works wonders. It's my grandmother's remedy."

Krüger forced a weak smile. "Thank you, Frau Hoffmann. I'll do that."

"You'll see. you'll feel much better tomorrow."

"Surely, I will." When the workday finally ended, he headed home. A biting wind cut into his face. The image of the Gypsy girl haunted him. He turned around several times, but saw nothing. He called himself a fool. She'd denounced him to the British, so why would she follow him?

Driven by inner restlessness, he reached his house in record time, with the pleasant side effect that he was thoroughly warmed up. Regardless, he put some coal in the stove before setting to work.

After lighting a cigarette, he systematically went through each room, examining every object through an investigator's eyes, looking for a connection to Hartmut Goslar. He found two photos of his wife. He put the photos in the burning stove and watched as the flames flared up, greedily consuming his past.

It was a strange feeling: sad and liberating at once. Nothing would link Erwin Krüger, a law-abiding clerk at the city hall, to the proud SS-Hauptsturmführer he had once been. A sigh escaped his throat.

He'd saved his desk for last. Deeply moved, he leafed through a photo album, the only memento from his time in Belzec. His adjutant had brought it to safety and hidden it in time. There he was resplendent in his SS uniform on horseback at the camp gate. Another photo showed him inspecting the barracks. Surrounded by his subordinates on a team outing. His thumb caressed the photo paper. Those had been good times. It was a shame Germany had lost the war.

His gaze fell on the bulging pocket in the back of the album. His fingers gently slid over the edges before he pulled out the object: the War Merit Cross First Class with Swords, awarded for the exemplary organization of camp contribution to the war economy, along with the accompanying certificate bearing the Führer's signature.

Instantly, he was transported to the height of his career. A festively decorated room, cameramen, a good dozen SS officers eagerly waiting like children at Christmas for their Führer to appear. When he did, the room crackled with nervous tension. Each officer in his gleaming black SS uniform wanted to please the man who loved and ruled his people with stern devotion.

Despite his simple uniform, the Führer outshone them all. He greeted them modestly, gave a short speech, and moved down the line to say a few personal words to each of his loyal followers as he awarded them their medals.

Hartmut Goslar instinctively snapped to attention, reliving his greatest triumph as Hitler stopped before him with the red velvet cushion and pinned the medal with the words: "For loyal service to the Fatherland."

He skimmed the certificate, his eyes lingering on Hitler's signature in rapt devotion. Stern and unyielding, yet at the same time loving toward people. How could he destroy such a testimony of history?

But it had to be done. He silently asked forgiveness as he fed the most precious piece of paper to the flames, which greedily devoured it. A yawning emptiness opened in his chest. Grief for what could have been overwhelmed his entire being.

His fingers twitched, closing around the shiny silver War Merit Cross. Destroying it felt like self-mutilation.

"Just the medal," he muttered. "And the picture on horseback, I'll hide those two."

He carefully removed the photo from the album, tossed the others into the stove and returned the half-empty album to its place. He looked around. There weren't many hiding places. The secret compartment in the massive desk he'd taken over from his landlord was too obvious.

Even up in the attic, things would be found quickly during a search. He paced the rooms until his gaze fell on the toilet tank high on the wall. Nobody would look there.

He wrapped the cross in wax paper, and climbed onto the toilet seat. With some effort, he lowered the bundle into the tank. Now just the photo remained. He prowled the house once more. In the bedroom, a smile tugged at the corners of his mouth. For weeks, a strip of peeling wallpaper next to the wardrobe had been annoying him.

He slid the photo behind the wallpaper and groaned as he pushed against the wardrobe to move it in front of the damaged spot. Unfortunately it didn't budge. So he smoothed the wallpaper with his hands until the unevenness was barely noticeable. Satisfied with his actions, he returned downstairs, lit another cigarette, and mourned the final demise of Hartmut Goslar.

CHAPTER 14

David was hammering at a stubborn copper pipe when a colleague bellowed across the hall. "Goldmann! Your wife is at the gate, says it's urgent."

Startled, David put his tools aside. Roxy had never come to the factory before. He wiped his smudged hands on his overalls —too impatient to go to the washroom and wash his hands with curd soap.

The gatekeeper pointed to the area in front of the factory gate, where Roxy was shifting restlessly from one foot to the other. Even from a distance, David could see her tension-clenched posture. The way her eyes were trained on the street assured him something was wrong.

"Roxy, what are you doing here?" He drew close, noticing her pale complexion. "Is everything okay?"

"No." Her voice was hoarse. "Do you have a moment to talk?"

He glanced at his watch. Half an hour until the end of his shift. "Can it wait until after work?"

She grabbed his arm. "It's important."

David felt her desperation and nodded. "A few minutes. Let

me just tell the gate." He informed the doorman and led her to a huge rock a few meters away. "So, what's going on?"

"I went to the British. They're not going to do anything," she said without preamble. "They won't arrest him."

David's stomach churned. "Why? What did they say?"

"It was Morrison. The lieutenant who's in charge of cases like this." Her voice turned bitter. "Do you know who that is? That's Mo. One of my best black market customers."

"That can't be." David felt the blood drain from his legs.

"Oh, it can. He must have bought the pendant from Goslar and then gave it to me." Roxy laughed without humor. "Now he won't touch the case because he's afraid his illegal business will come to light."

The implication rolled over David like a heavy truck. "That means..."

"That means Goslar walks free. He'll never pay for his crimes." Roxy's voice broke. "They're all in it together, David. The Nazis, the British, everyone."

David pulled her close and held her tight until her trembling subsided. "There must be another way."

"What way exactly?" She pushed away from him. "Morrison is right—it's my word against his. And who is going to believe a Roma?"

David's mind raced. There had to be a solution. Men like Goslar couldn't be allowed get away with this. After glancing at his watch, he said, "I'm sorry I have to get back to work. We'll talk tonight. Promise me you won't do anything rash."

"Don't worry. I'm not doing anything today, and tomorrow I have the job interview at the brewery."

He slapped his forehead. "Damn, I completely forgot that I'm meeting my colleagues for a beer tonight. You want to come along?"

She shook her head. "Thanks, but I'm not in the mood."

"Should I cancel?"

"No. You go ahead. I promise I'll go home and behave."

"You and behave do not go together." David chuckled and kissed her goodbye. But inside, he was agitated.

When he arrived at the smoke-filled corner pub after his shift, Bernhard and four other colleagues were already sitting at their regular table, each with an empty beer glass in front of them.

"Hey, Goldmann!" called Werner, an older machinist. "Perfect timing, we were just about to order another round."

"Great." David grabbed a chair from the next table and joined them. His colleagues talked about soccer and work until the conversation drifted, as it always did, to the food situation.

"It's the black marketeers and profiteers who are to blame," said Bernhard. "They're hoarding the stuff and waiting for better prices."

"Not all of them do that," David replied.

"Oh, really?" Werner eyed him. "Are you one of them?"

"No." David was about to shrug his shoulders and not get involved, but then he said, "Don't tell me you've never bought anything on the black market."

His colleagues shifted sheepishly, because it was nearly impossible to survive without bartering at least occasionally. Bernhard changed the subject: "Trouble at home? What did your wife want at the gate earlier?"

David took a sip of beer to buy time while he mulled about how much to reveal. Finally, he decided on a cautious version of the truth. Most of his colleagues knew David was half-Jewish and would automatically assume that Roxy was Jewish too.

"My wife recently learned that a high-ranking SS man lives here in Essen. Under a false name."

Everyone fell silent.

"What kind of man?" asked Heinrich.

"An SS officer. From the camp where she was."

"Bloody Nazis," muttered Werner. "They're all crawling out of their holes."

"Did she report him?" Klaus, a burly welder, wanted to know.

"Yes, to the British. They won't touch the case. They want proof."

Otto, the oldest, shook his head. "Leave it alone, David. The past is the past. No good comes from tearing old wounds open."

"Excuse me?" Klaus bristled. "You want that piece of filth to get away with it?"

"I just don't want David and his wife to get into trouble," Otto replied. "The old networks still exist, and stories like this one never end well."

Bernhard leaned forward. "What proof do they want?"

"Documents. More eyewitnesses. More than just her testimony."

"Then you'll have to find other survivors," Klaus said. "Your wife can't be the only one."

"How? She doesn't know of anyone else." David frowned. It was quite possible members of Roxy's family had survived. So far, she hadn't felt the urge to look for them.

"The Red Cross," Werner suggested.

"You have to have a name," Bernhard objected.

"I'm sure you can search for the camp she was in. And see how many people came back from there."

"And then knock on strangers' doors? Not smart," Bernhard cautioned.

"The churches maybe," Klaus said. "Many survivors register with parishes. Or the Jewish organizations. There's always a way."

Otto shook his head. "You're making a big mistake. Men like that are dangerous. If he figures out you're on his trail..."

"What can he do?" Klaus interrupted. "We're not at war anymore. The SS has no power now. He can't just shoot someone."

"Can't he?" Otto looked around. "My neighbor tried to

expose an old Nazi. Three weeks later, he was killed in a hit-and-run accident."

For a few seconds, a chilled silence hovered over their table, while the rest of the pub remained cheerfully noisy. David breathed against the pressure squeezing his chest like a vice. Just because Roxy was clever didn't guarantee she could avoid an all-out ambush.

"That guy needs to be put behind bars. If you need help finding witnesses or anything, my brother-in-law's in the police," Klaus offered.

"Thanks. I might take you up on that." David meant it.

"Those swine need to pay," Klaus said firmly. "My father died in Buchenwald."

Otto sighed. "You're all crazy. But if you insist on risking your lives, fine." He finished his beer and stood up. "I don't want anything to do with this."

When David got home, Roxy was already in bed. A cup of cold tea sat on the nightstand next to the lamp. She stared into space, her fingers clasped around the wooden horse.

"I'm back," David said gently.

"How was it?"

"Good. The guys say hello." He sat on the edge of the bed. "We talked about your situation; without mentioning names, of course."

"My situation." Her voice was flat. "Is that what you call it when a murderer walks free?"

David reached for her hand. It was ice cold, in spite of her being tucked under the thick feather duvet. "Can I get under the covers with you? It's freezing."

"I didn't make a fire. We're almost out of coal anyway."

He hoped this winter wouldn't be as bad as the last, when a cold snap in early January had brought Arctic temperatures to Germany, freezing transport routes and collapsing food supply. David hung his clothes over a chair, put on his pajamas, and slid under the warm blanket.

"What are we going to do?" she asked once she was snug in his arms.

"My colleagues think our best chance is to find more witnesses."

"Who? Hardly anyone survived. You know that."

"You survived." He stroked her arm. "There must be others."

"And how are we supposed to find them?" She chuckled bitterly. "Should I place an ad in the newspaper: 'Seeking survivors from Belzec'?"

"Not the worst idea." David grinned. "But too obvious. Goslar mustn't know that you recognized him."

"Why not? It might lure him out of hiding," Roxy turned in his arms, challenging him.

"Or you into an ambush. From the way you described him, he has no conscience. He's capable of anything."

"I can take care of myself." Her shoulders stiffened, signaling to David that he needed to tread carefully. She hated being underestimated.

"I know." He grimaced. "However, you have a tactical advantage if he doesn't know about you, and that'll help you catch him faster."

"Probably." She smiled a tiny bit. "I know you want to shield me from harm, but I'm going to bring Goslar to justice. Whether the British help me or not."

That was exactly what David feared: Roxy taking the law into her own hands. "Promise me we'll try the legal path first."

"Fine by me," she muttered, pouting. "Where are we going to find eyewitnesses?"

"We're visiting my parents over Christmas. We could start there."

"Why Berlin of all places?"

"You were in the Marzahn collection camp before they deported you to Belzec, right?" He'd heard only fragments of her story, never the whole thing, since she hated talking about that time.

Roxy was quiet, lost in thought. Eventually she agreed, "That's right."

"Maybe there are still records. Or someone who remembers."

"To Marzahn." Her voice became shrill. "I swore I'd never go back."

David waited. These moments when the past caught up with her like a dark wave tore at his heart.

"Do you know what the worst thing about it was?" she asked suddenly. "The stench. That awful reeking from the sewage fields. You never got used to it. Even Aunt Gisela's food tasted like feces." Her lips pressed tight as if she were fighting nausea.

David stroked her hair. "It's over, sweetheart."

"I don't know what's wrong with me. I'm not usually so squeamish. But lately I'm on the verge of crying all the time." She shrugged. "It's probably the situation with Goslar, which is weighing on me more than I expected. I thought I'd made peace with it, but suddenly it's all coming back. Every night I dream of the camps."

"You're safe with me. I won't let anyone hurt you," he whispered as he kissed her hair. And for once, she didn't contradict him, the way she usually did when he even hinted that she might need help.

After a while, she spoke again. "Tibor had an older sister, Eva. She was nineteen and heavily pregnant when we were sent to Marzahn. She was one of the few in the clan who managed to find a permanent place to live with an Aryan couple."

"What happened to her?" David asked.

"It didn't do her much good. I saw her later in Belzec. But the baby, Natalie, stayed with the landlords, who passed her off as their own."

"We could start there. Maybe someone from your family contacted them."

Roxy nodded thoughtfully. "I don't remember the street name, but I can find the address blindfolded." Her sense of direction was phenomenal, and after years of living rough, she'd come to know the city by heart.

"Why didn't you ever look for Natalie during your time in Berlin?"

"First, it was still wartime, and second..." Roxy swallowed. "...I didn't want anything to do with my clan anymore."

"When we're at my parents' house, we'll visit Natalie's foster parents. Maybe they can help us. Your clan was so big, someone must have survived."

"Possibly." A faint tremor shook her body and David tightened his grip.

"If you want, I'll come with you."

"We'll see. Let's talk about something else." Her hands slid over his stomach.

"Mmm," David purred. "Let your hands do the talking."

Roxy laughed, climbed on top of him, and pushed up his pajama shirt. Under the touch of her lips on his skin, all his worries melted away. There was nothing in the world but the two of them.

CHAPTER 15

The day before their departure for Berlin, Roxy woke up with a strange feeling. The nausea was back, stronger than before.

David noticed. "Are you okay?"

"Just my stomach." She waved it off. "No wonder, since all you can buy is swill."

David frowned but said nothing. After breakfast—which Roxy had trouble keeping down—he kissed her goodbye. "Good luck at the brewery today."

Roxy had gotten a tip from a customer that the city brewery was desperately looking for a stable hand. She didn't have high hopes, but it was worth a try.

The brewery's massive brick building sat on the edge of town. Even from a distance, the air smelled of yeast. In the walls, the original dark red bricks had been patched with mismatched rubble stones of various sizes to create a colorful mosaic.

"So peaceful," thought Roxy. "Why can't people of different origins and colors be like these stones?"

She walked around the main building to the stables. Yeast smell gave way to the warm, familiar scent of horses. Roxy took a deep breath and felt something relax inside her. She loved horses. They'd always pulled her family's caravans.

She introduced herself to the stable master, Wieland, a burly man with a gray mustache. He looked her up and down, incredulous. "You want to be a stable boy?"

Roxy squared her shoulders. "I'm good with horses."

"No offense, but..." He scratched his head. "You're a woman. And so slight. Being a stable boy is no walk in the park."

"I'm tougher than I look."

"Besides," Herr Wieland continued, as if he hadn't heard, "you're married. Shouldn't you be at home taking care of your husband?"

Roxy's fingers tightened around the strap of her bag. Those prejudices again. Women belonged in the kitchen, not in the stable. "I heard you were desperately looking for a stable boy. I'll be the best you've ever had."

He shook his head. At that moment, an eighteen-year-old backed out of the stable with a harried look on his face. "Boss, I can't get Baldur out of his stall."

"Can't Hans do it?" Wieland growled.

"It's his day off today."

"Have to do everything myself!" Wieland marched off, without paying further attention to Roxy.

Before she could think it through, Roxy sprinted after him, struggling to match his huge strides. "Please. Let me try."

The burly man stopped so abruptly she nearly bumped into him. "You?"

"Please. Give me a chance to prove how good I am with horses."

He sighed. "Fine. But don't come crying to me afterward." In the stable, he pointed to a powerful dun horse in one of the stalls. "Baldur has a mind of his own. Seems he's not in the mood for the midday round."

Roxy approached the stall. The horse whinnied nervously, while prancing restlessly back and forth. A magnificent animal with a shiny coat and a white blaze on its forehead. Almost as beautiful as her favorite horse, Chavo. She pushed the thought aside.

"He bites," Wieland warned. "And kicks. He's gotten three lads already. Better let me do it. I don't want trouble with your husband."

Roxy ignored him. She slowly opened the stall door and stepped inside. Baldur bared his teeth and threw his head back, his ears flat.

"Shh," Roxy cooed, standing just out of reach. "I won't hurt you. I just want to say hello."

His ears twitched, but otherwise he didn't move.

"I get it. You don't like wearing the harness. It's not exactly comfortable, is it?" Everything around her faded until there were only her and Baldur, to whom she spoke as if he understood her. She firmly believed he did. Horses were highly intelligent animals.

Since he seemed to respond to her voice, she continued talking. Low, humming, almost as if she were singing. That was how she had done it with her clan's horses. Just like her father and later her uncle Gottfried had taught her. Suddenly she felt connected to her family, sensed their presence, remembered everything they'd taught her about horses.

Little by little she moved closer. Baldur snorted again, this time it sounded less threatening. Roxy held out her hand and let him sniff her fingers. Then she gently placed her palm on his velvety muzzle.

"Good boy," she murmured. "You're just misunderstood, aren't you? The men here have no patience with you."

Her hands stroked the horse with gentle but firm movements, first on the muzzle, then on the neck. Gradually, Baldur relaxed and his ears pricked up.

"Unbelievable," the stable master said behind her.

Roxy didn't let herself be distracted. Without taking her eyes off Baldur, she reached for the halter with one hand, slipped it on, and led him out of the stall like a lamb.

"Where's the harness?" she asked.

Wieland pointed to a wall where various bridles and harnesses hung. The stable boy took down a collar and a bridle, handing her both without a word. Her fingers worked deftly, checking every strap, every buckle. She'd done this a hundred times, in another life.

"Done," she finally announced, patting the dun horse on the neck.

Wieland came close, inspecting her work. He tugged on the straps and checked the buckles. Finally, he nodded, clearly impressed. "Not bad. Where did you learn that?"

Roxy hesitated. Because the truth would only lead to new problems, she opted for a half-truth. "Before the war, my family owned horses. I grew up with them."

"Hmm." Wieland scratched his chin. "I don't usually hire women." He studied her. "But you've got a way with the horses, I'll give you that."

"Does that mean I got the job?" Roxy's heart leapt.

"As far as I'm concerned, you can start tomorrow."

The joy evaporated. "I... I'm going to Berlin to visit my family over Christmas."

"All right. You'll start on January 1. Six days a week, alternating shifts. Let's go over to the main building right away. They'll handle the paperwork."

As Roxy left the brewery, she felt light as a feather. She'd done it! A proper job, honest work. And something she'd enjoy.

"I got a job!" she announced as soon as she opened the door to her apartment.

David stood at the stove, stirring a pot of potato soup. He turned around, a broad grin on his face. "That's wonderful! I want to hear every detail!"

While they ate, Roxy told him about stubborn Baldur and how she'd calmed him down. Once she finished her story, David got up and danced with her around the apartment. "I'm so proud of you."

"Stop it, David, I'm getting dizzy," she protested, laughing.

"That's something new." He stopped and kissed her. "We'll find a solution for the Goslar mess, too."

"I hope so."

"But tomorrow we're going to visit my family. They can't wait to see us again."

After dinner, Roxy packed their suitcases, since they had to leave for the train station at dawn.

The next morning, the nausea returned. This time it was so bad that she threw up.

"Roxy, this isn't normal," David said. "Maybe you should see a doctor."

"And miss the train to Berlin? No way." She rinsed her mouth, trying to hide the wobbling of her knees. "I'm fine."

But David wouldn't let it go. "If you don't feel better in Berlin, you're going to see a doctor there."

She hated doctors. They reminded her of the time when Marek had threatened the Polish doctor with a knife to force him to stitch Tibor's wound. That was the last time she'd seen her cousin—a few days later, he'd died in the notorious Pawiak prison.

"All right," she said, letting David believe she'd comply.

CHAPTER 16

The station teemed with people. Travelers with heavy suitcases stood everywhere; children tugged at their mothers' skirts. The noise was deafening. David held Roxy's hand tight as they squeezed through the crowd.

"The train should be here any minute," he said, looking for the right track on the notice board.

No sooner had they reached the platform than the old steam locomotive puffed in, patched cars clanking behind. They found a compartment with two free seats, opposite an elderly man with a wooden leg and a woman with two small children.

The train jerked into motion. David watched the scenery slide by—industrial ruins, bombed-out factories, heaps of rubble where homes had once been. Beyond that, flat land.

"Not much has changed," Roxy murmured.

"Oh, but it has," David disagreed. "They're rebuilding. Everywhere."

The journey seemed endless. The train stopped frequently, sometimes in the middle of nowhere, for no apparent reason. Once, they stood still for nearly an hour with nothing to see but bare fields and a destroyed farmhouse. At the border to the

Soviet zone, Russian soldiers boarded the train, checked papers, and searched luggage.

Roxy had her eyes closed, but David could tell from the tension in her body that she wasn't asleep.

"We could have postponed the trip," he whispered.

"No." She opened her eyes. "The sooner we find witnesses, the better."

When they finally arrived in Berlin, a gray blanket of dust and smoke hung over the city. The train station was crammed—refugees carrying bundles, soldiers of all four occupying powers, travelers, businessmen. It was also just as bitterly cold as it had been in Essen.

"God, how I've missed this city," David said.

Roxy looked at him in surprise. "Really? I don't find it particularly inviting."

"It's my home." He took her suitcase in one hand, his in the other, and headed for the exit. "I told my parents not to pick us up because you never know exactly when the train will actually arrive."

At last they stood in front of the four-story townhouse. David let out a low whistle. "Nicely done!"

Most of the holes in the facade had been bricked up, though not plastered, and the roof also appeared to have been repaired. Even the front door, which David had fixed countless times, had been replaced with a brand new one.

"Julius must have used his connections," Roxy remarked.

After the terrible years of persecution, the Falkenstein Bank was returned to Julius shortly after the war and he'd quickly become one of the richest men in Germany again. He'd offered David's father the management of the bank—as well as an apartment in his prestigious townhouse, while he chose to live in his villa on the island of Schwanenwerder.

"Do you remember?" David looked at Roxy from the side. "How you lived undetected in the attic?"

"I didn't want to, because I didn't want to be dependent on

you, but the prospect of a permanent place to sleep was just too tempting." Roxy made a dreamy face.

"You used to climb up the facade and in through the roof window." He'd often watched Roxy in action, but he still couldn't understand how a person was capable of doing such things.

She grinned. "Only in emergencies. Normally, I took the staircase, which was much more convenient."

"You never told me."

"You don't need to know all my little secrets." She nudged him. "Come on, let's go inside."

Before he could ring—the torn-out bell panel had been replaced too—the door flew open and his sister Amelie threw herself into his arms. "Finally. Mother has been beside herself since you said you were coming."

"Sis." David hugged her before holding her at arm's length. "You look just the same as always."

"Only thinner." Amelie freed herself and hugged Roxy, less enthusiastically but just as warmly. "Welcome back. You must tell me all about Essen, what you're doing, how you're doing."

"It's nice to see you again," said Roxy.

"Amelie!" David chided his sister affectionately. "Let's go inside first." He grabbed the two suitcases and entered the stairwell.

"First floor," Amelie called after him, linking arms with Roxy.

"You didn't move back into our old apartment?" David paused just prior to the landing, where the apartment door stood wide open.

"No, that's where I live." She smiled. "It's a company apartment, so to speak, since Julius hired me as an accountant."

"That's wonderful! You didn't tell us anything."

"It's brand new, and I wanted to surprise you with it."

David couldn't follow their chatter anymore because his mother Helga appeared in the doorway. Her hair was almost completely gray, but that didn't make her any less beautiful.

"David!" Helga pulled him into a hug so tight he could hardly breathe. "My boy, finally!"

"Mutter." A lump formed in his throat. He hadn't seen his parents in over two years. Only now, in Helga's arms, did he realize how much he'd missed them.

Next it was Roxy's turn. Helga embraced her daughter-in-law, "Welcome home, Roxy." She stepped back and looked her over. "You've lost so much weight. Don't they feed you anything in the Ruhr region? Not that it's much better here, but dear Edith provides us with plenty of potatoes and vegetables."

"Edith has always been resourceful," said Roxy.

"Mutter, let us go inside first," David scolded in a loving tone.

"I'm so happy to see you again." Helga bustled. "Your father is still at the bank; he always works late. I'll call him right away to tell him you're here." She darted into the living room where the telephone stood. It was a novelty, and yet not really. The Goldmanns had owned one way before Hitler came to power, until they'd been forced to give it up. Just before she reached the telephone table, the kettle whistled in the kitchen. "Oh my goodness! The coffee water. You drink coffee, don't you?" She glanced at Roxy.

"Of course, Helga."

David's mother stood frozen, torn between the kitchen and the telephone. Amelie made the decision for her. "Mutter. Take care of the coffee, I'll call Vater."

Helga nodded and trotted off to the kitchen. Amelie remarked, "I told you she was beside herself with excitement. You'd think the prodigal son had come home."

"Very funny." David poked her in the side. "You better make the call."

The apartment had the same layout as their old one upstairs, yet everything looked different. New, secondhand furniture adorned the living room, curtains hung on the windows, and a small potted Christmas tree stood in the corner.

Helga entered the living room with a tray and busily placed cups and plates on the table. "First, let's have some coffee. I baked a cake; I've been saving sugar for it since David's call. Julius and Edith will be stop by later. They have an early flight to England tomorrow to visit Julius' sister Adriana."

"Frau Gruber and her husband stayed there?" David asked.

"Yes, I think Frau Gruber realized how badly the city had been destroyed during her visit a year and a half ago and prefers to stay at her country estate in England."

"I would do the same if I had the choice," said Roxy.

"Really?" Amelie hung up the phone and joined the conversation. "Wouldn't you miss your home?"

Roxy frowned. "As a child, we never stayed in one place for long. Home for me was always our wagon."

"Right, I completely forgot." Amelie sat down at the table. "Vater will set out in fifteen minutes, he just has to finish something."

"Then we won't wait for him." Helga said it with a weariness that had nothing to do with her guests' arrival and cut the cake.

David's parents loved each other deeply, the difficult years under Hitler's regime bringing them even closer together. Regardless, David detected bitterness in his mother's voice and cast a questioning look at Amelie.

She shook her head and silently formed the word: *Later.*

"Tell us," Helga urged after serving everyone a piece of cake. "How are you? What's new?" Her gaze lingered on Roxy for several seconds.

David reported on the situation in Essen, then the doorbell rang.

"That must be Edith and Julius." Amelie jumped up and opened the door. Shortly afterwards, she ushered them inside.

David flinched at the sight of the sixty-five-year-old man. Despite Nazi persecution, he remembered Julius as a distinguished gentleman who made even shabby, too-large suits look elegant. Today, however, not even the brand-new tailored English suit could lend him that old polish.

Julius Falkenstein was a broken man. Leaning on a cane, he dragged one leg and sank heavily into the upholstered armchair Helga had pulled to the table for him.

On the other hand, his wife Edith, fifteen years his junior, seemed unscathed by the years of deprivation. She looked stunning in a figure-hugging wool suit with matching shoes and handbag.

"David, Roxy, how wonderful to see you again." Edith greeted them with air kisses on both cheeks. "How do you like Essen?"

"Would you like a piece of cake?" Helga interrupted her. "With carrots from your garden."

"I'd love one. And coffee, if you have some," replied Edith.

"I'll put on another pot." Helga was the perfect hostess.

"Edith has turned the entire garden at the Schwanenwerder mansion into vegetable beds. She even had greenhouses built," Amelie explained.

"A very clever idea," Roxy praised. "Where did you get the glass? In Essen, we still have to board up the windows with wood."

"The Americans helped. In return, I supply a certain amount of the harvest to the transit camps for returning soldiers." Edith was positively glowing. For years, she'd been the pretty appendage of her powerful and wealthy husband, but it seemed she'd finally found her calling.

David glanced over at Roxy and saw something like envy in her eyes. How he wished that the job as a stable boy would give her the validation she so desperately needed.

Half an hour later, the door opened again and Heinrich, David's father, entered. He walked slightly stooped, exhausted from long hours at work, but his eyes lit up as he saw his son.

"David, my boy." The hug was short and firm. "And Roxy. Welcome. We've been waiting so long for you to visit."

"The British just recently started issuing travel permits to Berlin," Roxy apologized.

"It's complicated. The tensions with the Russians..." Heinrich waved her off. "Let's not talk about politics."

Long after the cake had been eaten, they were sitting at the table talking. Roxy leaned her head on David's shoulder.

"Are you tired?" he whispered.

"A little."

"Want to lie down?"

"I don't want to be rude," she said modestly.

David raised his voice. "Mutter, where are we going to sleep? Roxy's tired from the trip and would like to rest."

Amelie cast him a startled look, because Roxy was never tired. She had more stamina than anyone.

"I've prepared the guest room for you." Helga jumped up. "Come, Roxy, I'll show you."

Once again, she looked at her daughter-in-law with a strange expression that David couldn't interpret.

After his mother returned alone, David explained, "It's hard on her. She..." He looked around at the familiar faces of the people he loved. He trusted them unconditionally, and yet he was unsure whether he should reveal Roxy's secret.

"Maybe wait until she tells us herself." Helga said with shining eyes.

"No, it's probably better that she's not here." David wrestled with himself. "It's really weighing on her."

"Poor thing, some women have a hard time with it."

David looked at his mother in confusion. "You know she spent a few months in Belzec." He hesitated before blurting out, "Recently she recognized the camp commandant. He lives in Essen."

"Oh my goodness!" Edith and Helga simultaneously covered their mouths with their hands, sheer horror in their eyes.

"I hope she reported that filthy swine," Amelie exclaimed,

earning herself a stern gaze from her mother, who didn't tolerate swear words in her house.

"At least she doesn't have to be afraid of him anymore; he'll be behind bars for many years," Heinrich said, always the voice of reason.

"Unfortunately not," David leaned back dejectedly. "That's the problem."

Amelie narrowed her eyes. "You aren't telling us she didn't report him, are you?"

"She did. But it's complicated. Goslar, that's his name, now calls himself Erich Krüger and works for the city administration."

"A new identity," Julius chimed in. "That's common practice among incriminated Nazis. Those who can't or won't flee to South America create a new life for themselves under a false name, with the help of their old networks." He pushed his glasses up his nose.

Anguish spread through David's bones. "The British don't want to pursue the case. They sent Roxy away, citing lack of evidence."

Amelie's eyes flashed. "That's outrageous! Of course they have to do something!"

"Amelie," Heinrich admonished her. "Calm down."

"No!" She looked as if she wanted to storm off on the spot. "That man is a war criminal. He belongs in court, not in city government!"

"We agree on that, young lady," Julius interjected. "The British reaction is strange. They have special units, which investigate such cases and collect evidence. There must be more to it."

"Don't they believe Roxy because she's a gy… Roma?" asked Edith.

"That may play a role, but the main reason seems to be that Goslar has something on the British officer in charge."

"Blackmail, then." Julius nodded. "I suspected as much. People don't change."

"Does Goslar know Roxy recognized him?" Heinrich asked, his brows furrowed in worry.

"I don't think so. You know how good she is at staying unnoticed."

Amelie nodded. "She's given me quite a scare more than once, appearing out of nowhere. I swear, that woman has the gift of making herself invisible."

"Nonetheless, you shouldn't underestimate him. Goslar is fighting for his life. He'll stop at nothing to get what he wants. He proved that during the Nazi era."

Goosebumps spread across David's back, because Otto had said the same thing. "Are you suggesting that Roxy should drop her case?"

Once again, it was Julius who raised his voice. "Definitely not. But it's a tricky situation. If the officer in charge blocks it, her only option is to go up the chain of command."

"The regional commander doesn't receive German citizens without official positions," Edith objected.

Julius looked over his glasses at his wife. "I was thinking of Adriana."

"What does your sister have to do with it?" Edith asked.

"She's extremely well connected and knows everyone of rank in England. I'm sure she can establish an unofficial contact for Roxy."

"That sounds promising." Helga poured her guests some of the wine the Falkensteins had brought.

"Please don't tell Roxy yet," Julius asked. "I don't want to get her hopes up unnecessarily. We'll be in touch as soon as we return from our trip to England. Until then, she should try to gather evidence."

"Thank you very much, Julius." David was genuinely moved by the helpfulness of this man who'd already done so much for the Goldmanns.

"You're welcome."

CHAPTER 17

E rwin Krüger couldn't concentrate. The words swam on the documents in front of him. The name Roxana Goldmann circled in his head like a vulture over a carcass. She was a threat to his new life.

As soon as Weber left for his lunch break and Frau Hoffmann went to the archive, he picked up the phone and dialed the number for the residents' registration office.

"Krüger, Restitution Department," he introduced himself. "I need an address for a case. Roxana Goldmann, married, maiden name unknown."

"One moment, please," said the woman on the other end. He heard the scraping of a chair, footsteps, then nothing. After endless minutes, her voice sounded. "I've found her. David and Roxana Goldmann. Residing at Krupp-Steele Housing Estate, House 47, Apartment 12."

Krüger jotted down the address. "Thank you very much."

He blew an imaginary strand of hair out of his face. That had been easier than he'd feared. No prying questions, no annoying forms to fill out. His position in the city administration was already paying off.

The Krupp workers' housing estate. Of course. Where else would someone like her live? Certainly not in a respectable neighborhood. He spent the rest of the day feeling restless until he could finally make his way to Gunther's pub.

Gunther was polishing glasses. "Erwin, you're early today. I'm not open yet."

Krüger sat down at the bar. "I need your advice."

"In matters of love? Things not working out with Sonja?"

"On the contrary, we have a date for tonight. It's about my past."

Gunther was one of the few people who knew his real name. He frowned. "Bad?"

"Possibly. A Gypsy woman from the camp recognized me and reported me to the British."

"Shit." Gunther jumped up, and locked the door in a flash. "You have to get out of the country right now. I can—"

"Wait. The British officer refused to file the complaint. He sent her home."

Gunther's eyes narrowed to slits. "For what reason?"

"Let's just say he and I have done business from time to time that his superiors can't know about."

Gunther grinned. "Well done. A little blackmail often goes a long way. Still, you have to be careful. These Gypsies are like leeches—once they've latched on, they won't let go."

Krüger took a sip of the beer Gunther had set down for him. "That's what I feared. I got her address."

"Clever. Pay her a visit. Scare her. See how she reacts."

"I don't know. If I confront her, I can't deny it anymore."

Gunther shook his head. "God, how can you be so naive? That bitch is a walking time bomb. Even if you have the Brit in your pocket, he can be replaced at any time. You know how high the turnover rate is among the occupiers; they can't get back to their beloved England fast enough."

"You mean she'll try again?"

"It's a risk. Best to get rid of her right away." Gunther drew the edge of his hand across his throat. "Loose ends are dangerous. Never leave them behind."

Erwin shook his head.

"Since when do you have scruples?"

"That's not the point." Erwin hesitated. "As far as I'm concerned, that dirty Gypsy can go to hell. I should've ended her back then in the camp. Though now, with the occupiers everywhere... a murder is risky."

Gunther gave him his interrogation glare. "All right, then you have to find out what she's up to first. Scare her a little."

"I can't do that alone."

"You don't have to." Gunther grinned. "Luckily, your friend was one of the best Gestapo agents."

"Good, let's pay her a visit." Erwin wanted to get it over with. So they drove to the worker's housing in Gunther's rickety delivery van. The gray row houses looked dreary in the dim light of the few street lamps. The one where the Gypsy lived was as bleak as the rest, poorly repaired, with boards in the windows instead of glass panes.

They climbed the stairs to her apartment. Erwin knocked. Nothing. He knocked again, louder this time. Footsteps approached, though not from inside, from the neighboring apartment.

An elderly woman with curlers in her hair opened her door a crack. "What do you want?"

"Good evening, sorry to bother you. We're looking for Frau Goldmann," Erwin said politely, giving the woman a charming smile.

"The Goldmanns are away."

"Oh, that's a shame. Do you happen to know when they're expected to return?"

"No, I don't."

"And you don't happen to know where the Goldmanns went?"

"Why do you want to know?" The woman asked, suspicious.

"We're old friends, from before the war."

"I'm sorry, try again in the new year." The neighbor slammed the door in their faces.

Once they were back on the street, Gunther spat, "Old hag. She wouldn't have dared to do that in the old days."

"Times have changed, unfortunately." Erwin curled his lip. "No one respects us anymore."

"Don't worry, that'll change again." Gunther clapped his shoulder. "At least we know she can't do anything in the next few days. They're probably visiting family and won't be back until after the holidays. That gives us time."

"Time for what?"

"To plan her demise, of course." Gunther grinned, sliding behind the wheel. He reached across and opened the passenger door from the inside so Erwin could get in.

"You really want to get rid of her?"

"Better safe than sorry." Gunther started the engine. "Want me to drop you off somewhere?"

"That would be nice. I'm meeting Sonja for dinner." Erwin lit a cigarette, passed it to Gunther and lit another one for himself.

Gunther pulled up in front of the restaurant. "See you next week. Until then, find out everything you can about the Gypsy."

"Thanks for your help." Erwin got out of the car and strode into the restaurant where he'd arranged to meet Sonja. It was one of the few places still serving decent food despite food shortages.

Sonja was already there, her hair pinned up, wearing a dark blue dress that flattered her figure.

"Please accept my apologies for being late," said Erwin as he kissed her hand. "I was tied up at work."

She glanced at her watch. "To be honest, I was early. And it's much too cold to wait outside."

They chatted animatedly while they ate. Sonja told him about her late husband, a Wehrmacht officer who'd been killed in action during the final weeks of the war.

"He was a good man," she said with shining eyes. "Loyal, dutiful. He loved his country."

"You must be proud of him."

"Oh, yes. But it was hard, too." Her gaze flicked to his ring finger. "Were you ever married?"

Erwin hesitated. Hartmut Goslar had been married, or to be precise, he still was—if he hadn't died. His wife had borne him two sons, who'd been killed during the siege of Breslau. He felt a twinge of regret, because Grete had been the perfect wife for an SS Hauptsturmführer. Graceful, charming, gentle, with a pure Aryan ancestry documented five generations back.

It didn't matter anymore. She lived in Dresden now, believing her husband had died a heroic death. A beautiful, pliant woman like her wouldn't remain alone for long. It was better that way. If she knew about his transformation, it'd complicate things.

Gunther's warning echoed in his mind: *loose ends are dangerous*. Was Grete a loose end he had to take care of? He shoved the thought aside.

Sonja misinterpreted his hesitation. "Forgive me, I didn't mean to reopen old wounds."

He donned a sad expression, grateful for the way out she'd shown him. "Indeed, some pain remains." He placed his right hand over his heart and skillfully spun a half-truth. "I was happily married for twelve years until my wife and two sons..." He drew a breath showing Sonja genuine sadness, "...died in a bombing raid."

"I'm so sorry."

His years of practicing interrogation techniques told him that she meant it. This was a good starting point for moving on to the next step. "Thank you. That means a lot to me." He slid his hand across the table until his fingertips touched hers. Electricity crackled between them. "But that was a long time ago . It's time for me to look to the future." With a mischievous wink, he added, "I'm not too old to fall in love again."

As he had expected, Sonja blushed. Her voice was husky when she replied, "I too hope that there will be love for me once more."

After dinner, he walked her home. She lived in the same suburb as him, just five streets away.

"I had a lovely evening. May I invite you to dinner again?"

"I'd love to, I..." In the moonlight, he saw a shudder run through her body. "Would you like to come up for a coffee? Real coffee?"

Erwin briefly wondered if he ought to decline out of courtesy. But he hadn't wanted a suitable woman in so long that he couldn't resist the temptation. "I'd love to."

"Good." She fumbled in her purse for her house key to unlock the door. Her hands trembled so badly, she couldn't hit the keyhole.

A woman after Erwin's taste. She'd make a great wife, although she was probably too old to bear him children.

He gently took the key from her, opened the front door, and let her precede him. On the third floor she stopped.

"Here it is. The apartment is very modest." She seemed nervous.

"Understandable. The war spared no one. But if it's inconvenient..." He left the rest of the sentence hanging in the air.

"No, it's not." She straightened her shoulders and unlocked the apartment door, this time without trembling.

So she could pull herself together when it mattered. A useful trait in the wife of a high-ranking official—and he planned to be one again.

The hallway was spotless. A coat rack stood in the corner, a pair of slippers on a primitive shoe rack next to the door. She hung the key on a nail on the wall, took off her gloves, hat, and scarf, and hung them on the coat rack.

As she struggled to take off her coat, Erwin stepped behind her and helped her out of it before following suit, hanging both on the rack. Order and discipline were the foundation for a successful life. Yes, Sonja truly did have the character traits his future wife needed. Now he just had to find out if she was a good cook.

"Unfortunately, I don't have a second pair of slippers," said Sonja as she slipped into the felt slippers and put on a woolen cardigan.

"That doesn't matter." After taking off his coat and shoes, it was unpleasantly cold in the one-room apartment.

"I'll turn on the stove right away," she assured him, "then it'll be better. Please, have a seat."

He made himself comfortable in the only armchair, wrapped in a thick woolen blanket she brought him. Yes, this woman knew how to treat guests. A few minutes later, she served two steaming cups of coffee on a tray.

"Unfortunately, I don't have any sugar, but would you like some milk?"

"Black is fine, thank you." Erwin firmly believed you could judge a man's character by his preference for coffee. Milk was for weaklings and posers. Sugar for those who preferred pleasure over duty. Real men drank their coffee black. To his delight, Sonja drank her coffee black, too.

She fetched a chair from the kitchen and sat down next to him with an apologetic smile. "As you can see, I'm not prepared for visitors."

This was the decisive moment that would set the tone for the rest of the night. He pushed the blanket aside, leant forward, and looked deep into her eyes. "Thank you very much for the coffee. I should go." Then, using her given name for the first time, he whispered, "I don't want to impose, Sonja."

"You're not, Erwin." Again, a charming blush flitted across her cheeks. She definitely wasn't one of those hardened prostitutes who threw themselves at every man. "It's just... it's been a while."

"I'm afraid I'm a little out of practice myself."

Her lips trembled, not with fear, but with desire. That gave him the courage to pull her toward him and press a kiss on her full mouth. She responded hesitantly at first, then with a growing passion.

Her warm, soft body pressed against his. His hands found their way to her back. After a reasonable pause, he unzipped her dress. She flinched briefly as he slipped her wool cardigan and dress off her shoulders.

"You're beautiful," he whispered, lowering his mouth to her breasts, inhaling her scent. Then he scooped her up and carried her to the bed.

Later, as they lay next to each other, their bodies heated from exertion, Erwin stared at the ceiling. Sonja curled against him.

"That was lovely. I didn't expect..." She shivered under his hand.

He stroked her thigh absently. She'd have to learn not to engage him in conversation after the act. But today he'd be lenient "Me neither. It was a wonderful surprise."

She gazed at him with yearning. "You were so gentle."

So her late husband hadn't known how to satisfy a woman. Erwin shook his head at such stupidity. Every good interrogator knew that two things made women submissive: fear and desire.

He licked his lips. Sonja and he were going to have a lot of fun together.

"I'm sorry, my dearest Sonja. But I have to leave," he said after a while.

"Don't you want to stay?" He could see the plea in her eyes.

"I really can't." He kissed her. "Don't get up, it's cold. I can see myself out."

Outside on the street, he took a deep breath. Sonja had been surprisingly good in bed. He'd soon ask for her hand in marriage. Right now, his thoughts wandered to the Gypsy who'd denounced him. He thought again of Gunther's warning. *You can't leave any loose ends behind.*

In the icy winter night, his breath formed little clouds in the air as he hurried home. By the time he arrived, he realized Gunther was right. The Gypsy had to disappear. A regrettable accident. Nothing that pointed to him. It had been a stroke of luck that she hadn't been home earlier. That way, no suspicion would fall on him.

CHAPTER 18

Her heart pounding, Roxy stood in front of the gray apartment building. Two and a half years after the war, the facade was still blackened with soot and the windows boarded up.

A cold wind whistled through the streets. She pulled her coat tighter around her. Her hand hovered over the doorbell button marked Abel, yet she hesitated. An inexplicable fear held her back. Maybe it was better to leave the past alone after all.

"Shall I accompany you?" David had asked that morning.

"No. I have to do this alone," she'd replied.

Now, as she stood indecisively at the front door, she wished he were by her side. David would read her emotions and squeeze her hand. She felt safe in his presence. It had been that way from the first day she met him. She smiled just thinking about it. Of course, she hadn't let him see it then. Besides, it had been a completely irrational feeling, because there was nothing he could've done to protect her from the Nazis.

Her fingers clenched around the wooden horse around her neck. In her head, David's voice said, "If you don't ring, you'll never know if Natalie is alive. She may be your only living relative."

He was right—as he usually was. Roxy smiled again and immediately felt better. Finally, she pressed the doorbell. Shortly thereafter, a buzz rang out. Surprised, Roxy pushed at the door, which sprang open.

Someone called from above, "Third floor."

The paternoster didn't look like it was working, so Roxy took the stairs. A woman in her early fifties stood in the apartment door. She wore a simple brown dress, her blonde hair tied back in a ponytail. Her blue eyes scrutinized Roxy.

"Good day. What can I do for you?"

Roxy cleared her throat. She'd rehearsed her speech on the way there. "My name is Roxana Goldmann. I'm looking for Natalie. Her parents lived with you for a while."

The woman's friendly expression vanished. Her shoulders stiffened and her voice became cool. "What do you want with Natalie?"

"I'm a relative. Her mother Eva was my cousin. I—"

"Another relative, then." The woman snapped. "Did Herr Popa send you? I told him we won't give Natalie back. She's our daughter."

Roxy flinched. Popa was her maiden name. Someone from her family had survived. She composed herself. "No, nobody sent me. Honestly. Until just now, I assumed I was the only one in my family who'd returned from the camps." Roxy looked at Frau Abel imploringly. "Is Natalie alive?"

Frau Abel crossed her arms over her chest. "Are you here to steal the child from us? We won't give her up. We took the little worm in when her parents were deported, she was barely a few months old. After the war, we adopted her."

"Absolutely not. Please believe me. I have lost my entire family in the camps. I just want to see her, to know she's well. Then I'll leave." Dizziness swept over her at the thought of a family member coming here. "Please, it's very important to me."

"Are you feeling unwell? You look very pale." The woman's voice lost its harshness.

Roxy braced herself against the doorframe. The world spun around her. Waves of nausea rolled through her, the damn illness that had been plaguing her for weeks.

"You'd better come inside." The woman took Roxy's elbow and led her through the living room into the kitchen. "I'm a nurse. Let me take a look at you."

Roxy sat down on a chair that Frau Abel pulled up for her.

"Take a deep breath. When was the last time you ate?"

"This morning," Roxy replied mechanically.

Frau Abel knelt down and took her pulse. Then she leaned back, looking at Roxy with a knowing gaze.

"How long have you been feeling sick?"

"A few weeks. I'm fine now."

"Do you have any other symptoms?"

"Symptoms of what?" Roxy ran her fingers through her wild curls. "It's probably because I don't eat enough. Hard to fill your belly when there's nothing to buy?" She shrugged.

"You're pregnant, Frau Goldmann," the nurse told her.

"Me? No," Roxy stared at her. "It's just hunger."

"When was your last period?"

Roxy furrowed her brow, trying to remember. She hadn't noticed, but now realized it had been far too long. "It was still warm outside, maybe in September?"

Frau Abel palpated Roxy's stomach. "That fits. I'd guess you're in your third month. Haven't you noticed anything?"

"I... no... I... was so busy," stammered Roxy. In hindsight, it all made sense: the nausea, the fatigue, the mood swings. The realization hit her with a force that took her breath away. "So I'm really having a baby?"

"Yes." Frau Abel's gaze was kind. "May I congratulate you?"

"I think so. My husband..." Warmth pulsed through Roxy's veins until she thought she'd explode with happiness. "He'll be so happy. I... we... we had no idea."

"I'll make you some tea. It'll be good for your nerves."

While Frau Abel bustled about in the small kitchen, Roxy

folded her hands over her belly. How could she not have noticed? She had a reputation for keen perception. She'd always recognized when her cousins and aunts were pregnant, long before it was disclosed to the clan's youth. She'd seen it in them, just as Frau Abel had seen it in her.

A terrifying thought sent shivers down her spine. Roxy clenched her hands into fists. The Goslar case had taken on a sudden urgency. She had to get him behind bars before the baby was born—if the British continued to refuse, she'd have to take justice into her own hands.

Frau Abel placed a teapot of fragrant chamomile tea and two cups on the table. She poured the tea, handing Roxy a cup. "Drink up. It helps with nausea."

Roxy took a sip. The warmth revived her from within and took away some of her worries.

"I apologize for my behavior earlier," said Frau Abel. "My husband and I raised Natalie as our own child. After the war, when we learned that both her parents are dead, we adopted her." She sipped her tea. "I don't want to give her up. A few months ago, this man showed up and demanded her back. It broke my heart."

"Please, you don't need to be afraid. I truly just want to see Natalie." Roxy smiled. "I'll have my hands full with my own child soon."

"It's very difficult on your own. Does your husband have family who can help?"

"His family lives in Berlin, and we live in the Ruhr area." Roxy held the teacup with both hands. "Who was this man? Do you know his full name?"

"He introduced himself as her grandfather."

"Uncle Gottfried." A lump formed in Roxy's throat. Of all the family members, he was the one she least wanted to see. He'd betrayed her to Goslar—if not for him she'd have escaped that morning. Then she'd never been forced to work in the bloody Sonderkommando, and she wouldn't have been transferred to

Krychow, where they had drained the moor in sweaty slave labor.

Then you wouldn't have met Marek, whispered an inner voice. *Great consolation. He wouldn't have died to enable my escape,* replied a second voice.

"Gottfried, yes, that was his name." Frau Abel put down her cup. "He lives in Berlin. In Neukölln, I think. Would you like to visit him?"

"No way!" Roxy clenched her jaw so tightly that it cracked.

Frau Abel gave her a sympathetic look. "He's your family."

"You don't understand." Roxy gnawed on her lower lip. "He... we... we didn't part on good terms."

"A lot of time has passed. Maybe this is an opportunity to end old feuds? Your child needs a family."

"My husband's family will have to suffice. I want nothing to do with my uncle."

Frau Abel let the subject drop. "Natalie should be home from school any minute. Would you like to wait?"

"I'd love to."

About ten minutes later, the doorbell rang. Frau Abel rose. "That must be her. Please wait here."

Shortly afterward, footsteps pattered up the stairs and a bright child's voice called out, "Mutti! I got an A in German."

"That's wonderful, my dear." Roxy listened intently to the sounds indicating that Frau Abel was helping Natalie take off her school bag and coat, before she hugged her. "We have a visitor. Roxana Goldmann has come to see you. She's related to your biological mother."

"Really?"

A girl appeared in the doorway. Natalie was tall for her seven years. Roxy's breath caught in her throat. She was the spitting image of her mother, Eva. The same big brown eyes and wild dark curls. Even the way she tilted her head to one side as she looked at Roxy with curiosity.

"Hello, Natalie. I'm Roxy."

"How do you know my *Dej*?" She had the same voice as Tibor when he was a child.

"We lived together before you were born." Unexpectedly strong emotions overwhelmed Roxy.

"What did she look like? My Mutti says I look a lot like her."

"You do. She would be so proud of you."

"Mutti says that too. You know, sometimes I miss my *Dej*, even though I can't remember her. I only have one photo of her."

"Can I see it?"

Natalie looked at her mother. When she nodded, she rushed off and returned with a worn photo. Roxy took it carefully, the next moment her eyes welled up.

The photo showed the entire family on Eva's wedding day. It had been a beautiful celebration. Roxy pointed to a girl with wild, curly hair and bare feet. "That's me, when I was a little older than you are now."

"You're barefoot."

Roxy nodded. "I always wanted to go barefoot until my husband made me these." She pointed to the soft rubber shoes.

"Your husband made them himself?" Admiration spread across Natalie's face. "They are very pretty."

"Thank you."

Natalie thought for a moment. Then she asked, "Will you visit again?"

The question took Roxy by surprise. "I don't know if that's possible. I live far away and am only visiting Berlin."

"What a shame." Natalie smiled—a shy, delicate smile that melted Roxy's heart.

Roxy leaned forward. "I can't promise that I'll visit you again soon, but I have a gift for you." She pulled the wooden horse pendant over her head. "My father carved this for me when I was a child. I want you to have it."

"But... it's yours."

"I don't need it anymore." Roxy placed the leather cord

around Natalie's neck. "It's to protect you and remind you where you come from."

Natalie touched the pendant reverently. "Thank you."

Frau Abel put a hand on Natalie's shoulder. "Go play, dear."

Once the girl had disappeared, she turned to Roxy. "Natalie never stopped asking about her mother. We told her the truth, but it's not the same as hearing it from someone who knew her well."

"I never knew my mother either," Roxy confessed. "She died when I was born."

"I'm sorry to hear that."

"I'd better go. Thank you for everything. Natalie seems very happy with you."

"We love her so much." Frau Abel touched her chest. "It would break our hearts if we had to give her up."

Roxy didn't know what to say. "That won't happen."

Outside, she stopped and breathed the cold winter air deep into her lungs. She placed a hand on her flat stomach. A child. Quickening her steps she returned to David's parents' place, eager to share the happy surprise.

But halfway there, she stopped, gasping for breath. Fear constricted her throat. She had to protect this child from Goslar at all costs. That man had no scruples.

As she caught her breath, she turned on her heel and marched to Neukölln to find Uncle Gottfried.

CHAPTER 19

At last Roxy stood in front of the apartment building in Neukölln, which looked as if the war had ended yesterday. The front door stood open. She climbed the stairs until she spotted the name Popa scrawled on a piece of tape by a bell. Her heart thudded.

She'd asked her way from one Roma family to the next. Most had been suspicious until she'd revealed herself as one of their own. Then their faces had softened and the doors had opened a little wider. Yes, Gottfried Popa had returned from the camps.

For the second time that day, her hand hovered over a bell as she wrestled with herself, wondering whether she genuinely wanted to face her past. If it was just about her, she'd have turned on her heel and never wasted another thought on her uncle, who had so shamefully failed her.

But she had to think about the safety of her unborn child, and for that she needed a witness. Uncle Gottfried had been in the camp. He would recognize Goslar.

After much hesitation, she pressed the button.

Nothing happened. Waves of relief and panic alternately ran down her spine. She rang again. Just as she turned to leave, shuffling footsteps approached.

"Who's there?"

The voice. It was him. It had to be him. Roxy took a deep breath. She wasn't a child anymore, she hadn't done anything wrong. There was no reason to be afraid of the family patriarch. "It's me, Roxana. Your niece."

Silence. Through the closed door, Roxy sensed that her uncle was struggling with the same emotions rolling through her in waves.

It felt like an eternity, although in reality it took a few seconds, before the chain rattled and the key turned. The door opened a crack.

She recognized Uncle Gottfried immediately, though he'd aged beyond his years. His broad shoulders were slumped, his once thick black hair was thin and gray. Deep furrows carved his face. His eyes were marked by the inextinguishable torment of survivors.

"Roxana." His voice was rough. "You came back."

"Yes." She waited for his next move.

He opened the door wide and stepped aside. "Come in. It's good to see you."

The welcome was friendlier than she'd expected. He led her through a shabby hallway into a living room lit by a single bare light bulb; the windows were boarded up. The only furniture in the room was a crooked table, two chairs, and a worn-out sofa. A picture of the Virgin Mary hung on the wall—strange, since Gottfried had never been particularly religious.

There was no sign of a woman, so Aunt Gisela hadn't survived the camps.

At that moment, a man stepped out of the kitchen and asked, "Who was at the door?"

Before Uncle Gottfried could answer, the man stopped in his tracks, staring at Roxy as if she were an apparition. "Roxy? You made it."

"Yes, I did." She had last seen her cousin Romeo in Warsaw, the day after Tibor and Marek had been arrested. After a nasty row with hurtful words on both sides, Roxy had packed her bundle and disappeared, with the intention of never showing up again. Until today.

The three of them stood in the room, overwhelmed by their emotions.

"Come into the kitchen. It's warmer there," said Uncle Gottfried. "And tell us how you've been."

As if in a daze, she followed them into the kitchen, which was indeed warmer thanks to the roaring stove.

"We've been looking for you," said Romeo as he went to the stove and poured a dark brown, pungent-smelling liquid from a teakettle into three cups. The smell made Roxy gag. Regardless, she wrapped her cold fingers around the hot cup.

"The Red Cross had no information about you." She noticed Romeo was dragging his leg. He followed her gaze. "Stiff knee. An accident in the camp."

"We thought you were dead," Uncle Gottfried sank heavily onto a chair.

At last Roxy had the chance to look at him closely. His felt slippers had holes in them, his shirt was stained, and his thinning hair was uncombed. Aunt Gisela would never have tolerated it.

"How did you get out of Warsaw?" Roxy asked.

"I didn't." Romeo's head dropped. "I should have listened to you."

The belated vindication brought no triumph. Her cousin, once so full of life, resembled an old man.

"What happened?" Roxy asked, dreading the answer. In the months she'd spent in Belzec, she'd endured more than enough cruelty for a lifetime.

Romeo's face took on a distant expression. "They caught me after just a few days and deported me to Auschwitz."

Roxy flinched. After everything she had heard about Auschwitz, Belzec had been a walk in the park in comparison. "I'm sorry."

He looked at her with a strange mixture of remorse and reproach. "It was bad..." His whole body began to shake, even his teeth chattered. "I don't like to think about it."

"You don't have to tell me anything." Roxy understood his reaction; she also hated to think about her time in the camps. "Are there any other survivors in our family?"

"No one." Gottfried stirred his tea. One, two, three breaths before he looked up with a blank stare. "After you, Tibor, and Romeo escaped from Krychow, we prepared to spend the winter there. In the weeks that followed, Hans and Maria died, then Teresa, Harald, Letizia, Ariana, Sophia, and Gustav."

With each name of a family member he rattled off, Roxy felt the cold digging deeper into her bones. Even her fingers around the hot teacup seemed to turn to ice.

"Then the SS returned and transported the few survivors to Kulmhof."

Roxy gagged. Not even a handful had returned from the place where people were gassed on arrival.

"Me and about thirty other men were ordered to build roads. That saved our lives." Gottfried took a big gulp of tea and spat on the floor. "What a shitty life!" He picked up the spoon and stirred the tea in his cup forcefully. "We were forty-five when they sent us to Marzahn. Two are left."

Gottfried held his hand with two fingers extended in front of Roxy's face until he realized his mistake and extended a third finger. "Three as of today!"

"You can live with us," Romeo offered.

Roxy shook her head. "Thank you, but I'm married. My husband and I live in Essen."

"Our little Roxy got married. That calls for a celebration." Gottfried got up and took a bottle of schnapps from the shelf. "Which clan is your husband's?"

"He's not a Rom."

"A Sinto, then? Not Marek, that old man?" Romeo asked incredulously.

"Of course not." Roxy gnawed on her lip. "I loved Marek, he was like a father to me. He's dead." She locked eyes with Romeo. "Once we reached Berlin, he sacrificed himself so I could escape."

"Don't keep us in suspense. Who is your husband?" asked Gottfried.

"No one you know. His name is David Goldmann—"

"You married a Jew?" Gottfried was visibly shaken. "After everything they did to us?"

"The Nazis did that to us!" Roxy flared. "Not the Jews! Hitler and his henchmen put us in the camps and murdered our people!"

"Without the Jewish world conspiracy against Germany, none of it would have happened. We were collateral damage in the attempt to rid Germany of these parasites."

Roxy slumped back in her chair. Uncle Gottfried couldn't seriously believe the nonsense he was spouting.

"I won't allow my niece to be a Gadje's wife. You'll divorce him at once!"

"I'll do no such thing." Roxy glared at him. "You have no say over me anymore. I'm an adult."

"I am still the head of this family! And I decide who marries whom!" roared Gottfried.

"You couldn't protect your family from the camp, you've lost the right to call yourself head of family," Roxy snapped. "Of those who stayed with you in Krychow, you are the only one who survived."

"What are you implying?" He squinted his eyes.

Romeo intervened. "Don't fight. We wanted to celebrate Roxy's return."

"As long as she's married to a Gadje, she's not one of us." Gottfried refused to be appeased. On the contrary, he loomed over Roxy. "Get a divorce, or I'll disown you!"

But Roxy no longer feared him, not since she'd dealt with the SS. The thought of the SS automatically led to Goslar and the reason for her visit.

"I came because I need your help," she said, looking imploringly at Romeo.

"For what?"

"Goslar is alive." The sentence hung over them like a sword that might decapitate them at any moment. "He's living under a false name in Essen."

Gottfried's face turned pale. Romeo shivered uncontrollably.

"I recognized him." Roxy's voice trembled with suppressed anger. "I want to bring him to justice. He must pay for what he did."

"What do you need us for?" Gottfried was the first to recover from the shock.

"The British want evidence, photos, witness statements, anything. My word alone isn't enough." Roxy didn't mention that Lieutenant Morrison was pursuing his own agenda. If she came up with proof, he wouldn't be able to ignore her any longer.

Gottfried leaned back, his mouth a hard line.

"You were there," Roxy pressed. "You saw what he did. You can testify."

"No." The word fell like a stone.

"What?"

"I'm not testifying." Gottfried squirmed under her gaze. Her sharp instincts told her that he was racked by guilt... and shame. Suddenly, she realized that he'd always tried to do the right thing. He'd sacrificed Roxy in hopes of saving the rest of the family. He'd actually believed he could bargain with the Nazis. *Look, we're good camp inmates, so don't hurt us.*

Unlike her, he'd never managed to see behind the façade and recognize the Nazis' true motive: Extermination of every race they deemed unworthy.

Roxy sighed. "Please. Do it for Aunt Gisela."

"My wife is dead. My seven children are dead. The entire

clan—all dead." When he finally raised his head, Roxy saw a broken man. "A court ruling won't bring them back."

"It won't, but Goslar should pay for his actions."

"You've always been a rebel. Your father was the only one who could rein you in. After he died... I never managed to teach you discipline. You only ever did what suited you."

"That's not true," Roxy objected. "I always wanted what was best for the family. You adults never listened to me. You followed the Nazis' orders in the vague hope that things wouldn't get worse."

"And you knew, of course, that things would get worse?" Gottfried mocked her.

"It was so easy to see through the propaganda, you just had to pay attention to what wasn't said."

Gottfried suddenly looked very old. "The past is over. Let it rest. There's no point in reopening old wounds. Goslar won't be convicted. The old networks are still there."

"That's exactly why we have to fight. We'll show them that we haven't forgotten, that we—"

He dismissed her objection with a wave of his hand. "I don't want anything to do with it. Not with the Nazis, not with the Jews, and certainly not with the occupiers. I just want to be left alone."

"It's not just about you, or me." Roxy looked him straight in the eye. "I'm pregnant."

Gottfried showed no reaction to the news. "All the more reason to let it go. Goslar is living a new life; if you leave him alone, he'll do the same."

"It's too late for that. Eventually he'll hear about my complaint."

"Then you should leave Essen. Come to Berlin and stay with us. The Roma are a close-knit community; he won't be able to get to you here."

Roxy looked at her uncle with a frown. "I've spent years

living on the run. I'll never do that again. I'm going to make sure Goslar pays for his crimes!"

"Good luck with that." Gottfried twisted his mouth. "But don't come running to me crying afterwards."

"You're a pathetic coward." The words bubbled out before Roxy could hold them back.

Gottfried's hand shot out and grabbed her wrist. "Watch what you say, girl."

"Or what?" Roxy pulled away. "Who are you going to hand me over to this time?"

The silence that followed was deafening.

"You have no right—," Gottfried began.

"I have every right!" Roxy trembled with rage. "If you hadn't gotten in my way, I'd have escaped that day and nobody would have noticed."

"I had to protect the family. It wasn't just about you, it was about all of us." Gottfried turned his head away. "Go. And don't ever show your face here again."

Romeo cast her an apologetic look. "Uncle Gottfried has suffered a lot."

"We all have."

He shrugged helplessly. "You'd better go. He needs to rest. He never got over Aunt Gisela's death. He hoped until the very end, until the Red Cross confirmed that she'd been gassed in Kulmhof."

A chill crept into Roxy's bones. For all her strictness, she'd loved Aunt Gisela, who'd become a mother to her after Roxy's parents died.

"What about you?" she asked.

"Me? I'll manage."

"I mean, you were in Belzec too, and you'd recognize Goslar."

Romeo recoiled, horror etched deep into his face. A violent tremor seized him, forcing him to brace himself against the wall.

"I... no... I... I can't do it." He shook his head vehemently. "I can't... I can't face him."

A deep inner emptiness consumed Roxy. She'd held out so much hope that she'd find someone who'd testify to her story. If she brought witnesses, the British would have to pursue the case, and Morrison would no longer be able to stonewall.

"Goodbye!" She turned on her heel and stormed down the stairs. Outside, she leaned against the wall of the house, gasping for breath.

"Roxy! Wait!"

Romeo came running out in slippers and without a coat.

"Leave me alone," she muttered.

"No." He stood in front of her, a contrite expression on his face. "I need to tell you something. I'm sorry. What I said in Warsaw was a lie. I was so angry and afraid."

Roxy froze. "What are you talking about?"

"No one thought you were a burden. You were always one of us." He shrugged. "Except for Tibor, no one truly understood you, but... but... we loved you anyway. All of us."

Perplexed, Roxy fought back the tears welling up in her eyes.

"Don't be so hard on Uncle Gottfried. The camps broke him. He never got over their deaths. He doesn't talk about it, but I know. He drinks too much and screams at night when he's plagued by nightmares."

"None of us survived the camps unscathed," Roxy murmured.

"You're fighting. You're not giving up." Romeo smiled weakly. "Tibor would be proud of you."

The words hit her unexpectedly. She had to blink. "Thank you. That means a lot. I think about him often."

"Me too."

"My biggest regret is that we didn't properly reconcile before he died."

Romeo bit his lip. "That's why I wanted to apologize to you.

The unpleasant things I said in Warsaw shouldn't stand between us any longer."

His words gave her new hope, and she hugged him.

"I'm sorry, but I honestly can't testify. It... I... I can't handle it."

"It's all right. I'll find someone else. Take care of yourself."

Roxy set off for her in-law's, deep in thought. So many things had happened today, and she had to process them before she could face David.

CHAPTER 20

Like a caged tiger, David paced back and forth in his parents' apartment. Amelie wrapped Christmas presents at the table, while her mother prepared dinner in the kitchen.

"Stop it already," Amelie said without looking up. "You're making me nervous."

"She's been out for a long time." David glanced at the clock. "What if something happened to her?"

"Roxy can take care of herself, you know that." Amelie put the scissors aside. "She's probably the most capable person I know."

"Still." David stood at the window and looked out onto the street. "She should've been back long ago."

"She wanted to visit Natalie, a child she's never met before, who might be her only living relative. It's easy to lose track of time in a situation like that." Amelie joined him at the window and put a hand on his shoulder. "You'd better help me cut newspaper to wrap the presents."

But David was far too fidgety for such a task. He'd offered to accompany Roxy, but she had insisted on going alone. He understood her, he genuinely did. And while he didn't want to restrict her in any way, worry gnawed at his insides.

The afternoon hours dragged on. Heinrich came home from work, Julius and Edith stopped by on their way to the airport to wish them a Merry Christmas. And still no sign of Roxy.

"Maybe I should go look for her," David muttered as he peered out the window again.

"Don't be silly," his father said. "It's not even dark yet. Where would you start searching anyway?"

"I could—"

At that moment, the doorbell rang. David spun around and raced to open it. Roxy stood in the hallway, her cheeks reddened by the cold and her dark curls even more tousled than usual.

"Roxy! Thank God." David pulled her into his arms. "I was worried sick."

"I'm sorry." Her voice sounded muffled. "I lost track of time."

"I don't want to smother you," he said, knowing how much she valued her independence. "It's just so hard to sit at home and not be able to help."

They walked into the living room, where Amelie squeaked, "Roxy, don't look!"

"Why not?" Contrary to her usual attentiveness, Roxy didn't seem to notice Amelie was frantically hiding something under a newspaper.

"Amelie is wrapping Christmas presents," Heinrich explained. "She's been at it all day."

"For me too?" Roxy asked in surprise.

"Of course. I've made something for everyone." Amelie put her hands on her hips. "You're part of the family."

Roxy's eyes glistened, and she reached for David's hand.

"Is everything okay?" he whispered.

"Yes. I'm just a little overwhelmed. Can we talk? In private?"

"Sure." David led her into the guest room and shut the door.

Roxy walked to the window, turning her back to him. David stood beside her in silence, giving her time to gather her thoughts.

"I visited the people who adopted Natalie," she said at last. "She's... she looks just like her mother. And she has Tibor's voice." Her eyes glistened with tears. "She's happy there. They love her very much."

"That's wonderful news."

"Frau Abel is a nurse." Roxy drew a deep breath. "She told me something."

David's stomach tightened. "Yes?"

Roxy finally looked at him. Her eyes held a mixture of fear and hope that took his breath away.

"I'm pregnant."

Time stood still. The words penetrated his mind in fragments.

"You... we..." He couldn't form a proper sentence.

"I know. I was just as surprised." Roxy worried her lip. "She guesses I'm three months along."

A grin spread across David's face, so wide his cheeks hurt. "We're having a baby!"

He pulled her into his arms, savoring the love they shared. After everything they'd been through, they were going to start a family.

"Are you truly happy?" Roxy asked against his chest.

"Am I happy?" David pulled away from her and looked deep into her eyes. "Roxy, this is the most wonderful thing that's ever happened to me. Except you. I'm over the moon."

"Do you think I'll be a good mother?" She sounded uncertain. "My own mother died when I was born. I don't know how to do it."

"That's not true." David cupped her face. "You're good with people. Remember how you hid the Gerber children from the SS in the attic?"

"That was only for a few hours."

"They'd never seen you before, and yet they trusted you." His heart felt as if it would burst with joy. "You'll be a wonderful mother."

"Do you really believe that?"

"I don't just believe it, I know it." He kissed her gently. "Besides, you have me. My father did a lot with us kids. We went on family outings to Lake Wannsee, weekends with Aunt Feli, picnics,..."

Roxy leaned into him. "I'm scared. This child will change my whole life."

"Being parents will bring us so much joy. This child is the future. A future without racial hatred, in a world where a Romani woman and a half-Jew can live together peacefully."

She flinched as if his words had conjured up a bad memory. He stroked her back. When she still didn't say anything after a few minutes, he broke the silence. "What are you so afraid of?"

"Goslar."

An icy cold crawled into his bones. In his joy, he had completely forgotten about him. "We'll put him behind bars before the child is born. Our little one will grow up safe and sound."

Roxy turned in his arms and looked up at him with so much love it warmed his heart. He counted himself lucky that this extraordinary woman had fallen in love with him.

"I was gone so long because I visited someone else."

Her strained tone sent a chill down his spine. David's emotions were in turmoil, yet somehow he managed to keep his calm. "Do you want to tell me?"

She bit her lip before nodding bravely. "Frau Abel told me someone had showed up to get Natalie back. It was Uncle Gottfried."

"So he survived." The surge of anger toward Roxy's uncle hit him unexpectedly. A rollercoaster of emotions raged through David. Anger, worry, fear, pain, joy, and love followed each other in rapid succession.

"He and Romeo."

"That's good." David thought practically. "Now you have two witnesses, the British can't ignore that."

She buried her nose in his chest. "Unfortunately not.

Gottfried doesn't want to testify. He thinks it's better to let the past rest."

"He can't be serious!" David roared. "Should I talk to him?"

A soft chuckle escaped her. "Better not. He still believes the Nazi propaganda about the Jewish world conspiracy. Besides, he's a broken man. The camps destroyed him."

"That doesn't excuse anything."

"No. But I don't have the strength to deal with him. I just want to be happy and close this chapter of my life." She sighed. "Uncle Gottfried and I agree on that, we just have different methods: he wants forget the past, while I want closure by bringing the perpetrator to justice."

"That's why I love you so much. You always stand with justice and never give up." Something occurred to him. "Romeo is your cousin, isn't he?"

"Yes." Roxy let go of him and sat down on the bed.

"He was in the camp, too."

"I asked him. I think he wants to help me, but he can't. He nearly had a nervous breakdown when I mentioned Goslar." She lay on her back and stared at the ceiling. "He was in Auschwitz."

Just the name of that most terrible place on earth sent waves of dizziness through David's body. "We'll find another way. We won't let Goslar get away with it."

Roxy didn't answer. Instead she reached for his hand. "Hold me, will you?"

Touched by her trust, he lay down next to her and formed a protective cocoon around her. Eventually, a knock at the door startled them.

"David? Roxy? Dinner's ready," Helga called.

"We'll be right there," David replied. He looked at Roxy. "Should we tell them? About the baby?"

"Not today. Let's wait until tomorrow. Today, I want to keep the news... just for us."

"As you wish." David kissed her forehead. "They'll be delighted."

"I think your mother suspects. She gave me the same knowing look as Frau Abel."

"I wouldn't put it past her."

The next morning, David woke to the smell of freshly baked cookies, which awakened memories of Christmas celebrations during his childhood—before Hitler had taken power. A broad grin spread across his face. He couldn't wait to tell his mother she'd soon be a grandmother.

Next to him Roxy slept curled up like a cat. He looked at her lovingly as his thoughts wandered to a distant future in which their children stood in front of the Christmas tree with shining eyes, unwrapping their presents.

He got up quietly and got dressed. Contrary to her usual habit, Roxy didn't stir and continued sleeping. The day before must have exhausted her.

The kitchen bustled with activity. Mutter stood at the stove while Amelie set the table. His father read the newspaper.

"Merry Christmas," David greeted them.

"Merry Christmas, my boy." Helga hugged him. "Did you sleep well?"

"Very well, thank you."

"Where's Roxy?"

"She's still asleep. The past weeks have been hard."

The doorbell rang. Amelie jumped up. "That must be Aunt Feli!"

It was indeed Helga's sister Felicitas. He and Roxy had found refuge in her huge mansion in Oranienburg during the last months of the war.

She had hardly changed—the same upright posture, the same determined chin. Just her clothes were shabbier. She pressed a small box into David's hand: "I brought Christmas baubles."

David passed the box to Amelie so she and Mutter could

decorate the tree later. Then he helped his aunt out of her coat and hugged her. "Aunt Feli!"

"David, my dear. How wonderful to have the family together again."

She greeted Amelie and Heinrich, before she walked into the kitchen to join her sister. "Can I help with anything?"

Helga hugged her with her hands raised high, dough sticking to them. "Perfect timing. I need someone to glaze the cookies. But first, I'll make you a cup of coffee."

David turned around and saw Amelie unpacking the tree decorations. She was so absorbed in her work she didn't even notice him. He stood in the middle of the room, feeling a little lost, until his father patted the seat next to him.

"Come sit with me; you won't get any attention from the women until it's time to open presents. Amelie's been crafting Christmas decorations for weeks and has been waiting for the baubles so she can get started, and Helga and Feli will be chatting in the kitchen for hours."

"Aren't we celebrating in Oranienburg?" That's how they'd done it all the years past, even during the war. Despite being a party member from the very beginning, Felicitas had never abandoned her Jewish in-laws.

A shadow fell over Heinrich's face. "You don't know yet. The Soviets requisitioned the villa."

"They did that a long time ago. I helped Aunt Feli move into the servants' quarters."

"A few weeks ago, they kicked her out for good. Luckily, she found accommodations not far from here in the basement of a ruin."

"But why didn't you..."

Heinrich raised his hand. "You know how stubborn your aunt can be; she has that in common with your mother." Even after more than thirty years of marriage, his expression softened. "She flat out refused to move in and be a burden on us."

"That sounds just like Aunt Feli." David smiled at the

memory of how his aunt had berated a police officer many years ago when she had retrieved Helga's confiscated silverware. "She's a force to reckon with."

"Who's a force?" Felicitas entered the living room with a cup of coffee.

"You. Dad just told me about Oranienburg."

"Ah, those were the days," Feli's expression took on a dreamy look. "But that's over. It's time to roll up our sleeves and rebuild."

"I'm sorry," said David, who admired his aunt.

"You don't have to be." Feli sipped her coffee. "It's only fair. I believed in Hitler, in his promises. I really thought he would make Germany great again." She shook her head. "How could I have been so stupid?"

"You weren't the only one," said Heinrich.

"That doesn't excuse anything." Feli peered from Heinrich to David. "I turned a blind eye to the crimes committed in the name of this ideology. I knew about the camps, about the deportations. And I did nothing."

"You always helped us," David objected. "And you hid Roxy and me at your place when we had nowhere else to go."

"It was the least I could do." Feli put down her cup and folded her hands. "You're family. But what about all the others? The strangers I could have saved? I looked away because it was easier."

An awkward silence settled in the room. Then Amelie cleared her throat. "Shall we talk about nicer things? It's Christmas."

"You're right." Feli looked around. "Where's Roxy, anyway?"

"She's still asleep."

Feli raised her eyebrows. "I remember her as an early riser."

"The last few weeks have been exhausting for her." David wasn't sure whether he should bring up the Goslar situation. Fortunately, the decision was made for him when the door to the guest room opened and Roxy appeared. She wore the simple green wool dress Feli had given her when they had sought refuge at her house. It hugged her figure and contrasted perfectly with her black hair.

David couldn't take his eyes off his wife. He instantly fell in love with her all over again. Noticing the gentle swell of her belly, his heart stuttered.

"Merry Christmas," she said. Then she spotted the visitor. "How lovely to see you, Felicitas."

"I'm glad to see you too." Feli hugged her. "We've missed you. Two years is a long time."

Helga appeared in the doorway. "Come, sit down, Roxy. I'll get you a cup of coffee." When she brought the coffee, she said, "Feli and Amelie, will you help me with breakfast?"

Roxy immediately put her cup aside and started to rise, but Helga pushed her back into her chair. "That's not necessary. You and David should make yourselves comfortable. I haven't had you here with me for so long."

David watched as the corners of Roxy's mouth twitched. She found it difficult to let herself be pampered. Still, she obediently sat back down, took her cup of coffee, and leaned back.

Later, when the whole family was gathered around the table for a late breakfast, Heinrich raised his water glass. "We are so happy that we are all together again. Especially that David and Roxy finally got permission to travel to Berlin. Here's to the family!"

"To family," the others echoed.

David looked at Roxy, who nodded almost imperceptibly. He cleared his throat. "We have some more news."

All eyes turned to him.

"Roxy is having a baby."

For the duration of a heartbeat silence struck. Then a storm of joy broke out. Helga jumped up and hugged Roxy, tears running down her cheeks. Amelie squealed with excitement. Even Heinrich beamed from ear to ear.

"Oh, my God, a grandchild. I can't wait," Helga said, her eyes shining.

"When is it due?" Amelie asked.

"Around June, we don't know exactly," Roxy replied.

"When the time comes, I'd be happy to stay with you in Essen for a few weeks and help out," Helga offered. "If that's alright with you, of course."

"That... that would be very kind." Roxy was visibly overwhelmed. "In the old days... at home... we lived with so many women and children someone always helped. To be honest, I'm afraid of having to raise a child on my own."

"You won't have to. David will help." Helga shot her son a stern gaze. "And if all else fails, Amelie or I will take turns staying with you for as long as you need us."

"Or me," Feli chimed in.

"That's so sweet of you." Tears glistened in Roxy's eyes and David squeezed her hand.

"We're family. And family sticks together. Always." The words came from Feli, and she was the best proof of that. Even during the Nazi years, she'd stood by her Jewish relatives.

"Thank you."

Being a witness to his wife's happiness made David happy, too.

CHAPTER 21

Erwin Krüger sat in a small café in downtown Essen, waiting for Sonja. Through the fogged-up window, he observed people scuttle by, their collars turned up, their faces barely recognizable under scarves and hats. A barren year was coming to an end. Hopefully, the new year would bring more: more food, more coal, more living space... more of everything.

He stirred his coffee and looked around the café. It wasn't heated; the only source of warmth being the bodies of the people sitting close together, their hands wrapped around their hot cups.

Still, the owners had made the effort to decorate the room for Christmas. Straw stars stuck to the windows and thick paper angels dangled from the ceiling, spinning gently.

Erwin had never cared much for this holiday. A sentimental event that worshipped a Messiah who'd never existed. A Jewish invention to weaken the Germanic with fairy tales of charity and turning the other cheek.

Unlike Hitler. He had indeed existed. A man of flesh and blood who'd come to return Germany to its former greatness, to free the nation of the parasites sucking it dry.

Krüger sipped his coffee. It was bitter and strong, the perfect antidote for the nostalgic Christmas spirit prevailing in the city.

He couldn't say for sure what had gone wrong. Perhaps it was the Americans, controlled by Judaism, with their endless resources. Or the Russian Bolsheviks, squandering their soldiers as cannon fodder. Those two nations had conspired to crush the dream of a better world because they couldn't—or wouldn't—understand the vision.

But the fight wasn't over. Germany would rise again. It would just take time, patience, and men like him who worked in secret, weaving networks, waiting for the right moment.

The café door opened with a jingle. Sonja entered, lugging a huge suitcase that nearly crushed her under its weight. Her cheeks were reddened by the cold.

She looked around and he waved her over.

"Erwin." She set the suitcase down with a huff and kissed him on the cheek. "Please excuse me, I'm late. I came straight from the train station."

Punctuality was the mother of all virtues. Even the Gypsies in his camp had learned to be punctual. If he could teach that trash discipline, he certainly expected it from Sonja. Feeling generous, he decided to let it slide, just this once. "It happens. How was your visit to your sister's?"

"Wonderful." Sonja sat down opposite him and sighed contentedly. "You can't imagine how different Upper Bavaria is compared to here. No ruins, no rubble, just fields and forests. And the food." She licked her lips. "I must have gained two kilos while I was there."

"That'll do you good." He smiled. Sonja needed some meat on her hips. The hunger years had turned her voluptuous figure into a stick.

She pointed to the suitcase. "Irene sent so much food. Eggs, butter, even a huge piece of bacon. And homemade bread."

"That sounds like a feast."

"It will be." Sonja leaned over the table, her eyes sparkling. "I want to cook for you tonight."

"That would be delightful." Erwin placed his hand on hers. He hadn't tasted her cooking yet. It was an important skill he needed to check before taking the relationship to the next level.

His thoughts drifted as she recounted the little travel adventures, her brother-in-law's farm, the adorable children, and other trivial things. His mind drifted to the Gypsy, circling like a wolf ready to pounce.

An hour later, they were in Sonja's small apartment. She'd put a knitted smock and an apron over her dress and was cutting onions while a piece of butter melted in a pan. When she added the onions to the melted butter, they sizzled and a delicious aroma filled the room.

"Sit in the armchair," she said. "You don't have to stand around in the kitchen."

"I like watching you." Erwin leaned against the doorframe, admiring the skillful work of her hands. Efficient, without wasted movements. She'd run a tidy household. In his mind, he imagined them entertaining important dignitaries, each complimenting Sonja on the delicious food and the tidy apartment.

"My mother taught me how to cook," Sonja said as she cut a large piece of bacon into thin slices. "She always said the way to a man's heart is through his stomach."

"A wise woman."

Sonja laughed. "She was. Strict, but fair. She'd have liked you."

"You think so?" Her mother had died five years ago; he didn't care whether she'd have liked him or not.

"You're reliable. Decent." Sonja turned with a smile. "Rare character traits these days."

Krüger stepped closer and put his hands on her shoulders. "I try to be a good man."

She leaned against him. "You are."

Yes, he certainly was. He'd always served his fatherland, even when it hadn't been easy. He'd sacrificed so much. A pang of pain shot through his heart at the thought of his wife Grete.

More than once he'd been tempted to visit her. But he couldn't. She believed he was dead, and that was how it had to stay. Nothing must tie him to his old identity.

The dinner Sonja prepared from her sister's gifts was indeed a feast. He hadn't eaten so well in years. As he put a forkful of fried bacon into his mouth, he closed his eyes in delight. The smell alone made his mouth water, and the taste sent pleasurable shivers down his back. Sonja had hit the perfect note: the bacon was crispy yet soft, and superbly seasoned.

"Delicious. Absolutely delicious!" he praised. "You are a true master in the kitchen."

"Thank you." Her gentle blush was almost as delicious as the fried bacon taste lingering on his tongue.

As he leaned back, full and satisfied, Sonja asked, "Would you like dessert?"

"Dessert? Have I died and gone to heaven?"

"I hope not." Gleaming with happiness she disappeared into the kitchen. A few minutes later, she carried two small bowls of fragrant apple compote to the table.

He sniffed. Apart from the tart apple, he smelled a sweet, slightly pungent and spicy aroma that instantly created a cozy atmosphere. Memories of times past came flooding back. How he'd sat with Grete in front of a crackling fireplace while outside the snowflakes had created a winter wonderland.

A maid had served them the finest French red wine and little canapés. Longing filled his chest; he wanted that luxurious life back.

"That was excellent," he said as he pushed his empty bowl aside. "I can't remember the last time I ate so well."

Sonja beamed. "I'm glad you enjoyed it."

Then she cleared the table while Erwin made himself comfortable in the armchair, a blanket over his knees. Satisfied, he took in the domestic scene, which was almost intimate in its everyday normality. Yes, he could definitely imagine living with Sonja. In time, when the occupiers had left Germany, the old guard would be in charge again. Then they'd be able to afford a maid and Sonja wouldn't have to work so hard.

He picked up a newspaper and read while Sonja washed the dishes and tidied up. When she was finished, she appeared in the living room with slightly reddened cheeks.

"Come sit with me," he said. Seeing her questioning look, he added, "On my lap."

She did as she was told, and he put his arms around her hips, where the two extra kilos she'd gained were pleasantly noticeable.

"We're going to need a second armchair," he said.

"Am I too heavy for you?" She was about to get up, but he gently held her back.

"Not at all. I love being close to you, but it's a bit impractical in the long run if we only have one chair, don't you think?"

She nodded, confused.

He nibbled her neck for a while until she relaxed against him. Close to her ear, he whispered, "The last few weeks with you have been amazing. They've shown me what I've been missing. After my wife died, I thought I'd never..." He left the sentence hanging, a perfectly timed hesitation.

"Erwin..." she breathed.

"I'm not a young man anymore. I've experienced war, loss, deprivation. But with you, I feel alive again."

She turned her head, her eyes full of love. "I feel the same way. Through you, I found joy in life again. You've shown me there's a future worth living."

"Our love is a precious gift I never expected." He let the sentence sink in before continuing, "Sonja Schenk, will you be my wife?"

Conflicting emotions flashed across her face. "Erwin, I love you too. But this is so sudden. We've only known each other for a few weeks."

"That's true. I struggled with that. I thought long and hard about whether I wanted to propose to you." His hand caressed her hips and slowly moved over her stomach toward her breasts, stopping just before reaching them. She suppressed a sigh. "While you were at your sister's, I missed you every waking minute."

"You did?" Her eyes glistened with emotion.

"I realized how much I love you, and that I never want to spend another day without you. I want to fall asleep with you at night and wake up next to you in the morning." He removed his hand from her torso and cupped her cheek. "At my age, you know what you want. And I want you. I want to build a life with you, a future."

"I... I don't know what to say."

"Say yes." He gave her his most charming smile. "We've both lost so much. Let's not waste any time. Let's be happy again. Together."

Sonja swallowed hard. He could see the thoughts racing through her head. She was lonely, he knew that. A childless widow, whose husband and sons had been killed in the war. She longed for company, for someone to care for her.

"It's very soon," she hesitated. "Maybe we should get to know each other better first."

"What else is there to learn?" He turned her slightly toward him, gazed into her eyes, and took her hands in his. "I know you're kind, hardworking, loyal. That you're a good cook." A small laugh. "That you believe in traditional values, in family, and decency."

"And you?" She looked at him. "What do I know about you?"

"Everything that matters." Erwin lifted her hand to his lips and kissed it gently. "I am a man who loves and respects you. Who can offer you a safe home, a name, a future."

The silence stretched out. He waited patiently. He'd learned that silence was often more effective than words.

At last, Sonja took a deep breath. "I'm afraid of making a mistake."

"I understand." He brushed a strand of hair from her face. "But sometimes you have to take a leap of faith. Some people know each other for ten years before they get married and still find out it was a mistake."

"That's true." She nodded thoughtfully. "I know of a few cases like that. Some couples divorce after twenty or more years of marriage because their partners have changed."

"That won't happen to us. We're both middle-aged adults. We're not going to change our personalities anymore." He squeezed her fingers. "Please say yes. I want nothing more than to have you as my wife and love you for the rest of my life."

He noticed the exact moment when she cast her doubts aside and made her decision.

"My sister will think I'm crazy," she muttered to herself.

"Maybe you are a little bit. Crazy about me." He emphasized his words with gentle circular movements of his thumbs under the hem of her blouse.

"I am." She hesitated for a few seconds. "Yes." A radiant smile spread across her face. "Yes, I want to marry you."

He pulled her into a kiss, long and deep, with just the right mixture of passion and restraint that melted her.

"You just made me the happiest man in the world," he whispered against her lips.

"What happens now? My last wedding was almost twenty-five years ago."

"Luckily, I work for the city government and can take care of the paperwork in no time. If you want, we can be at the registry office next month."

"Now that I've made the decision, I can't wait to become your wife."

"And I can't wait to become your husband." Erwin wanted to

move quickly. The sooner they were married, the more firmly his new identity would be established. He nibbled on her earlobe. "But first we should practice for the wedding night, don't you think?"

"I'd love to," she whispered.

Now he just had to solve the problem with the Gypsy. But that would have to wait until tomorrow. Tonight, he wanted to devote exclusively to Sonja.

CHAPTER 22

Spurred by Roxy's courage David decided to retrace his own past. On the last day before their departure, he made his way to his old workplace. Standing in front of the entrance gate to the locomotive workshop, he took a deep breath. The big hall with the glass dome, visible from afar, no longer existed; in its place, charred walls towered into the sky. Regardless, he imagined he could hear the familiar clattering and hammering.

"Who are you here to see?" the gatekeeper asked.

"Baumann. Does he still work here?" The chances were slim, but it was his only lead in finding the man who'd taken him under his wing. An old communist who hated the Nazis like the plague. On David's first day he'd given him the nickname Kessel, kettle, because Goldmann sounded too Jewish.

"Yes. Herr Baumann works here. Shall I announce you?"

A grin tugged at David's lips. "Please tell him Kessel is here."

The gatekeeper picked up a telephone receiver and held it to his ear. "Herr Baumann, a Herr Kessel would like to see you." After hanging up, he handed David a pass issued to Herr Kessel. "Please sign here."

For a heartbeat David wanted to clear up the mistake, then he signed with a flourish: D. Kessel. "Here you go."

The gatekeeper cut the form in half, giving David one part along with a safety pin, and explained, "Please pin this to your jacket and wear it so it's clearly visible while you're on the factory premises."

"Thank you very much."

"Herr Baumann said you know your way around. He's waiting for you in the big hall."

David looked at him in astonishment. "You mean the bomb crater?"

"It looks worse than it is. A temporary wooden structure has been built inside the walls. Herr Baumann is waiting for you there." The gatekeeper pushed the heavy gate aside and let David enter.

Instantly, he felt transported back in time. He walked the familiar path past various sheds made of sheet metal, wood, and even cardboard covered with plastic tarpaulins. It was a shame to see this place so run-down. On the other hand, why should the locomotive workshop in the heart of Berlin have been spared from the widespread bombing?

As he pushed open the heavy door and stepped into the large hall, it took his breath away. In the middle of the huge building stood a comparatively small wooden box with windows made of milky plastic sheeting.

A deafening screech drowned out every other sound. *The circular saw urgently needs oiling*, David thought as he walked toward the door of the oversized wooden box. Just before he reached it, the saw fell silent. Instead, a soft hissing sound reached his ears. Probably the welding station.

He couldn't help grinning. Thanks to Baumann, Koloss, and the other "reds", the locomotive factory had long been a safe haven for David.

The door opened and Baumann stepped out. Wiry, stooped, with a gray beard, but unmistakably Baumann. He came up and clapped David's shoulder. "I never thought I'd see you again, Kessel! I feared the worst because you hadn't shown up."

David replied sheepishly, "I've been living in the Ruhr area for over two years."

"That explains it. And now you're back in Berlin?"

"Just visiting my parents. The British have finally issued travel permits."

"Well," Baumann scratched his head. "The occupiers aren't exactly on friendly terms."

"You can say that again."

"Come with me, I'll show you my kingdom. It's not the same as it used to be, but better than nothing. We're rebuilding." Baumann went to an open shelf on the wall and grabbed a helmet. "Put it on. New safety regulations."

"Just like ours. They're much stricter about safety now."

"It's a good thing. Fewer accidents, especially with the incompetent boys they send us. They know the entire Hitler alphabet by heart, but can't hold a hammer."

David laughed. He'd missed Baumann. His new colleagues were fine, but it wasn't the same as the close-knit community they'd been in Berlin.

The deafening screeching started again, accompanied by staccato hammering.

"Come with me!" Baumann shouted over the noise, leading David to a plexiglass box at the edge of the hall. On the way, he stopped at a safe distance from the welding station and gave the worker a hand signal.

As soon as Baumann closed the door of the Plexiglass container behind them, a soothing silence descended on David. He took a deep breath.

"Not used to it anymore, huh?"

"I'm responsible for fixing the machines. And while they aren't running, they don't make noise," David explained.

"It's a pleasant surprise to see you." Baumann poured coffee from a thermos on his desk into two reasonably clean mugs and handed one of them to David.

Taking a sip, David grimaced. Some things never changed. "You still drink lukewarm coffee?"

Baumann shrugged. The next second, the door opened and a mountain of a man ducked through the frame. As soon as he stood in the Plexiglass box, the room seemed to shrink to half its original size.

"Well, if it isn't our Kessel," the giant boomed, slapping David on the back with his shovel-sized hand.

The blow knocked the wind out of David, and he gasped, "Koloss, leave me in one piece, will you?"

"You've gotten soft in your old age," the giant teased.

"Man, I'm glad to see you alive." Warmth washed through David's veins. He hadn't realized how much he'd missed his former colleagues.

"I can hardly believe it. We thought you were... well."

"Dead?" David finished. "Almost. But as you see, I made it."

Baumann poured another cup of lukewarm coffee and handed it to Koloss. "Come, sit down. Tell us what has become of you."

"My wife and I started anew in the Ruhr area. I got a job in a cast steel factory."

"Your wife?" Baumann looked over at Koloss. "Our little one has grown up."

"Congratulations!" Koloss rumbled.

"And you?" David asked. "How did you fare?"

Koloss scratched his head. "I was lucky, if you can call it that. Those bastards drafted an old geezer like me, so I deserted."

That sounded like Koloss. Just like Baumann, he was a staunch communist and anti-Nazi.

"Well, the countess found an old friend on Lake Constance who let me stay with her—until she was arrested. Long story short," Koloss grimaced. "I swam across Lake Constance to Switzerland with another fugitive."

"You can swim?" David asked astonished.

"Oh, please," Koloss puffed himself up. "You're right, not

particularly well. Thanks to Judith's swimming lessons, I made it to the other side."

David narrowed his eyes. "You mean Judith Rosner? The Olympic swimming champion? The one who now lives in America and coaches the national team?"

"Exactly."

"Man, I read about that story in the newspaper. Quite an adventure."

Koloss drank the coffee in one gulp and placed the empty cup next to the thermos. "Phew, tell me about it. I'm still scared thinking back. Anyhow, the Swiss put me in a camp. Geneva Convention and all that. Being a prisoner of war in Switzerland was like a spa. Enough to eat, a warm bed, no bombs. We had to work, of course, but I'm used to that."

"Seems like you were lucky in your misfortune."

"I definitely was. After the surrender, it took another nine months before I finally made it to Berlin. First of all I looked for Baumann. The Russians made him foreman here. He hired me on the spot."

Baumann nodded. "Anyone would have. Good welders are in short supply."

"In the Ruhr area, too." David turned to Baumann. "And how have you been?"

Baumann's face darkened. "I certainly didn't have it as good as Koloss."

David waited patiently. Most people struggled to talk about their war experiences, he knew that first-hand from Roxy. If Baumann didn't want to talk, he wouldn't push him.

"Shortly after Koloss deserted, the Gestapo caught me. Someone in our cell betrayed me." His voice became bitter. "Interrogation. Trial. The usual."

David clenched his jaw, because he had a good idea of what "the usual" meant in the context of a Gestapo interrogation.

"The People's Court sentenced me to death for high treason and undermining military morale." Baumann spat on the floor.

"A sham. We were all dealt with en masse. Everyone except one pregnant woman was sentenced to death."

Koloss clearly knew his comrade's inner torment, since he poured the last of the coffee into Baumann's mug.

"Thanks. Dirty Nazi pigs. So I sat on death row and waited. It ain't funny, I can tell you that."

"I can imagine. Did you appeal for clemency?"

Baumann snorted indignantly. "No mercy. The Tommies saved my life."

"By accident, so to speak," Koloss chimed in, because Baumann was having trouble speaking. "The prison in Plötzensee was hit during a bombing raid. Baumann seized his chance and took off."

"Holy shit!" David groaned. He'd heard about the infamous Plötzensee Blood Nights, when the Nazis had summarily hanged close to three hundred men in four nights after the cell block was damaged.

"You can say that again. Only four of the fugitives weren't recaptured. I was one of them." Gradually, the color returned to Baumann's face. "The pastor hid me in the Swedish church until the end of the war. And now I'm back here."

"Almost like old times, except that half of our comrades are dead," Koloss said.

"That time is over. Finally, we have the chance to build a just society," Baumann said with conviction.

David raised his eyebrows. "In the eastern sector?"

"Sure." Baumann's eyes lit up. "The Soviet zone is our future. No more capitalists exploiting the workers. Everyone gets what he needs to live."

"And everyone is equal," Koloss added, albeit with less enthusiasm than his comrade.

David chose his words carefully. "Have you forgotten how the Soviets behaved after the capitulation?"

"That wasn't good," Baumann rubbed his chin. "But thank God that's over."

"We hear so many stories about arbitrariness, about people being kidnapped right off the street in broad daylight." David couldn't believe that the two men who'd fought so bravely against the Nazis didn't realize that the Soviets were pursuing the same goals, just in different packaging.

"The birth pangs of a new order," Koloss dismissed. "Yes, there are problems. Yes, some things go wrong. But it's better than what we had under the Nazis. And better than capitalist exploitation in the West."

"Are you sure?" David asked. "In the West, there is more freedom, more—"

"Freedom for whom?" Baumann interrupted him. "For the rich? For the old Nazis who assumed new identities and are back in office and in positions of power?" He shook his head vigorously. "No, Kessel, true freedom lies in equality. And only the Soviets can give us that."

Koloss cleared his throat. "It's not perfect, we can see that, too. For example, the Russians are taking everything that isn't nailed down. Factory equipment, machines, even railroad tracks."

"Those are reparations, they're entitled to them," Baumann replied sharply. "After what Germany did to them."

"True," David conceded. "But it doesn't make life any easier. People are starving while the Russians carry everything away."

"People are starving in the West, too," Baumann interjected.

"That's right." Koloss nodded his head back and forth. "Nowhere is good. But in the East, there's a vision of a better future for all."

"A dictatorship," David muttered. "We've had that before."

Baumann glared at him. "Communism isn't a dictatorship. It's difficult at first because a people don't just change overnight. But at least we're free from capitalist exploitation."

David didn't want to argue. His old colleagues would either realize for themselves they were on the wrong track—or they wouldn't. "Do you have a lot of work in the workshop?"

"The locomotives are all shit. We're repairing them from morning till night," Koloss said.

"We could use your skills. Don't you want to return to Berlin?" Baumann asked.

The idea was tempting, especially because Goslar would be far away. But he couldn't make such a serious decision without consulting Roxy first.

"I like it in Essen at the moment, but if I return, I'll get in touch, I promise."

After a few minutes of talking shop, he said, "I have to go, there's still a lot to organize before we leave tomorrow. It was nice to see you again."

"Me, too. I'll walk you to the gate."

"Keep your chin up, Kessel," Koloss called after him.

As David handed his visitor's pass to the gatekeeper and walked down the street to the tram stop, he felt a strange mixture of melancholy and relief. Some things had stayed the same, others had definitely changed.

On the train the next day, Roxy leaned her head on his shoulder and dozed off. David, on the other hand, watched the landscape roll by. His thoughts wandered into the future. To what would happen after they returned home. Ever since he'd learned Roxy was expecting a child, his concern about Goslar's existence had tripled.

"You're worrying too much," Roxy said without opening her eyes.

"How do you know?"

"From your heartbeat, it's gotten faster."

"I was thinking about Goslar."

She sat up. "What about him?"

"I want to see him. I need to know who we're up against." His secret ulterior motive was to find out if he could take the man on in a fistfight.

Once again, Roxy guessed his thoughts. "He's not particularly strong, but he's still dangerous."

David stroked her hair. "I don't plan on getting into a fight with him. Still, I want to know what he looks like so I'll be ready if we encounter him."

"That's a good idea. If you know your enemy, you're halfway to winning."

"Where did you hear that saying?" David asked with a laugh.

"I just made it up." She wrinkled her nose. "I have a bad feeling about this."

A shiver ran down David's spine, because Roxy's intuition was usually right. "Me, too. That's why I want to be prepared."

"Thank you for standing by me." She nestled close, intertwining her fingers with his. "I appreciate it very much."

"I love you, Roxy. No matter what you do, I'll always be by your side." He placed his other hand on her belly. "Especially now."

"You're worried about the baby."

"Yes. I won't sleep peacefully again until Goslar is behind bars."

A serious expression came into her eyes. "Me either."

An unsettled feeling came over David. "Please don't do anything rash."

"I won't."

Her statement didn't reassure him. Although he didn't possess her infallible intuition, he knew his wife well enough to sense she was plotting something he wouldn't like.

CHAPTER 23

JANUARY 1948, ESSEN

The first rays of morning sun falling on her face, Roxy stepped through the brewery gate into the stables. The cold winter air smelled of yeast, hops, and horse manure—a mixture that soothed her. After many rejections and humiliating conversations, she'd finally found a job. It wasn't carpentry, but at least it was work where she could be outside and use her hands.

"Good morning, Frau Goldmann," greeted the stable master, busy assigning the teams for the morning tour. "Punctual as always."

"Good morning, Herr Wieland." It was her second week at the brewery, and she loved every minute of it. Mucking out stalls, grooming horses, caring for harnesses, and hauling water was hard work, but she didn't mind. On the contrary, the physical exertion did her good and distracted her from constantly pondering how she could gather evidence against Goslar.

"Max and Moritz need extra attention today," said Wieland, pointing to the two black geldings harnessed to the heavy beer wagon. "They had a long trip yesterday. And Kasper needs to be taken to the farrier later; he lost a shoe."

"Will do." First though, Roxy went to Baldur's stall, the jittery dun horse who flinched at the slightest sound and lashed out at everyone but her.

"Good morning, my handsome boy." She held out a brown, shriveled carrot.

Baldur didn't take the treat from her hand like he usually did. He seemed to want to tell her something, nudging her several times with his muzzle while pawing at the ground with his front hoof.

"Is something wrong with your leg, Baldur?" She felt the leg and lifted his hoof, but everything was fine. No visible injuries.

"Or do you just want some cuddles?"

He whinnied as if to confirm.

"Don't worry, you'll get a thorough grooming later, but first I have to take Kasper to the farrier." She patted Baldur's neck and left his stall. Directly opposite was Kasper's stall, an old, placid gelding with gentle brown eyes who'd been working at the brewery for fifteen years and was not easily ruffled. But today he seemed nervous.

Since the farrier didn't open until later, she began mucking out the stalls. Her thoughts wandered to Goslar. If she wanted him in court, she needed allies. She wouldn't be able to do anything on her own. Morrison had made that clear.

Thankfully, Julius had kept his word and asked his sister Adriana for help. She'd given him the name of an acquaintance: Kate Johnson, the wife of a British major. She didn't live in Essen, but in Duisburg, which was only a good hour away by train.

"She loves to get involved," Adriana had said. "If anyone can help, it's her. Unofficially, of course."

Roxy had written down the address. Maybe she'd visit Kate Johnson once she gathered more proof. When there was no doubt that Erwin Krüger was indeed Hartmut Goslar.

"Frau Goldmann," Wieland called. "The farrier phoned. Can

you take Kasper to him right away? I need him for the midday tour."

"Of course." Roxy put down the pitchfork and walked to Kasper's stall. The old gelding whinnied softly in greeting. But when she put the halter on him, he laid his ears back.

"Come on, old boy," she murmured, scratching his forehead. "I know you've lost your shoe, so we're going to the farrier. You'll feel better afterward."

She led Kasper across the brewer's cobbled courtyard. It was a clear morning, at every step the frost crunched under her feet. Kasper usually didn't mind. Today though he was acting strangely. He fiddled with his lips at the halter, tossed his head back, and stamped his hooves. Roxy worried that he might have injured himself when he'd lost his shoe. She placed one hand on his neck and ran the fingers of the other hand along the halter, searching for a foreign object. But she found nothing. Then she repeated the procedure with his leg.

"What's wrong with you, Kasper?" she crooned.

He snorted, flaring his nostrils, but obediently followed her. Horses were living creatures that sometimes had a bad day. Roxy hadn't known him long enough to gauge the reason for his foul mood.

She continued walking, her senses sharp. Then she remembered that Baldur had also been off this morning. She'd ask the stable master later if anything odd had happened during the night.

Halfway to the farrier they stepped out of the building's lee onto the road, where the wind whistled directly into their faces. Kasper stopped dead in his tracks. He dug his hooves into the ground, his muscles taut like a drawn bow.

A sharp smell stung Roxy's nose. It seemed familiar, though she didn't have time to consider what it might be. Kasper threw his head up, the whites of his eyes shining. At the same time, he let out a shrill whinny and took a huge leap to the side.

It happened so fast Roxy couldn't react. The lead rope slipped through her hands, the friction burning her skin.

"Kasper! Easy!" With sheer willpower, she forced herself to remain calm so he didn't become even more frightened. Cautiously, she took a step toward him, reaching for the rope. For a heartbeat, she grasped the end. Then a loud bang cracked behind them, and the rope jerked with a force she couldn't hold.

In the next second, Kasper reared up. He stood elevated like a statue, his front hooves high in the air. Roxy smelled his pungent sweat, saw the muscles bulging under his coat, and felt his panic. Then everything happened at once. His massive body swung, and a hoof struck her arm.

A white-hot bolt of pain exploded in her arm, shooting through her body like lightning. She heard a dull crack that shook her to the core. One last tug and the rope slipped from her hand. Next came the pain. Her arm throbbed with a force that took her breath away. She lost her balance and hit her head on the cobbles.

At some point, she heard muffled footsteps, as if through water. Someone called her name. Roxy tried to answer, to lift her head, but her body no longer obeyed her. Then someone knelt beside her, picked her up, and carried her away.

"Easy," growled the farrier.

"Where's Kasper?" A bitter taste stung her throat.

"Wieland is taking care of him."

"What happened?"

"He shied. You're lucky he didn't smash your skull."

"But why?"

The farrier didn't seem to hear her. He set her gently on a crate near the fire. Heat soaked into her body. Her arm, which had been numb from the cold, came back to life. Waves of pain pulsed from her forearm to the tips of her toes.

She tried to move her fingers. The pain intensified, so she stopped. After looking at the sore spot, she gasped. There was a bend in the middle of her forearm that didn't belong. "What's wrong with my arm?"

"Broken, probably. I called a doctor."

"Did you smell it too?"

He looked at her as if she were imagining things. "I'll get you a glass of water. The doctor should be here any minute."

Gradually, the fog in Roxy's brain cleared. She placed the scent: pepper oil. That was what had made Kasper so nervous. It must have been on the halter. And Baldur had smelled it too. He'd pawed at the ground to tell her that something was bothering him, and she hadn't understood.

And then the bang. That alone wouldn't have been enough to spook a seasoned brewery horse like Kasper. But combined with the pepper oil, it had pushed him over the edge.

Roxy panted as the realization hit her like a punch to the chest. It wasn't an accident. Someone had orchestrated the incident. To send her a warning, or—she swallowed hard—to kill her?

She forced herself to breathe in and out until the nausea subsided. She had no doubt that Goslar was the culprit. A man without scruples. He must have found out about her complaint somehow and wanted her out of the way.

David stood at the workbench adjusting a valve when the foreman approached him. "Goldmann, your wife had an accident. She's in the hospital."

The valve fell from his hand, clattering onto the concrete floor. "What happened?"

"The caller didn't say."

David looked at his boss, the fear constricting his throat.

"Go ahead and leave. Come back tomorrow morning."

"Thanks." David put away his tools, grabbed his coat, and hurried away. Driven by fear for Roxy and the baby, he reached the hospital in record time. On the way, he imagined the worst-case scenarios in which his beloved wife was fighting for her life, pale as death. He forced himself to calm down. If she was dead, the police would have notified him, not the hospital.

"My name is David Goldmann. My wife is here, Roxana Goldmann. Can I see her?" he asked, out of breath, at the reception desk.

The nurse looked at her records. "Second floor, room 214. But you—"

David wasn't listening. He stormed up the stairs, taking three steps at a time. Room 214 was almost at the end of the hallway. He threw open the door and burst inside. He stopped abruptly in the middle of the room. Roxy was asleep, her eyes closed. She lay pale and lost in bed. Her left arm was encased in a bulky cast.

"Roxy, my darling," he whispered.

Her eyes opened. "David."

He was at her side in two steps, stroking her cheek. "Are you alright? What happened? The baby—"

"The baby is fine," she reassured him. "The doctor examined me."

Relieved, his knees went weak and he sank into the chair next to the bed. "Thank God. I was so scared for both of you."

"I broke my arm. And I have a concussion." She grimaced. "The doctor says I can't work for at least three weeks."

"That doesn't matter. The main thing is that you and the baby are fine." He brushed a strand of hair from her forehead. "What happened?"

Roxy's eyes sparkled. "I was supposed to take Kasper to the farrier, but on the way he shied and kicked me."

David's heart skipped a beat. The brewery horses were huge. And Roxy was so petite. He sought her uninjured hand and squeezed it. "You got off lightly."

"Yes, I did." She drew it out with an emphasis that sent shivers down his spine. The horror scenarios returned.

"It was an accident, wasn't it?" He clung to the more benign alternative because anything else was too disturbing to consider.

"No, David. It wasn't an accident. Not with Kasper. He's the oldest and calmest horse at the brewery. He never spooks. Not at steam whistles, not at rolling barrels, not at anything." She glanced at the door and lowered her voice. "He was nervous this morning. I didn't notice at first, but someone must have smeared pepper oil on his halter. And then there was a bang, directly behind us. At just the right moment. As if someone had been waiting for me."

David's stomach cramped. "You think someone did it on purpose?"

"I don't think so, I'm sure of it." She squinted her eyes. "There's no other explanation."

"You mean it was Goslar?"

"Who else?"

"It couldn't have been him because he's working at City Hall at this time of day," David objected.

Roxy rubbed her nose. "He could have hired someone to do it, instead of getting his own hands dirty."

Fear blazed through David's veins like wildfire until every cell in his body was burning. He didn't want to lose Roxy. "We have to call the police."

"And what am I supposed to tell them? Everyone thinks it was an accident—the farrier, the doctor, even the stable master. He said even the calmest horse can spook sometimes."

"Oh, Roxy. We have to do something."

"But what?" Her voice was filled with frustration. "The police won't help me, just like Morrison won't. Besides, the doctor has ordered me to stay in bed, so what can I do?"

"As long as you stay in bed, you'll be safe." David thought feverishly. "What about Julius' sister's friend?"

"Kate Johnson." Roxy turned her head toward the window, as if the answer lay outside. "I was going to visit her once I had solid proof."

"We can't wait for that. We'll go to Duisburg as soon as you're back on your feet." He leaned forward and kissed her forehead. "But first, you rest and get well. Promise?"

"I promise." She smiled. "Although resting isn't exactly my strong suit."

"I know." David smiled back, but inside he was seething. If Goslar had staged this accident, the situation was more serious than he'd thought. The man was still dangerous.

"I'm taking you home," he said. "I won't leave you alone. Never again."

"Thank you." She looked at him. "But what will we do tomorrow when you have to work?"

CHAPTER 24

His hands clenched tightly around a glass of water, Erwin struggled to come to terms with the events. His man had failed. The Gypsy had survived the accident. The plan had been to spook the horse and then finish her off. It was supposed to look like the horse's kick had killed her.

That son of a bitch had gotten cold feet and had run away instead of seeing it through. Erwin wished he could flay that useless bastard alive. Cold sweat beaded his forehead. That damn Gypsy. Why did she always survive? He cursed himself for not shooting her in the camp. Back then, he'd have gotten a medal, but today...

The petty criminal had been Gunther's idea. Erwin snorted. He couldn't wait to give his friend a piece of his mind. "If you want something done right, you have to do it yourself!" he growled.

Frau Hoffmann looked up from her typewriter. "Did you say something, Herr Krüger?"

"Nothing important." He forced himself to put on a friendly expression. "I'm just a little annoyed about this case."

"These cases can get under your skin. The hair-raising injustice…" She brushed a strand of hair from her forehead. "I had to learn to distance myself from them. When I first started here, I was so angry every day."

"The fates of the innocent are affecting me deeply," he lied without batting an eyelid. His gaze fell on the phone. He had to know how bad things were. "I need something to calm my nerves."

"Would you like me to make you some chamomile tea?" she offered, helpful as always.

"That would be extremely kind. If it's not too much trouble."

"Not at all, Herr Krüger."

No sooner had she left the office than he dialed Gunther's number with trembling fingers.

"Zur Eiche. Gunther Lanter speaking," he answered on the third ring.

"Erwin here. Any news?"

A brief silence. "Broken arm, concussion. She's in the hospital."

"Will she survive?"

"Looks like it. The doctor says she was lucky."

Erwin pressed his lips together. Lucky. The word tasted bitter on his tongue. "Were you there?"

"No, that would have been too risky. I know the head nurse."

Erwin smirked despite himself. Despite—or perhaps because of?—his rough-and-ready manner, Gunther was very popular with women.

"Does she suspect anything?"

"Head nurse, Gerda? No. No one else either. It was an accident. The horse spooked and kicked her." Gunther chuckled into the phone. "If you ask me, women shouldn't work with big horses. No wonder it went wrong."

Erwin's muscles loosened with relief. At least that part of the plan had worked; the police hadn't been informed and nobody would be investigating. "And the... you know? Does she suspect anything?"

"There are no signs of that. Though you can never be a hundred percent sure."

Erwin grimaced. That wasn't what he wanted to hear. "We should discuss the next steps in person."

"Yep, that's better. You absolutely have to bring this to a successful conclusion."

"Oh, so now I have to clean up the mess this guy made?" Erwin snapped. If he'd taken matters into his own hands, the Gypsy wouldn't be in the hospital with a broken arm.

She'd already be exterminated.

"I'll help you," Gunther said, his tone sympathetic. "I'm sorry the man lost his nerve."

The door opened and Frau Hoffmann entered with a steaming cup. The aroma of chamomile filled the office. As she spotted the phone receiver in Erwin's hand, she silently placed the cup on his desk.

"Thank you very much for the information," Erwin said all businesslike. "I am truly grateful."

"Did your colleague show up? She's a hot chick. Why can't you introduce us?"

Erwin thought it wiser to keep his private life and work separate. Nevertheless, he replied, "Gladly. I'll get in touch if I need any more information."

"Give the babe a kiss from me."

A barely perceptible trembling in his hand, Erwin placed the receiver back on the hook. The botched murder rattled him more than he wanted to admit. He'd believed it would be a clean job. A halter rigged with pepper oil, a loud bang at the right moment, a startled horse, and the troublesome Gypsy would be history with no one the wiser.

But she was alive. And worse, she might suspect something. Even if she believed it was an accident, she'd be jumpy now. Most people needed several weeks to process something like this. During that time, they made mountains out of molehills.

Staging a second accident was virtually impossible. He'd have to come up with a different plan.

He turned to Frau Hoffmann. "Thank you very much for the tea. I don't know how to thank you for your kindness."

"It's my pleasure," she replied. "You're such a kind man. Not like Herr Weber, who just barks orders at me."

"You don't deserve that." He smiled at her before turning his attention back to the file on his desk. Inside, he was so nervous the words blurred before his eyes. He had to eliminate the Gypsy once and for all. And this time he had to do it himself, then he could be sure she was actually dead. He needed a foolproof plan.

First, he thought about all the things connecting him to his past. He'd destroyed most of them and hidden the rest well. He clenched his jaw. As much as it pained him, he had to sacrifice the rest, too. Tonight after work, he'd destroy the medal and the photo.

Subconsciously, he ran his finger over his left forearm, where his blood type had once been tattooed. He'd had it removed after the war, leaving behind a thin scar that could have many explanations.

Regardless, anyone with half a brain knew that in ninety-nine out of a hundred cases, a scar in this spot meant one thing. He frowned. If necessary, he'd have to inflict more scars to hide the telltale one. He dismissed the idea because it would be too painful. Besides, he'd need a plausible excuse for Sonja explaining his injuries.

Sonja was his biggest trump card. She loved him. She'd testify for him without hesitation. If it came down to it, she'd swear he was Erwin Krüger and that the allegation was absurd.

"Frau Hoffmann," he said, following a sudden impulse. "I have to go to the registry office later to check some entries. I'll go straight home from there."

He had urgent matters to attend to.

CHAPTER 25

It was pitch dark when the alarm clock rang. Something felt different. Roxy's brain seemed to be stuffed with cotton wool. When she turned over to give David a good morning kiss, a bulky thing was in the way. She attempted to roll over it, until a sharp pain shot through her arm and up to her shoulder.

The memory of the accident came flashing back. The doctor had given her a sedative, then her arm had been put in a cast. A dull throb pounded in her bone.

"Stay in bed and rest." David brushed a strand of hair from her forehead and kissed her.

"I'll make breakfast."

"You stay in bed." He gently pushed her back onto the pillows. "Remember what the doctor said, you need plenty of rest, and you mustn't put any strain on your arm."

She wanted to protest, to tell him she'd experienced far worse than a broken arm, but couldn't find the words. Her eyes closed again. She noticed David pulling the blanket to her chin and wrapping her up like a mummy.

"I have to go," he whispered. "I'm working the early shift today so I can take care of you in the afternoon."

"You don't have to," Roxy murmured, but he was already

gone. She heard him moving in the hallway, then the door clicked shut and footsteps clattered down the wooden stairs.

Since she didn't have to go to work today, she could enjoy the cozy warmth under the down comforter a little longer. As she woke up again, daylight filled the room. The alarm clock on the nightstand read half past nine.

She rubbed her eyes, pushing herself up clumsily. The bulky cast hindered her every movement. Nonetheless, she struggled out of bed. With her good hand, she put the kettle on and rummaged for peppermint leaves in the drawer. It took three times longer than usual.

The kettle whistled, just as she dropped the leaves into the thermos. The apartment was freezing cold. Normally, it didn't faze her, having slept many nights in freezing temperatures because the only safe place was a bombed-out ruin or a wooden shed in an allotment garden. Today though, goose bumps covered her entire body and even her feet seemed to have turned into blocks of ice.

She decided to take the thermos and a cup to her bed, making herself comfortable under the blanket again—as comfortable as she could be with the annoying cast.

As she greedily sipped the hot tea, her right hand clasped around the warm cup. Gradually, the fog in her brain cleared, but the throbbing in her broken arm intensified.

She wasn't afraid of Goslar—at least not like she'd been when she'd stood before him at the camp with trembling knees. Back then, he'd been the master of life and death; with a snap of his fingers, he could send a prisoner to the afterlife. He was still dangerous. And just as ruthless, as yesterday's incident had shown. He knew who she was and wanted her dead.

Her thoughts whirled. As long as Goslar remained at large, she and the baby would never be safe. Unless she went into hiding. She could disappear, move to a remote corner of Germany, and change her name if necessary.

Yet, every cell in her body rebelled against this strategy. The

Nazis had tried for years to wipe her people off the face of the earth. Roxy balled her fist. No, she wouldn't hide again. She'd fight and bring Goslar down. But how could she do that? Lieutenant Morrison had made it clear that he wouldn't pursue the case. And she couldn't go to his superior until she had evidence.

An electrifying tension shot through her from head to toe as the solution struck her. She slammed the teacup on the nightstand and peeled herself out from under the thick blanket.

It took her a while to get dressed and slip on her shoes. The coat, however, presented an insurmountable obstacle: the cast wouldn't fit through the sleeve, and if she left it empty like a war amputee, she couldn't fasten the buttons. She tried a few test steps. Each time the coat slipped off her shoulder. So she wrapped herself in a thick wool scarf instead. That would have to do.

She pulled the door closed with a decisive click and locked it. As she pocketed the key, a shudder racked her because she knew David wouldn't like her plan. Probably rightly so. It was risky, but there were no other options. She needed proof of Krüger's true identity; only then would he be brought to justice—and she could live in peace with David and their baby. She wouldn't let Goslar destroy the life she had worked so hard to build.

Before leaving the house, she checked the street in all directions. Although nobody was in sight, she exercised caution and took a few detours until she was absolutely sure she wasn't being followed.

Only then did she take the direct route to Goslar's house. He'd be at work at this time of day and wouldn't return home until five in the afternoon at the earliest, when the office closed its doors to the public. That gave her plenty of time to search his house for evidence.

Normally, she'd have climbed the bare tree to assess the situation from above. With her arm in a cast, that was out of the question. So she crouched behind a trailer parked on the curb, to study the surroundings.

On both sides stood narrow, two-story terraced houses with small front yards. After every fourth house, a gap opened onto a path leading to the gardens behind.

Once she was assured there were no lights on in Goslar's house and no smoke rising from the chimney, she marched to the nearest path between the houses. As she had suspected, there was a green area with the meager remains of winter vegetables growing in the beds.

She peered in all directions again, and found nothing moving. The residents were probably either at work or busy with chores in the house. A sharp gust of wind swept through Roxy's scarf, making her shiver. In the bitter cold, no sane person stayed outside any longer than absolutely necessary, so she didn't have to worry about being discovered.

She crept across the frozen ground, which crackled softly under her soles. As she reached Goslar's house, she grinned. The broken basement window was covered with thick cardboard. Carefully, she pushed it aside, slipping through the opening, and pulling it back into place. It was child's play, even with a plaster cast on her arm.

The basement had that typical damp, musty smell that lingered in your nose for days. She turned around and saw the stairs leading up to the living area. The basement door creaked as Roxy opened it. She stood stock still and listened. But everything remained quiet. There was no indication that anyone was home.

There was a narrow hallway leading to the kitchen on the left and the living room on the right. On the kitchen table was an ashtray with a single cigarette butt in it. There were no dirty dishes in the sink, no objects lying around. Just a neatly folded stack of newspapers in a basket next to the stove.

Goslar was a stickler for cleanliness and order. In the camp, prisoners had been whipped if their caps sat crooked on their heads. Roxy entered the kitchen and inspected the cupboards. One by one she opened them to look inside: glasses, plates, cutlery. No sign of anything incriminating.

A dull throbbing in her temples distracted her. The doctor had instructed her to stay in bed for a few days to recover from the concussion. But Roxy couldn't be bothered with such details.

Next, she tackled the living room. In the corner stood a desk with a chair. Bookshelves hung on the wall, the sofa underneath. A huge painted landscape was mounted above the fireplace. More pictures adorned the other walls, each one carefully aligned.

There was nothing on the solid oak desk except a silver cigar case. Roxy opened the top drawer: letters, receipts, a small leather case. Nothing incriminating. She continued to the next drawer. Inside was a photo album. It was only half full. Mundane scenes, landscapes, portraits from the previous century.

Then a ray of sunlight shone through the window and illuminated the wall. Frowning, she moved closer, squinting her eyes. Sure enough, rectangles in several places on the wallpaper were slightly darker than the rest. She ran her finger along the wall until she felt a tiny hole. A nail had been there. Excited, she bit her lip.

Goslar had taken down the pictures. There was only one explanation: they contained clues to his past.

Her excitement evaporated and she sighed. Goslar was fastidious to the extreme. If he'd combed his house for suspicious items, she'd find nothing. Disappointed, she sat down on the staircase leading to the upper floor. She'd bet a month's worth of food coupons that he'd destroyed everything that could be used against him.

Her plan had been a failure. With her shoulders slumping, she stood up and automatically touched her chest seeking the comfort of the horse pendant, until she remembered that she'd given it to Natalie.

Strangely enough, the thought gave her new hope. If Goslar had kept this materially worthless trinket for so many years, there must be other things that he considered too valuable to destroy. There must be something in this house that connected him to his past; she just needed to look harder for it.

The living room was too obvious. The basement and attic were also out of the question. So she tried her luck in the bedroom. It was clean and tidy, only the wallpaper, which was peeling in places, disturbed the perfection. The furnishings were just as frugal as on the ground floor: a bed, a wardrobe, a bedside table with a lamp on it. Nothing was hidden here.

Roxy was about to leave the room when she noticed a bulge in the wallpaper next to the wardrobe. She stepped closer, running her finger over the seam, feeling a tiny edge in the wall.

She slid a finger inside the wallpaper, finding something smooth behind it. Her heart pounded with excitement. Carefully, she pulled the object out. It was a photo. Its jagged corner got caught on the wallpaper, so she couldn't remove it completely.

It featured a man in an SS uniform on horseback. In the background, hundreds of prisoners stood in rows, staring straight ahead, shoulders squared, hands holding caps placed neatly on their chests.

Dizziness washed over her as a vivid memory transported her back in time. She was standing on the roll call square. One hour, two hours. All around her, prisoners fainted, unable to stand at attention in the scorching heat. Once again, the count didn't tally. The numbers never seemed to match. So for the fourth time, the SS marched through the ranks, generously distributing blows left and right with the bone crusher—a rubber truncheon filled with stones.

During the fifth count, another two hours later, Goslar himself rode through the rows, cracking his whip down on the prisoners' bare heads from high above. Two rows away, a man collapsed under the treatment, writhing in pain on the ground.

Roxy blinked several times to dispel the grim memory, sweat trickling down her forehead. She examined the picture more closely. Goslar's face was clearly visible under the cap with the imperial eagle, along with the insignia of an SS Hauptsturmführer on his uniform. She'd finally found proof of Goslar's true identity. He couldn't deny this photo.

Then, the sight of Marek, her fatherly friend, in the front row froze her blood. Grief and fury surged so hard her knees nearly buckled. Her fingers eased the edge of the photo free until the paper resisted and began to tear. She stopped. One more pull and she'd destroy the only evidence left to bring Goslar to justice.

Carefully, she pressed the photo back into place and let her eyes wander around the room in search of something she could use – anything—but there was nothing that wouldn't risk more damage.

She took one step toward the door to fetch a knife from the kitchen before a brittle crack stopped her. The sound of metal on metal. Frantically she gazed around. Then the scrape of a key. As Roxy flinched, light flared across the landing downstairs. Footsteps followed, and the glimmer of light died away as the front door closed with a thud.

Her fingers shaking, she slid the photo back behind the wallpaper. Leaving it there tore her heart, but if Goslar found her inside his house...no. She couldn't risk that. At least she knew where it was, and could return with the police to fetch the evidence.

But first, she had to escape. Now. The only staircase led straight into the living room, where someone was standing. A man capable of anything. Her pulse hammered. The cast dragged at her arm, slowing her movements. If Goslar caught her red-handed, her fate was sealed.

Once more, her gaze wandered across the room, weighing

her options. Hiding in the closet or under the bed would be foolish. In both places he'd discover her in no time.

The only viable option was to escape through the window. Her mouth went dry. Under normal circumstances, that would have been child's play for her, but with the cast? Heavy footsteps wafted up from the living room. A drawer in the desk was pulled open.

She didn't have much time left.

CHAPTER 26

S hutting the door behind him, Erwin leaned against it for a moment. The soothing silence enveloped him. He was safe in his house; here he could be himself without having to fear being recognized.

He took off his coat and hung it on the hook in the hallway. With trembling fingers, he loosened his tie. The Gypsy was still alive. The thought drilled into his skull like a red-hot nail. All the planning, the risk he'd taken, had been for nothing. Gunther had hired a damn bungler, and the fool botched the job. Erwin clenched his fists. If he got his hands on the man, he'd show him what happened to losers.

In the living room, he took a bottle of cognac from the shelf and poured himself a generous amount. The amber-colored liquid sloshed around in the glass. Despite his usual habit, he didn't swirl the fine spirit, nor did he inhale the woody cedar aroma with relish. He raised the glass to his lips and downed it in one gulp.

The cognac burned down his throat, warming his stomach. Slowly, a calmness spread through his body. His nerves, which had been stretched to the breaking point, relaxed. He took a deep breath and let his gaze wander around the room. Everything was in its place. The books were lined up straight on the shelf, the sofa cushions were neatly fluffed up, and the landscape painting above the fireplace was adjusted with precision.

Yet a subtle uneasiness nagged at him. Something was different. He couldn't put his finger on it, couldn't name it, but the atmosphere in the room seemed to have changed. As if someone had been here and disturbed the air.

"Ridiculous," he muttered, pouring himself a second cognac. "Your nerves are playing tricks on you."

He took a coaster from the shelf and sat down at his desk, where he placed the coaster about a hand's breadth away from the cigar case, set the shot glass on it, and opened the middle drawer.

The half-full photo album lay inside, along with neatly sorted stacks of letters. Everything was where it belonged. His hand hovered over the album. Then he paused. It was half a centimeter too far left. That was odd, because every object had its spot. The album belonged precisely on the right side of the drawer. An icy shiver ran down his spine.

"Nonsense," he said aloud into the silence. "I moved it myself. Yesterday, when I was going through the bills."

But had he really done that? His memory was blurred. The stress of the last few days, the constant tension, the wedding preparations, the failed action against the Gypsy. It was taking its toll.

He pulled out the album, flipping through the pages. The pictures stared back at him. Landscapes from the Black Forest he'd photographed years ago on a trip. A few pre-war views of Munich. Nothing incriminating. Nonetheless, they had to disappear. Every single one of them.

The devil is a squirrel. Erwin rubbed his temples. He had to be thorough. Nothing could be overlooked. If the Gypsy dug into his past—and she undoubtedly would, having survived the accident—she mustn't find anything.

He'd need fabricated photos. Pictures of family gatherings,

trips, mundane moments in the life of ordinary citizen, Erwin Krüger. A carefully constructed past that left no room for doubt.

His gaze was drawn to the album again. He drank the second cognac, waiting for the calming effect to kick in. Of course, no one had been inside his house. How could they get in? He'd found the front door double-locked, as it was every day when he came home.

Besides, who could have been here? The Gypsy woman was in the hospital with a broken arm and a concussion. Yet the doubt gnawed and wouldn't let him relax.

He got up, pacing the living room. He opened every drawer, checked every shelf, inspected every corner. Nothing had changed. Nothing was missing. Nothing had been added. He ran his finger along the top shelf. A thin layer of dust covered his fingertip.

"I'm going crazy," he muttered.

Still, he couldn't shake the dread that someone had been in his refuge. In his safe space. It was an outrage. How dare this person violate him that way?

Fear slid up his spine like a slithering snake. There was no point in putting it off one more second; he had to destroy the incriminating photo. And the medal. Any indication of his true identity posed a threat. The bloody Gypsy had survived, and as long as she lived, he was in danger of being exposed.

The thought of destroying a piece of his glorious past hurt far more than he ever thought possible. The photo showed him in his prime, at the peak of his power. Hartmut Goslar, SS Hauptsturmführer, on horseback in front of hundreds of prisoners trembling at the sight of him. It was intoxicating, the feeling of being omnipotent, invincible, a god on a horse, ruling over life and death.

But the war cross was his greatest pride, awarded for his heroic efforts and loyal service to the Third Reich. All these years, the piece of metal had given him support when times were hard. The medal had been held in the hands of the Führer. It was his everlasting connection to Germany's savior.

Sentimentality was a luxury he couldn't afford.

Erwin took a deep breath and walked to the stairs. His slippers clacked on the wood as he climbed the steps. His inner turmoil intensified with every step. It was as if the house was trying to tell him something.

As he reached the hallway at the top, he stopped to listen. There was no sign that anyone was in the house. Only the old beams in the roof creaked softly with the rhythm of the wind whistling outside.

As always, the bedroom door was closed. His heart pounding, he pushed it open. The room was empty. The bed was neatly made, the closet closed, the nightstand untouched.

A gust of wind swept through the room and blew the window open. It slammed against the wall.

Erwin froze.

The window had been ajar. Not closed, but ajar.

Every single hair on his body stood on end. He never left a window ajar. Especially not in winter. Windows were either shut or open. Nothing in between. Never.

So someone had been here after all. He wasn't crazy.

He rushed to the window and peered out. The garden lay deserted, the bare flower beds covered in frost. There were no footprints in the frost, no movement. But that didn't mean anything, an intruder could have sneaked across the concrete slabs by the house.

Erwin needed three attempts to lock the window, his hands were shaking so badly. The cognac had lost its calming effect. Panic gnawed at his guts. He had to destroy the photo. Right now.

On the wall, where the wallpaper bulged, his fingers felt their way over the rough surface, found the edge, and slipped behind it. Smooth paper caressed his fingertips.

Relieved, he tugged out the photograph.

It was still there. Whoever had been here hadn't found it. Still, that thought didn't calm him. On the contrary. The certainty that his refuge had been broken into disturbed him deeply. Thick beads of sweat trickled down his forehead.

From the photo in his hand, his younger self looked back at him, proud and dignified in his immaculate SS uniform. His peaked cap was perfectly aligned, the badge gleaming. It was the image of a man aware of his own greatness.

"Farewell, Hartmut," he whispered affectionately. Then he hurried into the kitchen and took a box of matches from the drawer.

His hands were surprisingly steady as he struck a match. The small flame flickered orange and yellow like a playful dervish. He held the photo over the sink, touching one corner with the flame. It immediately ate through the paper. The fire crept across Hartmut's face, the prisoners in the background, the horse, over everything he had been. The paper curled, turned black, and crumbled to ashes.

Erwin watched as the last remnants burned and fell into the sink. Black flakes that had once been his past. He turned on the tap and rinsed the ashes down the drain. Hartmut Goslar was gone for good.

Just his War Merit Cross remained. He fished the precious item, wrapped in wax paper, out of the toilet tank. He couldn't burn the medal or throw it in the trash. For a brief moment, he toyed with the idea of giving it to a comrade who worked as a steelworker and have him throw it into the smelter.

The notion tightened his throat. The Merit Cross, which Hitler himself had awarded him, melting like ice in the sun. No. That would be sacrilege. It was already afternoon and dusk would soon fall. Erwin put on his coat, pocketed a spoon, and left the house.

The cemetery lay ten minutes away. He chose the most beautiful and largest grave: that of General Alaric von

Hohenfeld, a glorious field commander from the early 19th century. A row of polished marble stones surrounded the grave, behind which rose the majestic headstone made of shiny black marble, reflecting the last rays of sunshine. Two angels looked down benevolently on the deceased. Beneath them, a raised sword was displayed above a laurel wreath and the inscription:

"To the hero of the fatherland, who united bravery and honor."

This was a dignified place to bury his War Merit Cross 1st Class with Swords. He dug with the spoon. The frozen earth yielded reluctantly, but he continued working until the hole was about twenty centimeters deep.

One last time, he took out the Merit Cross and unwrapped it from the wax paper, gazing at it reverently in the fading light. The black cross, the white background, the red ribbon. It had been his anchor, the reminder of his true identity.

"I'm sorry," he whispered, not sure exactly who he was talking to. To the medal? To his former self? To the Reich lying in ruins? Or to his Führer in the afterlife?

He wrapped the Merit Cross once more, gently dropped it into the hole, and shoveled earth over it. Then he covered the loose soil with an ivy vine.

As Erwin stood up, his knees ached. Though the pain in his heart was worse over the demise of his glorious past. Darkness settled over his soul as it had over the cemetery. Street lanterns cast ghostly shadows between the markers. A crow cawed somewhere in the distance.

He banished the gloomy thoughts and straightened his shoulders. It was time to merge completely with his new identity. From now on, only Erwin Krüger existed, and he would create a bright future for himself.

On the way home, the wind tugged at his coat. Surprisingly, he felt lighter with every step. It was so soothing to let go of his former identity that he wondered why he hadn't severed ties long ago.

A smile tugged at the corners of his mouth. In a few weeks,

he'd marry Sonja; then his happiness would be perfect. Nothing and no one could harm him.

Not even the Gypsy woman—because she'd meet her maker soon.

CHAPTER 27

David left work two hours early to tend to his sick wife. He hurried home, lengthening his strides threefold.

As he stepped into the hallway, he called out, "Darling! I'm back!"

But Roxy didn't answer. She must be asleep. He took off his shoes and coat and slinked into the apartment. But a glance at the bed told him she wasn't there. He walked into the tiny bathroom, which was also dark and empty. There was no sign of Roxy.

He'd urged her to stay in bed and rest. The doctor had said not to underestimate the concussion. What could have prompted her to leave the apartment?

He returned to the bed. The covers were thrown back. On the nightstand stood a thermos and a half-empty cup of peppermint tea. It looked like she had left in a hurry. Did she have to hide?

"Roxy. It's me, David. There's no one else here," he called into the empty apartment. Still nothing moved.

Where could she be? In this dog-cold, with a broken arm and a concussion? His mind raced. Maybe she'd felt sick and gone to the neighbor's? Or to the hospital? Or—and this thought made his blood boil—Goslar had kidnapped her.

He swallowed the rising nausea, because he needed a clear head. Roxy wasn't easily intimidated. If someone had taken her, there'd be signs of a struggle. Something. But apart from the unmade bed, the room was tidy. Nothing pointed to force.

He sat down on a kitchen chair and waited. The minutes crawled by like thick syrup. His hands shook as he lit a cigarette. David inhaled the smoke and tried not to picture horrifying scenarios about what might have happened.

After what seemed like an eternity, he heard a creak on the stairs. Roxy's light footsteps were inaudible except when she stepped on the half-broken third step from the top. He instinctively held his breath until the key clicked in the lock.

Rushing into the hallway, he saw her. A woolen scarf hung lopsided around her shoulders as she shivered from the cold. But she didn't seem to be hurt.

"My goodness, Roxy! You scared me half to death. I thought I'd never see you again!" Relief gave way to deep anger. "Where have you been?"

She flinched at the sharp tone. "I—"

"The doctor ordered you to stay in bed!" His voice was louder than he intended. "You have a concussion, Roxy. You shouldn't have left the apartment."

"I know, but—"

"But what?" He loomed over his wife, his head bursting with the images of what could have happened. Inhaling, he struggled to regain his calm. "Do you know how scared I was? I came home and you were gone. I thought something had happened to you. I thought Goslar had..." His voice broke.

Roxy put her good hand on his arm. "I'm sorry, David. Truly. But I had to check something."

"What was so important for you to take a risk like that?" Gradually, his agitation subsided and he put his arm around her shoulders. Compared to him, she was small and petite, which led most people to underestimate her. "What was so urgent it couldn't wait until you were well?"

"Come with me. I'll tell you everything, but I need to sit down."

"Oh, Roxy." Instantly, he felt guilty. She could barely stand on her feet, and he was lecturing her. He stroked her cheek. "You're freezing. Get into bed right now."

She obediently let him put her to bed and cover her up. He poured the rest of the tea from the thermos into two cups and held one out to her. Then he sat down on the edge of the bed. "So, what couldn't wait?"

"You're not going to like it." She looked up at him, guilt written all over her face. "I was in Goslar's house."

The words hit him like a punch to the jaw. "You broke into his house?"

"So to speak."

David stared at her in disbelief. Then anger began to boil up inside him, and he had to take several deep breaths before he could speak. "You broke into the house of the man who just tried to kill you? Please tell me that's not true!"

She grimaced. "I had to do it."

"You didn't have to do anything." He ran both hands through his hair. "My God, Roxy. That wasn't just dangerous, it was illegal! Imagine if he'd come home and caught you?"

"Nothing happened."

"That's not the point." David jumped up and paced back and forth in the small apartment. "The point is that you took an incredible risk. You put your life on the line. And our baby's life."

Roxy flinched at his words. "I know. But understand me, David. He'll never stop. As long as he's free, he'll always be after us. After me. After our child."

"And that's why you're breaking into his place?" His voice dripped with sarcasm. "That makes everything better? If he reports you to the police, you're the one who'll go to jail, not him. What will become of our child then?"

"No one saw me," she said wearily.

"You don't know that for sure." He stopped in front of her. Her desperate expression broke his heart. "Roxy, please. I can't lose you. I can't lose both of you."

"I'm sorry, I didn't mean to scare you." She put down the teacup, placing her hand on his. "But it was worth it."

David frowned. "What do you mean?"

"I found something." For the first time since she'd come home, a spark of triumph lit her face. "A photo. Hidden behind the wallpaper in his bedroom."

Despite his anger, curiosity flared. "What kind of photo?"

"It shows him in his SS uniform, on horseback. In the background, prisoners are standing at attention." She held his gaze. "This photo identifies him beyond a doubt. It's him. Erwin Krüger is Hartmut Goslar."

The words hung heavy in the air. David sat back down on the edge of the bed. "Can I see the photo?"

Roxy grimaced. "I had to leave it behind."

"You found it, but didn't take it with you?" His jaw nearly dropped to the floor.

"Just as I found it, Goslar came home. In broad daylight. What kind of hours does this guy work?"

David groaned.

"The photo's edge was caught and I would have ripped it in my hurry, so I put it back and escaped out the window."

"Out the window. In your condition," David repeated, unable to fathom her words.

"I had no choice. I couldn't risk him catching me."

David forced himself to take a deep breath. The thought of Roxy climbing out of a window with a broken arm and a concussion while Goslar was in the house all but keeled him over.

"Does he suspect anything?" he finally asked.

Roxy shook her head. "I don't think so. I was very careful and left everything exactly as I found it."

"You think." David sighed. "That's not exactly reassuring."

"There's no reason for him to be suspicious," she insisted.

"If I had assumed a new identity to cover up my crimes, I'd always be on my guard." David rested his elbows on his knees. His head hurt. "And now? What do you want to do now?"

"We have to return with the police and get the photo," Roxy said as if it were the most natural thing in the world.

"You do realize what that means, don't you? You'll have to admit you broke into his house and searched his belongings." He ran a hand down his face. "They'll put you in jail. What becomes of our child then?"

The color drained from her face. "I found proof that he's a war criminal, so that has to account for something."

"It doesn't matter. You committed a crime. Don't you understand? The police will arrest you. And the photo? It won't be much use in court if the only witness is in jail for burglary. What judge will believe you?"

"But... but then..."

"Then we have nothing," David finished the sentence for her. "Worse still, what will become of our baby if his mother is in prison?"

Roxy pressed her hand against her mouth as she grasped the significance of his words. "What are we supposed to do then? There must be a way. He has to face justice."

David stroked her cheek. His anger had evaporated, leaving only concern for Roxy and their common future. "I don't know," he said honestly. "We have to think of something."

They sat in silence for a few minutes, their fingers intertwined, while the wind howled around the house like a pack of hungry wolves.

"I could ask Sergeant Wilson," Roxy suggested. "He offered to help."

"He has to report the incident." David sank back into his thoughts until an idea came to him. "Only Kate Johnson can help us now."

Roxy frowned.

"That woman Julius' sister recommended, the British major's wife in Duisburg."

"She's our last chance." A glimmer of hope lit up Roxy's face, but it faded immediately. "The photo is still in his house. I can't show her."

"But you can tell her where it is. You can describe what you saw. Maybe she has options we haven't considered. Julius' sister said she loves solving puzzles. And she certainly has no sympathy for Nazis."

"Do you really think she'll help us? When my only proof is hidden behind wallpaper in a house I broke into."

David chuckled. "When you put it like that, it doesn't sound very convincing."

"Exactly." She hung her head.

"But what do we have to lose?" David asked. "At worst, she hears you out and sends you away. At best, she believes you and does something about it."

Roxy mulled it over. He could literally see the wheels turning in her head as she weighed the alternatives. Finally, she said, "You're right. It's worth a try." She tilted her head, looking at him earnestly. "If we can't convict him, my only option is to go into hiding and assume a new identity somewhere far away."

David had entertained similar thoughts, but ended up pushing them aside. "Then I'll come with you. We'll start a new life together as Hans and Maria Müller."

Roxy giggled. "You make it sound so easy." She became serious again. "We would have to cut ties with your family and never see them again. Are you willing to do that?"

"You are the most important person in my life, and I'd give up everything to be with you and our child." He kissed her on the lips. "Of course I'd miss my family, very much so. But I'd miss you a thousand times more. I love you, Roxy. At our wedding, I vowed to always stand by your side, in good times and bad."

"I love you too, David." Her eyes glistened with tears. "I'm sorry I scared you today."

He squeezed her hand. "We'll get through this together. But please promise me you'll never do anything like that again. No more solo runs."

She nodded. "That's what Tibor always said."

"Your cousin was right. Together, we can achieve much more." David spoke from experience. His mother, along with hundreds of other housewives, had achieved the impossible: after a week of protesting in front of the building on Rosenstrasse, the Nazis had released their Jewish family members. If only all Germans had shown such courage as those housewives.

"I'm hungry," Roxy said. "Should I cook us something?"

"You stay in bed while I make us some hot soup. We'll plan the visit to Kate Johnson over dinner."

CHAPTER 28

ONE WEEK LATER

The passing landscape blurred as the train rumbled to Duisburg. The monotonous clicking of the wheels on the rails had a calming effect on Roxy. David had walked her to the station; he couldn't come with her because he hadn't been able to get time off on such short notice.

"Be careful," he'd said, hugged her tight. "Come back safe."

By now, she'd gotten used to the cast and was moving almost as nimbly with it as without it. The trip took a good hour. Enough time to come up with a strategy.

Adriana had praised her friend to Julius in the highest terms. "A remarkable woman," she'd said. "Smart, brave and with excellent connections." Thanks to Adriana's recommendation, Kate Johnson had agreed to meet Roxy right away.

As the train pulled into Duisburg, a thousand butterflies fluttered in Roxy's stomach. Mrs. Johnson was her only hope. If she couldn't help, Roxy would be forced into hiding and have to live with the fact that Goslar would get away scot-free. That was unthinkable, because Roxy had sworn to herself that one day he'd pay for what he'd done to her people. And she always kept her promises.

The area around the train station in Duisburg looked just as bleak as Essen. But the closer she got to Mrs. Johnson's address, the more upscale the neighborhood became. The occupation officers had requisitioned the cream of the crop in every city, preferably undamaged properties in villa districts.

Roxy glanced down at herself nervously. She'd dressed up for her visit to the Englishwoman, putting on the fine green wool dress. She'd paired it with hand-knitted black wool stockings and David's shoes. Over this she wore her only—rather shabby—coat. She'd unpicked the sleeve's seam so that her plaster cast would fit through. Surrounded by the elegant turn-of-the-century houses, she felt inadequate.

After stopping in front of a three-story mansion, she took a deep breath, ran her fingers through her wild curls, and rang the bell.

A maid in a starched apron opened the door. "Good afternoon. You must be Roxana Goldmann. Mrs. Johnson is expecting you."

Roxy followed the young woman through an entrance hall with a high ceiling and shiny marble floor. Magnificent paintings in gilded frames adorned the walls. A chandelier hung from the ceiling, bathing the room in bright light. There seemed to be no electricity rationing in this neighborhood. Fresh flowers stood in elegant vases, their scent mingling with the floor polish.

The maid knocked on a door before opening it. "Roxana Goldmann is here, ma'am."

"Wonderful! Send her in." A warm and inviting voice, with an unmistakable English accent, calmed some of Roxy's nerves.

Roxy stepped into the bright and spacious room. Tall windows flooded the room with natural light. It was luxuriously yet simply furnished: a sofa with cream-colored covers, armchairs with embroidered cushions, a low table made of dark wood. Watercolors depicting landscapes that reminded Roxy of English postcard motifs hung on the walls.

And standing in the middle of this room was Kate Johnson.

She was smaller than Roxy had expected, about the same height as herself, wearing an elegant dove-blue suit and a pearl necklace. Her chestnut brown hair framed her face in soft waves. Her friendly blue eyes sparkled. Roxy guessed she was in her early fifties.

"Frau Goldmann!" Mrs. Johnson held out both hands. "How lovely to meet you. Adriana has told me so much about you." She noticed the cast. "Oh, how did that happen?"

Roxy was still thinking about how to respond, as Mrs. Johnson waved her toward the sofa. "Please, have a seat. Maria, bring us some tea."

"Right away, ma'am." The maid slipped out.

"My German isn't as good as it used to be. May I call you Roxy?"

"Of course. Gladly." Roxy agreed, a little confused, as she hadn't expected such a warm welcome. "Your German is excellent."

"Please call me Kate." Kate sat down on the armchair next to the sofa where Roxy had settled. "I spent a year at a boarding school in Switzerland. That's where I met Adriana. Poor thing, it wasn't easy for her to give up everything and emigrate to England with virtually nothing."

Roxy forced herself to nod sympathetically. Nothing was a gross exaggeration. Adriana and her husband had left Germany in time and taken a large part of their considerable fortune with them. However, from Kate's perspective, Adriana's situation may have been challenging.

"Good grief, listen to me with my minor complaints… and to you of all people! Julius told us about the Nazi harassment. All those years, Adriana was constantly worried about him, especially when the war started and there was no more correspondence with Germany. When we heard that he'd been refused permission to leave..." She sighed. "Well, you know all that. Julius said you were in one of those horrible camps. Is that true?"

"Yes." Roxy seized the opportunity to address her concern. "That's why I'm here. I recently recognized the former camp commandant."

"Oh, good heavens!" Kate's face contorted into a grimace of horror. "Unimaginable. I hope you reported him. We have a special unit for criminals like him."

Roxy took a deep breath. "I tried."

At that moment, Maria returned with a tray. On it was a fine porcelain teapot, two cups, and an étagère with pastries that made Roxy's mouth water. Maria set everything on the table and disappeared as silently as she'd entered.

Kate poured a dark, strong-smelling tea. Bitter, Roxy guessed. She preferred coffee, or peppermint tea made from leaves she grew in a pot on the windowsill.

"Marks and Spencer Gold Blend," Kate explained with pride, handing Roxy a cup. "My mother sends it from England. It's the only brand worth drinking. And believe me, I've tried them all." Kate added a dash of milk to her cup, stirred it carefully, sipped her tea, and rolled her eyes in pleasure.

Roxy raised her cup to her mouth. The tea was bitter and very strong. She grimaced involuntarily.

"I can see you're not a tea drinker," Kate said with a smile.

"It's not that, it's just very strong. I'm not used to it," Roxy apologized, not wanting to be rude.

"You need to add some milk." Without waiting for a reply, Kate poured a dash of milk into Roxy's cup and handed her a spoon.

In fact, the addition of the milk made the brew almost palatable. Her attention, however, was occupied by the étagère with pastries. It drew Roxy's gaze like a powerful magnet.

Kate followed her gaze and pointed to the top tier. "That's shortbread. Help yourself."

"Really?" Roxy took a piece and put it in her mouth. The shortbread instantly dissolved into fine crumbs, and the intense flavor of sugar and butter exploded on her tongue. "It's delicious. Thank you very much."

"Feel free to eat them all, Maria can bring more."

Roxy didn't need to be told twice and tasted the next pastry, a small tart filled with dried fruit. Even if Kate couldn't help her with Goslar, the delicious treats made the visit worthwhile.

"You were quite hungry," Kate said after Roxy polished off all the pastries. "But now tell me how I can help you."

Roxy told her about running into Goslar, who now called himself Krüger, her unsuccessful attempt to report him, and the horse accident that wasn't an accident.

Kate listened attentively, interrupting only occasionally with a question. Her eyebrows drew closer together with every passing minute.

"That's outrageous," she said at last. "Absolutely outrageous. That this man is walking free as if nothing happened."

"The British officer said he couldn't do anything without proof," Roxy replied cautiously, not wanting to disparage Kate's compatriot.

"Typical." Kate snorted contemptuously. "Men and their rules. My husband is just the same. Everything has to be done by the book, everything has to be documented." She leaned back. "We'll have to take him down some other way."

"So you believe me?"

"Of course I believe you." Kate's voice was firm. "Why would you invent such a story? You have nothing to gain and everything to lose." She leaned forward. "Adriana hinted at terrible things. I want him to pay."

"Why are you doing this?" asked Roxy, hardly believing her luck.

"Most people think I'm a spoiled upper-class lady, and I suppose I am. But I also understand the terrible side of war." Kate's gaze drifted into the distance. "I was in London during the Blitz. It was the most horrible experience you can imagine. The whistling of the bombs, the explosions, the buildings collapsing like houses of cards. I was one of the few women with a driver's license, so I volunteered to drive an ambulance."

Roxy looked at the older woman with new respect.

"So many people died. My colleagues and I worked day and night…" She paused and sipped her tea. "We kept ourselves awake with hot tea and adrenaline while we dug out the buried with our bare hands, splinted arms and legs, stopped bleeding, and treated burns. And in the midst of all the chaos, I raced my ambulance from the ruins to the hospital and back. Every time it was a race against time, and far too often we lost." She put her cup down.

"I'm sorry," Roxy said.

"I'm not telling you this to get sympathy. You've suffered worse," Kate continued. "I'm telling you because I understand you. I understand what it means to be afraid and helpless. And I understand what it means to fight." She looked Roxy straight in the eye. "You are very brave. Braver than most people I know. You survived and built a new life for yourself, and now you're fighting for justice. I admire that."

"I admire your courage too," Roxy said quietly. "The bombing was terrible."

Kate waved her hand dismissively. "War is hell. For everyone, in their own way." She reached for a cookie from the étagère, which the maid had refilled. "But enough of that. Let's talk about the present. What can I do?"

After a brief hesitation, Roxy opted for the truth. She sensed that Kate wouldn't report her. "I found a photo in Goslar's house showing him in SS uniform at the camp. But I had to leave it behind."

Kate leaned forward with interest. "You broke into his house?"

Roxy hesitated a little. "Sort of. I climbed in through the basement window, but I didn't steal anything."

"Fascinating." Kate's eyes lit up. "It's like a scene out of an Agatha Christie novel. Do you know Agatha Christie?"

Roxy shook her head.

"Oh, you absolutely must read one of her books! Crime novels. Hercule Poirot, Miss Marple. Brilliant detectives who solve the most difficult cases." Kate rubbed her hands together. "I've always dreamed of being like them. Using my gray cells to expose a criminal."

Roxy didn't know who Miss Marple was. It didn't stop her from being infected by Kate's enthusiasm.

"So," said Kate, walking over to the window. She stared out, her hands clasped behind her back. "The photo is still in his house?"

"Probably. Unless he's destroyed it in the meantime."

"Possible." Kate turned around. "But if he kept it, it was for a reason. Sentimentality, perhaps. Or arrogance. Some men just can't let go."

"I can't fetch it. I promised my husband I wouldn't break in again." Roxy always kept her promises.

"You don't have to. That would be foolish. We'll get the evidence legally. I'll pay him a visit and confront him with the allegation."

"He won't just hand over the photo."

"True." Kate poured herself a third cup and rang for the maid to brew a fresh pot. Then she sat silently for a while, frowning.

Roxy didn't dare interrupt.

After a few minutes, Kate turned around and announced triumphantly, "I'll pay him a visit under a pretext. Once I'm in the house, I'll ask to use the bathroom and retrieve the photo from its hiding place."

Roxy jumped up. "That's insane. If he gets suspicious, he might hurt you."

"I'm the wife of a British major. He'd never dare to lay a finger on me."

Every fiber in Roxy's body screamed that this was a bad idea.

It was too risky. Something could go wrong. If something happened to Kate, she'd feel responsible. "It's far too risky. I'm coming with you."

"He'll recognize you", Kate objected.

"He hasn't seen me since the camp. I'll change my hairstyle, put on lipstick and eye makeup."

"If he's responsible for your accident, as we both assume, he knows by now that you survived and will definitely be suspicious when he sees your cast."

"That's true." Roxy hadn't thought of that. "Still, it's too dangerous. My husband—and yours too—will give me hell if anything happens to you."

Kate rang for the maid. "Maria, please bring me the black cape."

"Yes, ma'am."

"What are you up to?" Roxy asked.

"We're going to put you in a disguise, so Goslar won't be able to recognize you."

Shortly after, Maria returned with the garment. "Here you are, ma'am."

As soon as she left, Kate put the cape on Roxy and said, "Something's still missing. Come with me."

Obediently, she followed Kate into the foyer to the huge wardrobe. Kate took a hat from the shelf and put it on Roxy's head.

After regarding her a few moments, Kate muttered, "Not perfect yet."

On the fourth attempt—Roxy was amazed at how many hats a woman could own—she nodded with satisfaction.

Then she fetched a dark red scarf, which she draped elegantly around Roxy's shoulders. When she'd completed the look, she clapped her hands. "Perfect. Even your husband wouldn't recognize you. Turn around."

Curious, Roxy obeyed and stared at the elegant lady in the

mirror. "Unbelievable. I hardly recognize myself. And the cast isn't noticeable at all under the wide cape."

"Miss Marple would be proud of us." Kate was visibly pleased with her work. "While you engage Goslar in conversation, I'll ask to go to the bathroom, sneak into his bedroom and get the photo."

The thought sent a shiver down Roxy's spine. "Shouldn't we inform your husband after all?"

Kate waved her off. She took a pastry and thoughtfully put it in her mouth. "He's not in charge of Essen and won't want to interfere in the affairs of another department."

"Please, it's too dangerous," Roxy pleaded. "This isn't a game."

Kate looked at her sternly. "Don't be silly. If you don't want to come with me, I'll do it on my own."

"I'm definitely coming with you," Roxy assured her hastily. "I'm not going to let you go into the lion's den without backup."

"Then it's settled. We'll meet in front of his house tomorrow evening."

CHAPTER 29

David was on pins and needles, constantly checking the clock on the wall. Every minute dragged on like chewing gum. Why wasn't Roxy back yet? How long could her conversation with Kate Johnson possibly take?

He reminded himself to breathe to calm his nerves. Roxy was smart and resourceful, and since the accident with the horse, she'd been doubly on her guard. However, that thought didn't reassure him. Goslar must have found out about the failed attack and was surely planning a second attempt. David gasped for air, expecting a knock on the door at any moment and two serious-looking police officers delivering the bad news.

At last he heard a creak on the stairs. His heart leapt with joy. Before Roxy could slide the key in the lock, he threw open the door and pulled her into his arms. "Thank God. I was so worried."

"I'm fine." She leaned against him, and he could feel the tension in her muscles. "But we need to talk."

Just now David noticed the elegant cape and hat. "Where did you get that?"

"I'll explain in a moment."

An uneasy feeling stirred in David's stomach as he helped her out of the cape, under which she wore her own coat.

She snuggled under the thick down comforter while he poured her hot coffee from the thermos. After sitting down next to her, he couldn't control his curiosity any longer. "So? Tell me."

"Kate lent me these things." Roxy rubbed her face with her hand. "She wants to confront Goslar tomorrow evening."

David didn't quite understand what the garments had to do with the visit. "What exactly is she planning?"

Roxy's face contorted into a pained grimace. "She plans to access his house under a pretext and retrieve the photo from its hiding place while I distract him."

Goosebumps crawled down David's spine like ants on fire. "You're planning to confront the man who tried to kill you?"

"Hence the disguise, so he won't recognize me."

"It's still too dangerous." David shook his head.

"I can't let Kate go there alone," Roxy groaned. "She has no idea who she's dealing with. If something happens to her, I'll never forgive myself."

"And what if something happens to you?" David stood up and paced the room. "Roxy, this is madness. You're pregnant, you have a broken arm, and this man wants you dead."

"Kate is convinced that her status as the wife of a British officer will protect us. He won't dare lay a finger on her."

"And you believe that?" David fought against the rising panic.

Roxy was silent for a moment before admitting, "No, I don't. If Goslar feels cornered, he's unpredictable." She sipped her hot coffee, looking at him for help. "Believe me, I've tried to talk Kate out of her plan with the most convincing words I could muster. Unfortunately, it was a waste of time. You might as well try to teach a donkey to dance. If I don't accompany her, she'll go alone."

David leaned against the headboard. "Then I'll come with you."

"That won't work." Roxy shook her head. "If we show up with a man, Goslar will never let us into the house."

"I'll follow you at a distance. I'll stay out of sight, but nearby. In case something goes wrong."

She looked at him gratefully. "That's sweet of you, David, but you can't help once we're inside his house. Or do you want to break down the door?"

David shrugged. He was prepared to do anything to protect Roxy. "If I have to."

Roxy put her hand on his. "Is this the same man who yelled at me for sneaking into Goslar's house?"

"Come on, this is completely different! I'd only do it if he threatened you."

"Which you can't see from outside."

"You could scream for help."

Roxy wrinkled her nose in thought. "Do you remember the black soldier I told you about? Sergeant Wilson. He was visibly upset that Morrison refused to process my complaint and offered to help if I needed anything."

David nodded.

"We'll go see him tomorrow morning and ask him to accompany you. Then he can intervene if necessary."

"Do you believe he'd do that?" David still didn't like Kate's plan, but with Sergeant Wilson as backup, the risk for the two women would be manageable.

"I don't know. We have to try. He's probably our best chance."

David nodded. "At what time do you want to visit Goslar?"

"Tomorrow evening at seven o'clock."

"I'll be there. With or without Wilson." David was already pondering which colleague he might take along in case Wilson refused.

"Thank you for doing this for me."

"I love you, Roxy."

"I love you, too." She kissed him. First gentle and tender, then more passionately.

Much later, when they turned off the lights, she asked, "Do you know who Miss Marple is?"

"What makes you ask?"

"Kate said she wants to be like Miss Marple, only twenty years younger."

David chuckled. "Miss Marple is a character in Agatha Christie's novels. She's a lovable, slightly quirky older lady who solves criminal cases on her own. My mother has read all the books about her."

Roxy yawned. "Now I understand. Kate thinks she can follow in Miss Marple's footsteps and solve this case. I think she's bored in Duisburg, so this is a welcome distraction."

"Then it's good we'll be with her. Reality isn't a crime novel. People get hurt."

Roxy didn't answer. She'd fallen asleep next to him. David hated the plan, but he counted on Sergeant Wilson coming along. No matter how unscrupulous Goslar was, he wouldn't dare attack a soldier of the occupying power.

The next morning, David woke up exhausted. Every time he'd fallen asleep, he'd dreamed that Goslar was about to kill Roxy and had jolted awake. Then he'd carefully fumbled around on the other side of the bed to make sure she was lying safe and sound next to him. He wouldn't be able to sleep peacefully again until that man was in prison.

At work he was barely able to concentrate. Twice he burned his fingers with the soldering iron because he wasn't paying attention.

Herr Murr cast him concerned looks. "Goldmann, is everything okay?"

"Yes, boss. It's just... my wife. I'm worried about her."

"Go home early today. We can manage without you."

"Thank you." David took off his heavy apron and hung it on the hook. Then he headed for the British administration.

Finding Sergeant Wilson was easier than he'd feared: the Brit was standing in front of the entrance smoking.

"Sergeant Wilson?" David approached.

The man turned around. "Yes? Can I help you?"

"My name is David Goldmann. My wife, Roxana, was here a few weeks ago to report an SS-Hauptsturmführer."

Wilson frowned. After a few seconds, recognition flashed across his face. "Ah, yes, I remember. The young Gypsy. How is she?"

"Not well." David glanced around and lowered his voice. "There was an incident at her new job at the brewery, that was made to look like an accident."

Wilson's eyes narrowed. "And you think it wasn't?"

"I'm certain." David said. "Someone must have warned the man she was going to report. And now he wants to silence her."

"I had nothing to do with it." Wilson raised his hands defensively. "Just because I'm black, you want to pin it on me? You think I warned this guy?"

David looked at the Brit in bewilderment. "On the contrary, my wife sent me because you offered your help."

"I'm sorry. My nerves are on edge." Sergeant Wilson calmed down as quickly as he'd lost his temper. "But how can I help you?"

"The case is a bit unusual. An acquaintance of my wife's, an Englishwoman, is determined to see justice done by getting Goslar to confess. She wants to visit him tonight."

"Damn it! An Englishwoman, you say? Why the hell does she have to get involved? Do you know what complications that'll cause?" the sergeant roared.

David struggled to remain calm. "Apparently, she's not used to being contradicted. My wife couldn't talk her out of this reckless plan. So she decided to accompany Kate, the Englishwoman."

"Damn it all to hell!"

"That's why I'm asking for your help."

Wilson shook his head. "There's no way I can be a part of the plan. If it comes out that I had anything to do with a break-in—"

"No break-in," David interrupted him. "Just as backup. In case something goes wrong and he gets violent. You don't have to go into the house, just wait nearby. Please."

Wilson stayed quiet, while his brown eyes scrutinized David as if trying to size him up.

"And this Kate is really English?" he finally asked.

David nodded. "The wife of a major from Duisburg."

"What a bloody mess," Wilson cursed. Then he sighed. "I'll be there. But I'll only intervene if one of the women is in mortal danger."

"Thank you so much." David handed him a note with the address and time. "We'll meet about ten minutes early. I'll scout out a place where we can watch the house without being seen."

"Why does this have to happen to me?" Wilson grumbled, pocketed the note, threw his cigarette on the ground, and stamped it out with his boot. Then he turned and disappeared into the building.

David shook his head as he watched him go. He hoped Wilson would keep his word and indeed show up that evening.

As he arrived home, Roxy sat at the table drinking coffee. Her hair was pinned up, and she was wearing make-up. David's heart contracted painfully, as if it were being squeezed by a giant vice.

"You look beautiful," he said, kissing her.

She put down her cup. "I don't want Goslar to recognize me."

"He won't. You look so different with that hairstyle."

"Kate will introduce herself as a representative of a charitable organization. She's supposedly collecting donations for war orphans."

David rubbed his chin. "Good idea. Goslar won't be suspicious. But he'll likely try to brush her off."

"She said that if he doesn't let us in, she'll pretend to faint."

"I wonder if it was a mistake to involve Kate."

Roxy stood up. "It's too late for that now. We have to see this through."

"I have a bad feeling about this."

"Is Wilson coming?" Roxy tilted her head.

"He promised he would." David still wasn't sure whether the Brit would keep his word. He planned on bringing a crowbar with him just in case, but he wouldn't tell Roxy.

"See, then nothing can happen." She kissed him. "I have to go. Kate is capable and will ring Goslar's doorbell on her own if I don't arrive on time."

"I'm coming with you." David grabbed his coat.

"David—"

"I'll keep my distance. I promise. But I'm not letting you go alone."

Roxy looked at him, and he saw the gratitude shining in her eyes. She took a deep breath. "Then let's go."

At every step, David was tempted to catch up with Roxy and forbid her from putting herself in danger. But he knew she'd never speak to him again if he did. As hard as it was, he had to let her do this. Her and Kate Johnson. The double responsibility for the well-being of the two women weighed on his chest. Unlike Kate, he didn't believe for a second that Goslar wouldn't hurt her just because she was English—especially since she planned to pose as an employee of a German organization.

As he finally reached the street where Goslar lived, the blood rushed in David's ears louder than a beehive. Kate Johnson already waited, an elegant apparition in her dark blue coat and hat. She held a leather folder in her hand.

David hid behind a parked truck and watched as Roxy walked over to greet Kate. The two women spoke briefly, then rang Goslar's doorbell.

David held his breath.

The door opened. A man stood in the light—tall, broad-shouldered, with graying hair. Without a doubt, it was Goslar, or Krüger, as he now called himself.

He couldn't hear their conversation. Goslar hesitated for a moment, then stepped aside and let the two women enter.

The door closed behind them. David's hands clenched into fists. Roxy was in the house. With the man who'd tried to kill her. With the man who killed people for his sadistic enjoyment.

"Keep calm," he muttered to himself. "You can intervene at any time."

"Mr. Goldmann?"

When David spun around, Sergeant Wilson stood behind him.

"You can't imagine how relieved I am to see you."

Wilson nodded toward the house. "Are they already inside?"

"Yes. They just went in."

"Then we wait."

CHAPTER 30

Erwin sat on the sofa with Sonja, a glass of red wine in his hand. A fire crackled in the fireplace, the glow of the flames bathing the room in soft light. Tomorrow was the big day. The thought filled him with contentment. With her by his side, his new identity was perfect.

He raised his glass. "To my beautiful bride, whom I will marry tomorrow."

Sonja smiled happily. "I love you, Erwin. I can hardly wait."

"Me neither, my love." He patted her thigh. "Do you have the whole day off tomorrow?"

"Yes. My boss was very understanding."

"Once we're married, you won't have to work anymore."

Sonja leaned against him. "I'm still undecided about what to wear. The blue dress or the gray suit. What do you think?"

"The blue one suits you better," Erwin said automatically. His mind drifted to practical matters. After the wedding, Sonja would move in with him. He'd cleared two shelves in the wardrobe for her. They'd sell her furniture, since there was no room for it in his little house, but she insisted on keeping the crockery. He should be happy because he didn't have enough crockery, but then they'd own two incomplete sets, which he found deeply repugnant.

"Erwin, are you even listening to me?" Sonja's voice snapped him out of his thoughts.

"Of course, my dear. The blue dress."

She laughed. "I was asking where we should invite our colleagues for drinks."

"Ah, yes. Of course. The little café next to the registry office."

At that moment, the doorbell rang.

Erwin glanced at his watch. Hopefully, it wasn't one of his friends trying to sweeten his farewell to bachelorhood.

"Who could that be?" Sonja stood up.

"Stay seated, I'll get it." Erwin put down his wine glass and opened the door. Two women stood on his doorstep. The older one, perhaps in her early fifties, wore a dark blue coat and an elegant hat. She clutched a leather briefcase in her hand. The younger one seemed small and petite beneath her wide cape. A hat covered her pinned up hair and she wore too much make-up for his liking.

"Good evening," said the older woman with a slight but unmistakable accent. "Please excuse us for bothering you. We're collecting donations for war orphans. May we briefly explain our cause to you?"

Erwin eyed the two women. Something about the younger one seemed familiar, even though he couldn't say what it was. Perhaps it was the way she stood, leaning slightly to one side, as if she were ready to flee at any moment.

"It's late," he replied curtly. "Come back tomorrow."

"Who is it, Erwin?" Sonja called from the living room.

"Fundraisers, dear. I'll send them away."

But Sonja was already standing next to him. "For war orphans? Oh, those poor children. Please, come in. It's so cold."

"Sonja, this really isn't—"

"Nonsense, Erwin. We can spare a few minutes." She opened the door wide. "Please, come in."

The two women exchanged a brief glance, then the older one stepped over the threshold. The younger one followed with hesitation.

Erwin gritted his teeth. Why must Sonja have such a soft heart? He didn't feel like dealing with charity collectors. But how could he contradict Sonja on the eve of their wedding? Besides, it was too late anyway, since she'd led the women into the living room.

"Please, have a seat," said Sonja, gesturing to the sofa.

"That's very kind of you." The older woman sat down, while the younger one remained standing, her eyes darting around the room.

Erwin watched them closely. That accent. Was it Polish? No. It sounded more Swiss, mixed with something else. French perhaps, or English. It could also be Swedish. And the younger one... the longer he looked at her, the stronger the eerie feeling that he knew her.

He would give them a few marks and show them out.

"Sonja, darling." He tried to sound casual. "Would you please go upstairs and get my wallet from the bedroom? I think it's in my jacket."

She stood up. "Of course, Erwin. I'll be right back."

As soon as he heard her footsteps on the stairs, Erwin took a mark note out of his desk drawer.

"Here," he said, holding it out to the older woman. "For the war orphans. And now please excuse us. My wife and I would like to be alone."

She didn't take the money. Instead, the brazen person glared at him. "We're not here to collect donations. We know who you are."

Erwin's heart skipped a beat. "I beg your pardon?"

"We know that you are actually Hauptsturmführer Hartmut Goslar."

The world seemed to stand still. His stomach flipped over. Self-control honed by years of being an interrogator kept his expression neutral, "Madam, you must be confusing me with someone else. My name is Erwin Krüger."

The black-haired woman glared daggers at him. "I'm not confusing you with anyone else. I'd never forget you. Does the name Kate Mundaren ring a bell?"

Kate Mundaren. The name struck like a whip. He'd searched for that woman for weeks after a nurse was caught trying to smuggle a letter to her, written by a prisoner in the camp.

But nobody had heard of or seen Kate Mundaren. It was as if she'd never existed. The memory of the Gypsy who'd written the letter hit him with full force. Erwin furrowed his brow and tried to remember how he'd killed the man, but he couldn't recall.

In a fraction of a second, the pieces of the puzzle fell into place as he recognized the black-haired woman. The treacherous bitch had survived the horse accident. This time, he'd take matters into his own hands, and he'd guarantee she wouldn't survive. Neither would the other one. But first, he must send Sonja away, because her heart was too soft.

"I'm sorry, I don't know any woman named Kate Mundaren!"

Her face contorted with rage, the Gypsy hurled at him: "Because she doesn't exist. Kate Mundaren means, 'Here they kill people' in the Sinti language!"

He was speechless for a few seconds, then laughed heartily. "You're the cheeky brat who sneaked into my camp. I took your pendant, remember? Do you know that I received a medal for the efficient extermination of the gypsy plague? From the Führer himself. He knew you were an inferior race that had to be eradicated." Erwin talked himself into a rage. "Do you know what I regret most? Not killing you then, you piece of filth!"

"You should have done that, because now you're going to pay for your crimes, as sure as I'm standing here."

"I'll pay? Don't make me laugh!" He straightened to his full height. "You can't touch me. I work at City Hall. I'm a respected citizen. And you? You're just a lying, cheating, Gypsy."

"I saw the photo," the Gypsy said. "The photo of you on horseback in your SS uniform. In the camp."

Erwin's heart skipped a beat. The realization hit him unprepared. The open window. The moved album. She had been here. As soon as he recovered from the shock, he said, "You broke into my house. You little bitch. I'll report you. Then we'll see who ends up in prison."

"You won't do anything of the sort," said the older woman, who'd been sitting silently on the sofa, in an imperious tone. "My husband is Major Johnson, the city commander in Duisburg. I will personally see to it that you are brought to court."

Erwin's eyes widened in horror. An Englishwoman. That changed everything.

At that moment, Sonja walked down the stairs. "Erwin, I can't find your wallet. Did you—" She fell silent, sensing the tension in the room. Her eyes flicked from him to the women. "What's going on here?"

"This man isn't who he says he is," said Mrs. Johnson.

"Don't be absurd," Sonja said with a shaky laugh. "Of course he is. Who else would he be?"

"He's Hartmut Goslar. SS-Hauptsturmführer and former camp commandant in Belzec," claimed the Gypsy.

"That's ridiculous." Sonja turned to Erwin. "Tell them that's not true."

"It's a vicious slander." Erwin would deny everything until his last breath. It was his only chance to avoid the gallows.

"There's a photo of him in SS uniform," the Gypsy said. "Hidden behind the wallpaper in his bedroom."

"But how...?" Sonja clutched her head with both hands. "I'm calling the police."

"No!" Erwin grabbed her arm. The police were the last thing he needed right now. "The photo doesn't exist. It's a fabrication.

We can go upstairs and check. Then you'll see this woman is lying."

"You destroyed it, you rotten rat!" The Gypsy lunged at him. He dodged her just in time.

"That won't help you anymore," Mrs. Johnson said in a firm voice. "There are fingerprints, dental records, witnesses. If you are Hartmut Goslar, our specialists will expose you, I am absolutely certain of that."

Unfortunately, she was correct. The British needed only to track down his wife, Grete, and his carefully constructed identity would collapse like a house of cards. All the effort wasted, because the bloody Gypsy had survived. Gunther had been right warning him that loose ends were risky. This one had returned to drag him down.

With nothing left to lose, he aimed an uppercut at Mrs. Johnson. She staggered backward, hit her head against the wall, and sank to the floor in a daze. With one leap, he flattened her, wrapped his hands around her slender neck, and squeezed.

The Gypsy shrieked louder than a siren. He ignored her, he'd deal with her next... and then with Sonja.

"Erwin! Stop it!" Sonja cried in horror. "What are you doing? You're innocent."

At that moment, the front door burst open. Boots thundered in the hallway. A man in a British uniform stormed into the living room, his drawn pistol pointed at Erwin. "Let go of her immediately!"

Behind him a younger man appeared, a civilian.

It was over. Defeated, Erwin, or rather Hartmut, raised his hands.

"Hands behind your back." The soldier ordered.

Erwin obeyed mechanically. The cold metal closed around his wrists with a bloodcurdling click.

"Tomorrow is our wedding day," Sonja wailed, her voice choked with tears. "We were supposed to get married tomorrow."

"There will be no wedding," the soldier said, handing Erwin over to the other man before turning to the Englishwoman.

"Ma'am, are you all right? Do you need a doctor?"

"I'm fine," she croaked. "Honestly. Thanks to your quick intervention."

"It's my honor, ma'am." The soldier looked at her respectfully. "I'm Sergeant Wilson. Mr. Goldmann informed me of your plans."

"I'll tell my husband you saved my life," Mrs. Johnson said. "He'll see that you are rewarded for your bravery."

"That's very kind of you, ma'am."

Sonja sank onto the sofa. "I don't understand. Erwin, please tell me this is all a misunderstanding."

Hartmut Goslar shrugged. Poor Sonja. She'd had no idea. She'd genuinely believed he was Erwin Krüger.

CHAPTER 31

T he imposing facade of the district court gleamed in the sun. Roxy placed a hand on her belly, bulging under her summer dress. It could happen any day now, but first she had to make sure Goslar could never harm her child.

"Are you all right?" David's caring voice penetrated her thoughts. His arm rested on her shoulder.

"Yes." She took a deep breath. "I'm just nervous."

"That's normal." He gently pulled her close. "You don't have to worry. You're strong, Roxy. Stronger than anyone I know."

Grateful she smiled at him. Without David, she wouldn't have been able to get through the last months. At first, Goslar had been arrested for attacking Kate Johnson, but once he was in prison, the special war crimes unit had finally picked up the trail.

Lieutenant Morrison had vanished overnight—officially transferred to England, but Kate had delivered the real story. He'd been dishonorably discharged. Back home, he was indicted on black marketeering, extortion, and embezzlement.

Sergeant Wilson, on the other hand, had been promoted on Major Johnson's recommendation.

So many thoughts tumbled through Roxy's mind; today she'd finally close the book on her past.

"Shall we?" David offered her his arm.

She hooked her arm through his and together they climbed the stairs. The heavy wooden door swung open, revealing an entrance hall with high ceilings and marble columns. Their footsteps echoed through the room.

"Roxy!" A familiar voice made her turn around.

Kate Johnson approached them, looking elegant in a cream-colored costume. Despite the earnest situation, she beamed from ear to ear. Miss Marple had solved her first case.

Even her husband had grudgingly congratulated her—after lecturing her for putting herself in unnecessary danger.

"Kate!" Roxy broke away from David, shaking her hand. "I'm so glad you came."

"I wouldn't miss it for the world. I want to see that monster convicted." Kate took a step back, eying Roxy. "When is the baby due?"

Roxy stroked her belly. "Any day now."

"Then let's hope it waits until after the trial." Kate winked at her.

"Mrs. Johnson," David greeted her. "It's good to see you again."

"Herr Goldmann." Kate shook his hand. "Take good care of your wife and the little one."

"I will." Roxy's insides warmed at the loving look he cast toward her. "Every day."

A court clerk appeared in the entrance hall. "The trial of Hartmut Goslar will begin in ten minutes. All witnesses and spectators, please proceed to courtroom three."

Roxy's heart beat faster. The time had come. After all these months of waiting, she'd face him again. Finally, she'd testify against the man who'd destroyed her life and that of her family.

"Ready?" David squeezed her hand.

"Yes." She squared her shoulders. "Let's go."

They followed the bailiff down a long corridor. Other witnesses were also there, some of whom Roxy knew from the interviews over the past few months. It was a motley crew of survivors, civilian neighbors to the camp, and former SS guards hoping their testimony would mitigate their own sentences.

As they entered the courtroom, Roxy felt small and insignificant. The room was much larger than she'd expected. High windows let in daylight, reflecting off the polished wooden benches. At the front, on the dais, sat three judges in black robes. To the left and right were the seats for the lawyers, behind them the spectator benches.

And in the middle, in the dock, was he: Hartmut Goslar.

Roxy stopped in her tracks. The months in prison had changed him. His face was gaunt, his cheeks hollow, his skin sallow. His hair had turned completely gray. Just his eyes—those cold, merciless eyes—looked the same.

Their gazes locked. For a heartbeat, she was transported back into the camp. She, the frightened prisoner, and he, the almighty commandant.

At just the right moment, David squeezed her hand, pulling her back to the present. The camp was no more. She was free. Goslar was the one in captivity.

She lifted her chin and returned his gaze.

"Roxy." David's voice was gentle but firm. "Come."

He led her to a bench in the front row. Kate sat down next to her. The hall filled up quickly with many onlookers coming to watch the trial. Some because they stood for justice, others out of pure curiosity. On the prosecution side there were a few diehards who continued to claim Erwin Krüger wasn't Hartmut Goslar, even though he'd been clearly identified by his dentist's records. The specialists had explained to Roxy that a person's teeth were as unique as their fingerprints, and the extracted teeth didn't change anything.

"All rise." The bailiff's voice echoed through the courtroom. The audience rose. The three judges took their seats. The presiding judge, an elderly man with a gray beard and a serious expression, banged his gavel on the table.

"The trial of Hartmut Goslar is open," he announced. "You are charged with crimes against humanity, murder in at least a hundred cases, as well as aiding and abetting murder in thousands of cases, torture, and inhumane treatment of prisoners."

Roxy listened to the charges. With each crime read aloud, the atmosphere in the courtroom became more stifling. Some members of the audience began to cry. Others sat there as if petrified.

"The prosecution will now present evidence," the presiding judge said.

The prosecutor, a middle-aged man with sharp features and a piercing gaze, rose to his feet. He held a folder of documents in his hands, clearing his throat, he began in a firm voice:

"Your Honor, ladies and gentlemen. Before you sits a man who for years pretended to be Erwin Krüger. A man who believed he could escape justice by changing his name and starting anew." The prosecutor paused dramatically and let his gaze wander around the courtroom. "But the truth cannot be buried. The dead cry out for atonement and the survivors thirst for justice."

Goslar sat in the dock stony-faced. Only the constant grinding of his jaw betrayed his tension.

The prosecutor droned on, but Roxy was no longer listening. The man's abhorrent deeds may have been new to the audience, but she had experienced them firsthand. She observed the proceedings in a haze until she was called to the witness stand.

Roxy's heart pounded in her chest. This was it. She'd been preparing for this moment for months yet her legs felt like jelly. David gave her a gentle push.

As she walked forward, she felt Goslar's angry glare on her

back. Instinctively, she wanted to duck her head, but caught herself at the last moment. She was no longer the frightened girl. Goslar no longer held any power over her.

The court clerk handed her a Bible. "Place your hand on it and swear to tell the truth, the whole truth, and nothing but the truth."

"I swear," Roxy said firmly and took her place in the witness box. From there, she could see the entire courtroom. David sat in the front row, winking at her. His support gave her strength. Kate sat next to him, upright and dignified. So many people had been waiting for this day—and even more hadn't lived to see it.

"Frau Goldmann." The prosecutor stepped closer. "Can you tell us when and where you first met Hartmut Goslar?"

Roxy took a deep breath. "It was in June 1940, when my family and I were deported to the gypsy camp in Belzec."

"Can you describe what you experienced in the camp?"

The memories flooded Roxy like a dark wave. She closed her eyes for a second, collected her thoughts and began to speak. "It was hell on earth. We were treated like animals. Beaten, starved, forced to work until we collapsed." Her voice grew firmer. "But the worst was Goslar's cruelty. He greeted new arrivals in the same way each time."

"How did he do that?"

"He drew a line in the dirt with his riding crop. And then he said that anyone who crossed the line would be shot. In every group, at least one person doubted his words and wanted to test it out." Roxy looked Goslar straight in the eye, the memory making her blood boil. "I had to watch several times as this man shot them in cold blood."

A horrified murmur went through the room.

The prosecutor nodded solemnly. "Thank you very much, Frau Goldmann. No further questions."

Roxy rose from the witness stand on trembling legs. As she reached her seat, a heavy weight lifted from her heart. She'd done it. She'd told her story.

"The prosecution calls Gottfried Popa to the witness stand."

Roxy flinched. Uncle Gottfried? When she'd visited him in Berlin, he'd refused to testify and advised her to let the past rest. A broken man limped into the witness box. His hands shook as he took the oath.

"Herr Popa," the prosecutor began, "you were interned in Belzec?"

"Yes." Gottfried's voice was little more than a whisper.

"Herr Popa," the prosecutor continued, "did you ever meet the defendant, Hartmut Goslar, in person?"

"Every day." Uncle Gottfried avoided looking in Goslar's direction. "He rode through the camp on his horse, whip in hand. Whenever something wasn't to his liking, he struck out. Once I saw him beat a prisoner to death."

"Can you tell us more about that?"

Gottfried nodded. "The man was very weak. He could barely stand. When Goslar rode past on his horse, he stumbled. Goslar dismounted and whipped him, kicking him with his boots. He didn't stop until the man lay motionless."

"What happened next?"

"He ordered two prisoners to carry the body away. As if nothing had happened. As if he hadn't just killed a man."

The silence in the courtroom was so absolute one could have heard a pin drop.

The prosecutor paused for a moment before continuing. "Thank you, Herr Popa. No further questions."

Gottfried made no move to stand up. His Adam's apple bobbed frantically up and down. "I'd like to say something else."

Since no one objected, he continued: "I was just trying to protect my family. I thought if we followed the Nazis' rules, if we obeyed, they wouldn't hurt us." He shook his head. "I was a fool." At that moment, Uncle Gottfried gazed at Roxy. The pain in his eyes hit her like a punch to the gut. She gasped.

"I'm so sorry, Roxy, that I betrayed you." Tears welled up in his eyes. "I thought... I thought that if I informed the commandant about your presence, he'd see how loyal we were and spare our family. I thought then he would hurt our family."

Interrupted by sobs, he went on. "But I was wrong. So wrong. I should have listened to you. But you were just a child... Mature for your age with a vigilance like no other, but still a child. It was never my intention to hurt you. I believed that obedience would ensure our survival. Not even in my worst nightmares could I have imagined how cruel the Nazis are." He stood up. "Please, Roxy. I know I have no right to ask you for anything. But I ask you anyway: Forgive me. Forgive an old fool who mistook cowardice for wisdom and obedience for survival."

Roxy sat frozen. All eyes in the courtroom rested on her. David squeezed her hand.

The judge cleared his throat. "Herr Popa, please return to your seat."

Gottfried wiped his face and left the witness stand. The trial continued. Other witnesses were called, evidence was presented. Roxy hardly noticed any of it as Gottfried's confession echoed through her head.

He'd betrayed her in the camp. All these years, she'd hated him. And now he was asking her for forgiveness. It was the vindication that she'd been right all along. But it tasted stale. Millions had died before Uncle Gottfried realized what she had known at the tender age of twelve: that the Nazis aimed to eradicate the Roma and Sinti.

"The court will recess to deliberate," the judge announced at last. "We'll return in two hours to render the verdict."

The crowd rose, drifting toward the exit. Roxy remained seated, dazed by the events.

"Roxy?" David's voice reached her. "Are you all right?"

"Yes. I... I just need to think."

Kate Johnson produced a thermos and poured an aromatic golden-brown liquid into a cup, which she handed to Roxy. "Black tea. It'll do you good."

"Thanks." Roxy couldn't help but smile. For Kate, tea was the cure for everything. And indeed, the bitter taste, softened by a dash of milk, melted the patch of ice in her soul. Gradually, her essence thawed from within.

"Maybe you should talk to your uncle," Kate said once Roxy finished her drink.

"That's exactly what I was thinking."

Roxy found Gottfried outside on the steps in front of the courthouse, where he sat with his shoulders slumped, looking at his folded hands.

"Uncle Gottfried," she addressed him softly.

He jerked, fear appearing in his eyes. "Roxy, I—"

"It's okay," she interrupted him, sitting down by his side. "I forgive you."

"You do?"

"You did what you thought was best. You wanted to protect our family. I know now that, as the head of the family, you had everyone's well-being in mind, while I was mainly concerned for myself." She laid her hand over his.

"You were a child. Wise beyond your years, but still a child. I'm so sorry." He stared at his shoelaces. "Because of me..."

"Because of Goslar," Roxy corrected him. "He's the guilty one, not you. He forced us into an impossible situation. He forced us to make decisions no one should have to make."

Gottfried began to cry. "You and Romeo are the only family I have left. Of more than forty."

"And Natalie, Eva's daughter," Roxy added.

"I've accepted that she's better off with the Gadje than with me and Romeo. I just hope I'll be allowed to visit Natalie from time to time."

"I'm sure you will." Roxy had no doubt that Frau Abel was listening to the trial on the radio and had heard his confession.

"Congratulations to your pregnancy. If you ever visit Berlin again, I'd love to get to know my grandchild." Gottfried hugged her awkwardly. "We are family. We must stick together."

She felt David's presence behind her, and Uncle Gottfried noticed him, too. "Is that your husband?"

"Yes, this is David Goldmann." Roxy introduced the two of them.

The two men shook hands. "Take good care of my niece and her child. She's very special. Braver than everyone I know."

"I know," David replied. "I promise, I'll always be there for her."

Gottfried nodded. "Good. That's good."

The bailiff appeared at the door. "The court will reconvene in ten minutes."

Together, they returned to the courtroom. The atmosphere crackled as the judges took their seats.

The presiding judge cleared his throat. "Defendant, rise."

Goslar got to his feet. For the first time that day, Roxy saw a hint of fear in his eyes.

"The court has found you guilty on all counts," announced the judge. "Guilty of murder in at least one hundred proven cases. Guilty of aiding and abetting murder in several thousand further cases. Guilty of torture, inhumane treatment, and crimes against humanity."

He paused. The silence in the courtroom was absolute.

"The court sentences you to death by hanging."

A collective sigh of relief swept through the courtroom. On the bench behind them, Sonja slumped, sobbing uncontrollably.

She had repeatedly assured the interrogators that she loved this man, regardless of what he had done in a previous life. People could change. Why would no one give him a second chance?

EPILOGUE

TWO WEEKS LATER

The summer sun hung high in the sky as Roxy stepped into the forest. The shade of the trees provided a pleasant temperature, in contrast to the sweltering heat in the city. Little Marek lay in a sling in front of her chest, his dark hair glinting in the subdued light filtering through the canopy of leaves.

As she reached the clearing, she stopped and gently placed her hand on the sleeping baby's head. Then she knelt in the grass, careful not to wake little Marek. She'd woven a wreath of daisies, dandelions, and poppies and placed it on the bare earth in front of a beech tree.

"For you," she whispered. "Now you can rest in peace. Goslar has paid for his crimes."

The tears she'd held back for so long ran freely down her cheeks. She closed her eyes and let the faces appear before her inner eye.

First Tibor, her cousin and best friend, who'd died on the flight in Warsaw. "No going it alone," he'd always said. How often had David repeated those words?

Next, her many cousins. Maria, Hans, and Christian, who'd

died shortly after arriving in Belzec because they weren't allowed to give him medicine.

Livia, her only friend in the camp, killed by typhus. Until her death, she'd brought a ray of sunshine to the camp with her blonde hair, bright blue eyes, and friendly nature.

Aunt Gisela, with her unshakeable dignity, even as the world around her descended into chaos. She'd never stopped caring for every single member of the family. Eva, Teresa, Markus... and her many relatives. Only Gottfried and Romeo had survived.

And lastly, she thought of Marek. When she'd met him in Belzec, he'd become cynical as a result of the Nazis' cruelty. Regardless, she'd grown fond of him, just as he had of her. Against his declared will, he'd taken Roxy under his wing and become a surrogate father to her.

"Marek," she whispered and opened her eyes. New tears streamed down her face. "It's only thanks to you that I'm standing here. You saved my life by sacrificing yours."

She looked down at the baby in the sling. Little Marek blinked and looked at her with an alert gaze, as if he understood why they'd come to this place.

"I named my son after you. So that your name will live on. You will never be forgotten." Roxy wiped the tears from her cheeks. "I'll tell him about you. About your courage and your inner strength. I'll tell him how you protected me, how you fought for all of us."

Little Marek made an approving gurgling sound. Roxy gently stroked his cheek.

"I'll tell him about everyone," she continued. "About our people, our culture, our music. The Nazis wanted to wipe us out. They wanted us to be forgotten. But we won't be. As long as I live, as long as my son lives, you will be remembered."

She sat up, lifted little Marek out of the sling, and cradled him in her arms. He was so small and fragile, yet so strong. He'd survived the birth and the first weeks of his life. He was a fighter, just like his namesake.

"Look at him, Marek," she said, lifting the baby a little higher. "He bears your name, and he'll do so with pride. I promise you that."

The sun broke through the canopy of leaves, bathing the clearing in golden light. A gentle breeze ruffled her hair, and for a moment she felt as if someone were with her. As if all the people she'd lost were standing next to her, watching her.

"I did it. Goslar has been convicted. He has paid for his crimes."

A weight lifted from her shoulders. The vow she'd made to herself had been fulfilled. The man who'd caused so much suffering had paid for his crimes.

"But this is not the end. It is a beginning. A beginning for me, David, and our son. We will build a life together, a good life. Not because I am forgetting you, but because I carry you in my heart. Always."

Little Marek gurgled and Roxy smiled through her tears.

"I promise you, my little one, I'll never leave you alone. I'll always be here for you. I'll protect you, love you, show you how beautiful life can be. And I'll teach you to be proud of who you are. A Rom. A German. A human being. Part of something bigger."

He sucked on her finger. At that moment, Roxy felt a deep sense of peace wash over her. Despite everything that had happened, despite the unspeakable suffering she'd endured, she was here. She was alive. And she had created something wonderful—new life.

She put her son back in the sling and looked at the wreath of flowers in the grass. Then she turned and walked home. With every step she took, she felt lighter, until she seemed to float with happiness.

LETTER FROM THE AUTHOR

Thank you for reading **Hiding in Plain Sight**. If you enjoyed the book, I would be delighted to receive a short or detailed review —any feedback not only helps me as an author, but also other readers who become aware of my books.

If you would like to be the first to know when a new book is published, I invite you to subscribe to my newsletter: https://kummerow.info

After reading **The Berlin Wife's Vow**, many readers wrote to me about how much they love Roxy, and that her story felt unfinished.

I felt exactly the same way. Thus I wanted to give her the ending she deserved. After all the terrible things she had been through, she should get the satisfaction that, sadly, so many real people didn't receive.

Of course, it couldn't be too easy, but anyone who knows Roxy knows that she always comes up with something.

At the time when the camp in Belzec was used as a so-called "gypsy camp," SS-Sturmbannführer Hermann Dolp was the camp commander. Contemporary witnesses describe Dolp as brutal, irascible, and addicted to alcohol. His moods determined life, suffering, and humiliation.

Even within the SS, he was considered problematic, not because of moral outrage, but because he attacked the wrong person. There are reports of him being demoted after allegedly attempting to rape the Polish girlfriend of a German official.

Little is known about his fate. Hermann Dolp is said to have fallen in Romania in 1944. Whether this is true cannot be proven.

However, it is historically documented that numerous Nazi perpetrators went into hiding after the war, assumed new identities, or were protected by political interests. Hermann Dolp might therefore have slipped into a new identity, as did the character Hartmut Goslar in the novel, who was modeled after him. This possibility isn't pure fiction, but reflects historical reality.

Unfortunately, very few perpetrators were actually prosecuted and held accountable for their crimes after the war. The fictional Hartmut Goslar is no exception. Many real perpetrators evaded justice, including well-known criminals such as Klaus Barbie, the so-called "Butcher of Lyon," who was considered useful by US authorities at the beginning of the Cold War and was protected from a death sentence in France.

The corrupt British Lieutenant Morrison is a fictional character. However, there is ample historical evidence that individual Allied soldiers were involved in the black market. Poverty, chaos, moral decay, and abuse of power are unfortunate parts of the historical reality of the postwar period.

Since many of you have asked me what happened to Baumann and Koloss after the war, I have decided to include their stories and give them a conclusion as well. Perhaps there will be a happy ending for Koloss and Judith in a future book, but I need to think about that first. Until then, Judith will remain in the US and train the women's Olympic swimming team.

I also wanted to reconcile Roxy with her family. My editor repeatedly criticized the fact that Uncle Gottfried in particular was portrayed too negatively in the book **The Last Train Home**. That was not my intention, because he was by no means evil.

As a teenager, Roxy simply didn't understand that he was acting out of fear. He truly believed he was doing the right thing in the interests of the whole family, even if his decisions were tragic and wrong.

And finally, a personal note:

Kate, the tea-drinking Englishwoman, got her name from another tea drinker I met on a hike through the Pyrenees. As soon as we arrived at the mountain hut in the evening, her first action was always the same: she ordered hot water to make herself a proper English tea. She had brought the "only true" tea bags with her from home.

At that moment, I decided that one day I absolutely had to have a "lovably crazy tea-drinking Englishwoman" in one of my books. With the kind permission of the real Kate, Kate Johnson was finally created.

Thank you again for reading **Hiding in Plain Sight**.

The next book in the series is called **No Applause in Theresienstadt**. When Sophie learns that Eugen, the Jewish theater director she loves, is alive in Theresienstadt, she is determined to rescue him.

Order here: https://kummerow.info/escaping-reich/no-applause-in-theresienstadt/

Sincerely,

Marion Kummerow

Inspired by true historical events, From the Ashes is the unforgettable story of a tortured man, torn between his ideals, the iron fist of Stalinism and the woman he loves.

Marlene has no love lost for the **Soviet occupying forces**. Living in constant fear of the Russian soldiers, she works in a hospital to make ends meet, where she meets Werner, a cold-hearted career politician.

ISBN: 978-3948865252

ALSO BY MARION KUMMEROW

Love and Resistance in WW2 Germany

Unrelenting

Unyielding

Unwavering

War Girl Series

Downed over Germany (Prequel)

Blonde Angel: War Girl Ursula (Book 1)

War Girl Lotte (Book 2)

War Girl Anna (Book 3)

Reluctant Informer (Book 4)

Trouble Brewing (Book 5)

Fatal Encounter (Book 6)

Uncommon Sacrifice (Book 7)

Bitter Tears (Book 8)

Secrets Revealed (Book 9)

Together at Last (Book 10)

Endless Ordeal (Book 11)

Not Without My Sister (Spin-off)

Second Chance at First Love (romantic spin-off)

Berlin Fractured

From the Ashes (Book 1)

On the Brink (Book 2)

In the Skies (Book 3)

Into the Unknown (Book 4)

Against the Odds (Book 5)

Margarete's Story

Turning Point (Prequel)

A Light in the Window

From the Dark We Rise

The Girl in the Shadows

Daughter of the Dawn

Standalone

The Orphan's Mother

German Wives

The Berlin Wife

The Berlin Wife's Choice

The Berlin Wife's Resistance

The Berlin Wife's Vow

The Last Safe Place (spin-off)

Escaping the Reich

Three Children in Danger

Dark Shadows Looming Ahead

Perilous Journey to Freedom

Find all my books here:

http://www.kummerow.info

CONTACT ME

I truly appreciate you taking the time to read (and enjoy) my
books. And I'd be thrilled to hear from you!
If you'd like to get in touch with me you can do so via

Facebook:
http://www.facebook.com/AutorinKummerow

Website
http://www.kummerow.info